THE WATERKEEPER'S DAUGHTER

Best wishes,
Joan Mauch

JOAN MAUCH

WHISKEY CREEK PRESS
www.whiskeycreekpress.com

Published by
WHISKEY CREEK PRESS
Whiskey Creek Press
PO Box 51052
Casper, WY 82605-1052
www.whiskeycreekpress.com

eISBN: 978-1-63355-602-7
Print ISBN: 978-1-63355-731-4

Cover Artist: Molly Courtright
Editor: Dave Field
Printed in the United States of America

Dedication

For my sister, Peggy – often in my thoughts, always in my heart

ACKNOWLEDGEMENT

I owe a debt of gratitude to my family, especially my son, Benjamin, who have encouraged my writing aspirations over the years.

Thanks to: Art Norris, the Quad-Cities Waterkeeper who helped me understand the function of the Waterkeeper's Alliance; to author Wayne Sapp who explained the features of a Cessna 150 airplane; and to alpha readers Kristal Shaff, Renee Busha, Wayne Sapp and Rich Miller for their generous time and insightful critiques.

I also gleaned technical information from the following sources: *The Riverkeepers* by John Cronin and Robert F. Kennedy, Jr. (Scribner, 1997); *From the Bottom Up* by Chad Pregracke with Jeff Barrow (National Geographic, 2007); *Silent Spring* by Rachel Carson (Houghton Mifflin Company, 1962); and *Lake Okeechobee, Wellspring of the Everglades* by Alfred Jackson Hanna and Kathryn Abbey Hanna (The Bobbs-Merrill Company, 1948). In addition I made use of the Internet to do extensive research on the Acoma and Seminole Indian Tribes.

I am grateful to my publishers Whiskey Creek Press and Start Publishing, my editor, Dave Field, and talented cover artist, Molly Courtright, for their work in making me look better than I am.

Chapter 1

It wasn't unusual for Craig Whitaker to be late for dinner or, for that matter, to arrive home long after his wife was asleep. So when the doorbell rang and there was an empty spot on the pillow where her husband's head usually rested, Lisa didn't think anything of it. She glanced at the nightstand where the clock radio blinked five-thirty. An early riser, he was probably in the kitchen. He could get the door, unless what she'd heard was only the screech of a sandhill crane.

She yawned, turned over and started to go back to sleep, when she heard it again. This time, the bell called out sharply in rapid succession followed by a loud banging. Wide awake now, she wondered why Craig hadn't taken care of it.

As she made her way down the hall, Lisa gritted her teeth. What was she going to do with that man? He stayed out till all hours, rarely making it home for supper, and now he wouldn't even answer the damn door? It was beyond inconsiderate. Prepared to give her husband what for, Lisa poked her head in the kitchen. In the predawn gloom, she could see it was empty. He must have gone out and forgotten his house key. He'd done that more than once lately. She threw the door open, her face screwed up in a frown.

The man standing in the porch light wore a police uniform. It was Pete Hansen, the sheriff's deputy. She'd often seen him around town. With his friendly grin, big brown eyes and loose-limbed frame, he reminded her of a loopy old hound dog. At the moment, however, his welcoming smile was missing.

"I'm sorry to disturb you, Ma'am," he said, "but is your husband home? I need to speak to him."

Lisa gave him a vacant stare. "Craig?" She glanced over his shoulder to the driveway. The space where his car should have been was empty. "He must've gone out before I got up." She pulled the belt on her robe a little tighter. "Why do you need to talk to him?"

"Does he drive a Jeep Cherokee?"

"Yes," Lisa said with growing concern. "Is there something the matter?"

Instead of answering, Pete countered with, "Can you think of any reason he'd be parked by the lake at this hour?"

The man's barrage of questions, in addition to his solemn countenance, sent a thrill of fear down Lisa's spine. She trembled, but not from the morning chill. "He's over there all the time, Officer. It's his job. He's Lake Okeechobee's waterkeeper. You may have heard about him."

A glimmer of hope sparked inside her. There was nothing wrong. This cop was only doing his job—checking on a car that seemed out of place. Craig probably wanted to get an early start. He often did that.

She was glad to know the police were so conscientious, but rousting someone from bed to check on an abandoned car seemed excessive.

Pete turned his hat over and over. He seemed at a loss for words.

"What is it? What's wrong?" Lisa said.

"Why don't we go inside?" He put his hand on the screen door.

"Was Craig in an accident or something? Is he all right? Tell me." The words tumbled out one after another.

Please God, please let him be okay. I'll never complain about him coming home late again. Please, please let him be all right.

But the tone in Pete's voice and the look on his face said Craig wasn't all right, not all right at all.

"Please, Mrs. Whitaker, let's go inside," he said, adding, "It would be better that way."

Better? How could having a policeman in your house be better? Lisa stepped aside and they walked into the living room. She switched on a lamp and sat down. Pete remained standing.

For a brief second neither one spoke. In the distance an owl hooted. Then, as if there was no way to put it off, Pete said, "Mrs. Whitaker, I'm sorry to have to tell you this but your husband's boat was found over on the lake, capsized. Todd Johnson from down the street spotted it and called us. Even as we speak, efforts are being made to find him. We'd hoped some kids, fooling around, set it free and that he was safe at home with you." He hesitated and looked past her out the window. A Sega palm swayed in the breeze. The sun was beginning to rise, dispelling the darkness. In another few minutes there'd be no need for the lamp. "I guess we were wrong," he added softly.

Speaking in ragged, bite-sized chunks, Lisa said, "Take me. Over there. Please."

* * * *

The scene at the lake was like something from a movie. Spotlights from several crafts skimmed the surface and the shore, breaking through the mist like ghostly apparitions. Rescuers called out on bullhorns in the early morning quiet: "Craig Whitaker;" "Craig Whitaker." Their voices echoed back and forth across the lake, blending in with the occasional screech of a crane or a bittern's distinctive "oong-ka-choonk." Craig's motorboat had been flipped upright and towed back to shore, where it looked forlorn. And very empty.

Lisa couldn't breathe. A fifty-pound weight had dropped on her chest; her legs were rubbery. She trembled, her teeth chattering.

Pete said, "Mrs. Whitaker, you need to sit down. Here, let me help you." He removed his jacket and draped it over her shoulders. "Is there someone I can call? You shouldn't be alone at a time like this."

Call? Her thoughts immediately went to Annie, their twenty-one year old daughter. She'd planned to drive down from Gainesville today and was probably already on her way. Lisa could reach her cellphone, but didn't think telling her as she drove would be a good idea. Besides, as Pete mentioned earlier, some kids probably dumped Craig's boat over. He was more than likely somewhere having an early morning meeting. That had to be it.

Please, God, let him be all right, please, please.

Lisa shivered and drew the jacket tighter, searching for comfort wherever she might find it. "It's too soon…" She let the balance of her thought evaporate.

Pete shifted his weight from one leg to the other. "Is there something I can do? How about some coffee?" He looked as though he preferred to do anything except stand there and wait as this drama played out.

"No," Lisa said, "I'll be all right."

Two hours later, she witnessed a sight no one ever wants to see: a body pulled from the lake. She had to be restrained from rushing down to the dock as the boat approached. That corpse couldn't be her husband, she told herself. She took several steps and then collapsed.

When she came to, Lisa was confused: Who were these people? What was she doing on the ground? Then it came back to her in a sickening rush. Craig's boat had capsized. They'd found his body. Her husband was dead.

Chapter 2

Annie Whitaker was giddy with excitement. Not only did she have the whole summer ahead of her, but she'd been accepted as a waterkeeper intern. That meant she could work alongside her dad for the next few months, get college credit and earn a little money as well. How cool was that?

And to top it off, last night Nate had asked her to marry him. She'd almost called her parents right then and there, but it was late and she didn't want to wake them. Besides telling them in person would be more fun. She couldn't wait to see the look on her dad's face when he heard the news. Too bad Nate and his buddy already left for their camping trip or he'd be coming with her.

Around four, unable to sleep, she'd gotten up and headed south. Three and a half hours later, Annie glanced at her watch—the one her father had given her for high school graduation. The wristband was tarnished from constant wear. Gainesville to Moore Haven in less than four hours. Not bad. She grinned. Her dad would ask how long it took. She'd have to fudge a little or get one of his lectures about not speeding.

Pulling into the double driveway, she noticed the place seemed quiet, which was odd since her parents were early risers—a frequent source of annoyance as she grew up. Now she wondered why no one had thrown the front door open and greeted her with the usual hugs and kisses. Were they out of town? She'd told them she was coming home this weekend, so they knew to expect her. Maybe they forgot. Sure, like that would ever happen.

Annie got out of her Honda with the Gator's sticker on the bumper. Rubbing the spot on her back that let her know when she sat too long, she decided to leave her stuff for later and gave the house an appraising glance.

Nothing had changed since she was here for the Chalo Nitka Festival. It wore the same appearance of benign neglect as before. Did she really think that because her life had changed so radically her childhood home would also be transformed? Not really, but a coat of paint would have been nice. Unfortunately that wasn't her dad's strong suit, or her mother's either, for that matter. A surge of warmth flowed inside Annie. Peeling paint couldn't dispel her happy memories of the place.

She'd reached the front door and started digging around in her purse for her house key, when a police cruiser pulled up and an officer got out. Puzzled to see her mother open the passenger side door, she called out, "Mom," and sprinted over to the car. Then she noticed Lisa's anguished expression and ghostly pallor. Her clothes looked disheveled as though she'd fallen out of bed and thrown on the first thing her hands could find.

"Annie," she began, her voice scarcely above a whisper.

"Ma, what's wrong?" Over Lisa's shoulder she could see the officer, his face mirroring her mother's somber expression. "Where's Dad?" Panic bullied its way inside her.

When Lisa's mouth opened but nothing came out, the policeman came to her rescue. "I'm afraid there's been an accident, Miss. Why don't we go inside?"

Chapter 3

The unexpected passing of a prominent citizen in a community of any size is noteworthy, but in Moore Haven, where most everyone knew everyone else, news of Craig Whitaker's death was devastating. His efforts to protect the local waterways in and around Lake Okeechobee had been widely publicized, so he was well-known and respected. As a result, his wake and funeral were especially somber and well attended. Even in the Florida heat, some mourners felt the need to wear black.

The service was held at the local Catholic church. The small brick structure wasn't intended to hold the overflow crowd that showed up. Annie sat with her mother in the front pew and cried her way through the Mass for the Dead. When she thought her eyes were empty of tears, a phrase or hymn would strike a chord and her wellspring of grief again overflowed. She knew she should be strong for her mother's sake but, oddly enough, Lisa—whose ashen face seemed devoid of emotion—appeared to be holding up quite well.

Reflecting on it, Annie realized she'd never seen her

mother cry, not once. Oh, she and her dad had had their fights: There was the usual screaming, yelling and slamming of doors, but she didn't ever remember seeing her mom in tears. Instead of hugging her and saying things would be all right, she preferred to see Lisa break down and weep—demonstrating that she loved her father as much as Annie did.

She remembered the time her dad took her out on the Caloosahatchee. When she'd said, "Caloosahatchee River", he corrected her. "The Indian word for river is 'hatchee'. 'Caloosa' is for the Caloosa Indians that once lived around here. If you say 'Caloosahatchee River', what you're really saying is 'Caloosa River River.'" They'd had a good laugh over that. It had become a private joke between the two of them. One or the other would say "river river" and they'd invariably crack up. Now it made her cry.

Annie never considered her dad's job especially dangerous. Authorities claimed his boat capsized and he drowned. Maybe it was caused by the wake of a passing boat, they said, or perhaps he dropped something in the water, leaned over the side and lost his balance. It all seemed odd to her. He was too careful to allow something so mundane to take his life.

She touched the tarnished watch which suddenly became her most prized possession. It was as though his spirit communicated to her when she stroked it, which she did frequently throughout the service and burial. Her head hurt from crying. She was sick of talking to all those people and would be glad when it was over so she could grieve in private.

If only Nate were here. His image floated before her mind's eye, warming her inside. He'd taken off on that trip a few hours after he proposed. It had been planned for a long time so he couldn't get out of it. The site was so remote there was no cellphone signal so she couldn't call and tell him her sad news. He'd be upset when he found out about her dad and wasn't there to comfort her. She sighed. He was such a good man.

At the post-funeral luncheon, Annie noticed a couple standing with her mother across the room. The man bore a striking resemblance to her father. He was tall with a slight stoop and thick white hair, a deeply wrinkled face and startling blue eyes. The woman was petite, with salt and pepper hair done in a short bob. Her gaze moved rapidly from her companion to Lisa and back, reminiscent of a nervous ground squirrel. Their clothes were expensive, almost ostentatious.

Her mother waved Annie over. "Meet your father's parents." She gestured first to the man and then to his wife. "This is Craig Whitaker, Sr. and his wife Noreen. They flew in from Boston." Lisa's tone and expression said these people meant nothing to her.

By turns the Whitakers hugged their granddaughter. "It's so good to meet you at last," Craig said. Noreen gave her a sad smile and nodded. Their manner of speech reminded Annie of a girl she knew from Boston who swallowed her 'r's" saying "cawn" instead of "corn," or "skwea" instead of "square."

Annie was so stunned she could scarcely respond. These people were her grandparents? She'd never seen their photographs or received so much as a birthday card or visit from them. Now they'd materialized as if from thin air.

How was she supposed to react to these outsiders who suddenly took up space where family and close friends belonged? She knew she should experience something—warmth, friendliness, curiosity—anything, but there was only a cold emptiness inside. To her they were no different than those other people who'd come out of curiosity or to express their condolences—they were strangers, nothing more.

She recalled periodically asking her parents where they grew up and who their families were. It was a natural enough question. Aren't most kids curious about such things?

Once, back in grade school, a class project involved making family trees. When Annie asked her parents for information so she could complete the project, they'd been vague. They told her Craig was from New England and Lisa from New Mexico. That was it. No more information was forthcoming. They didn't want to talk about it.

At the time she assumed they were in some kind of trouble with the law or in a witness protection program. So she did what any kid in a similar situation might do—she made it all up. Over the years she'd almost come to believe those fictional relatives were real. It was more comforting than to think that, except for her parents, she was alone in the world.

Now, instead of feeling comforted, looking into the face of a man who so resembled her cherished father, Annie's loneliness and heartbreak only grew more intense.

Chapter 4

In the days that followed, Annie did her best to help her mother put their lives back together. It wasn't easy. They had to go through her dad's things and decide what to keep and what to throw out. But whenever they tried, they inevitably ended up reminiscing—and her tears would flow again.

One afternoon, sorting through a closet, Annie came upon a box of odds and ends. Thinking it was more outdated junk, she started to toss it on a pile headed for the dump when she noticed a photograph peeking from beneath some papers.

The faded picture was of a boy, not more than ten, standing beside a man whose arm was around the child's shoulders. They stood in front of a small plane. It looked like the crop dusters she'd seen fly over area fields. On the side of the plane, painted in large letters, was the name, "Whitaker & Son."

Whitaker & Son? That boy must be her dad and the man his father. She looked closer. There was a strong resemblance to the man she'd met at the funeral.

"Mom," Annie called. "Look what I found."

Lisa, her arms full of Craig's old clothes, came in the room and deposited them on a chair. "What is it dear?" she said.

"A picture of Dad as a kid. Look." She put the photograph in her mother's hand.

Lisa scrutinized it. "You're right, it is him." She handed the picture back.

"Can I have it?" Annie said, half expecting her mother to say "no." After all, a photograph of her husband as a child was precious. Didn't she love and miss him as much as Annie did? Judging from her lack of tears, you wouldn't think so.

"Of course," Lisa said and started to pick up the bundle of clothes.

Pricked by curiosity, Annie said, "So, his father had his own plane?"

Lisa nodded. "More than one."

"Why would he need more than one airplane?"

Lisa's face looked pinched, like she really didn't want to talk about it. "Because he owned a crop-dusting company. You know, for spraying pesticides." Her lips clamped shut. She started to leave the room.

"Mom, wait," Annie was puzzled. For as long as she could remember, her dad had been a staunch environmentalist. Did his father really earn a living by spraying chemicals? She'd read Rachel Carson's *Silent Spring* for a class assignment and was shocked to learn what went on.

"Is it true? Was Dad's father really involved spraying poison?"

Her mother had already left the room, so Annie went after her. She wanted answers and now was as good a time as any to get them. She caught up with her on the patio.

"So, Mom, is it true?"

Lisa sighed. "Yes, it's true. Your grandfather grew rich working for chemical companies, spraying problem insects and weeds."

"I read about that. They killed birds and fish, poisoned the water, even destroyed trees and flowers."

Lisa nodded. She looked so tired.

"How awful." Annie paused. Now that the subject of her grandfather had been broached, she pushed ahead. Who knew when, if ever, she'd get another opportunity like this?

"Can I ask you a question?"

"Would it make a difference if I said no?" Lisa gave her a weary smile. "What is it?"

"Well, first off, I was surprised when you introduced me to Dad's parents. I mean, I thought they were dead. Neither of you ever talked about them."

"Yes, well, I'm sorry about that, honey. I can see how it must have been a shock."

"It was. Then, after the luncheon was over, they just up and left, didn't stick around or anything. And you didn't urge them to stay either."

"Maybe I should have invited them to stay, but I was in no condition to entertain. Besides they could have stayed if they'd wanted to. Nothing was stopping them. There are plenty of motels around."

"But Mom, you ever think I might've wanted to get to know them? After all they *are* my grandparents and I never even knew they existed. Then after meeting them, they leave? What's going on? Why have they never bothered to come visit all these years? It's not like they're poor or at least they didn't look like it. And how come we never went to see them or even have their picture around? Why didn't Dad ever mention them?"

"Before you were born, your dad and his parents had a falling out and went their separate ways. This is the first time I've seen them since before we were married."

"So how'd they find out about what happened?"

"I called. It seemed the right thing to do."

Annie stood up and rubbed her lower back. She glanced around the yard. Between the flowers and the fruit trees, it was a riot of color. It was obvious the yard needed serious attention or it would look as neglected as the house. This had always been a nice neighborhood, filled with people who took care of their property. It didn't seem right to just let the place go. She could pitch in and do some yard work, maybe even paint the house. It'd be one way to get her mind off things.

She turned back to where her mother sat. "What did they fight about?"

Lisa's body drooped. "Do we really need to go into all that?"

Annie hadn't meant to upset her mother, but she wanted answers and knew if she let it go, that would be the end of it. The door was open a crack and she wasn't about to let it slam shut.

"Mom, I have a right to know."

Lisa hesitated, as if to respond, then pushed her chair back, and went inside.

Taken unawares by her mother's abrupt departure, Annie was at first puzzled then angry. She was no longer a child. Whatever happened before she was born was ancient history, that much was true. But she'd been led to believe she had no living relatives. Her parents hadn't actually said so but by withholding information, they'd let her draw her own conclusions. At this point she didn't much care what the truth was. Maybe her grandparents were bank robbers—or terrorists. It didn't really matter, but the more the truth was hidden from her, the more determined she was to ferret it out. She got up, knocking over a chair in the process.

She found her mother in the living room holding a small pottery bowl. When she was little, Annie had disobeyed her and took it from the shelf for a closer look. The fragile bowl slipped from her tiny hands and smashed on the kitchen floor. She never forgot her mother's stricken look at the sight of the ruined dish. Expecting a severe punishment, what Annie got instead was worse. Pursing her lips, Lisa stooped down and gathered the pieces of the shattered bowl. Then retrieving her glue and tweezers, she spent the next hour meticulously putting it back together. She never said a word about the matter. For Annie that hurt more than any scolding she could have received. Now Lisa sat alone tracing and retracing the almost invisible cracks with her finger.

Annie tried to dial back her anger. "Mom," she said. "Why can't we talk about it? Or don't you love Dad? Is that it? You just want to forget all about him and whatever happened?"

Lisa carefully replaced the pottery on the shelf where it had reposed for years. Then, her face contorted in anger, she drew back her hand and smacked Annie across the face.

"How dare you!" she said. "I gave up my life—my people—for that man. Who are you to suggest such a thing?"

Rubbing her cheek, Annie ran from the room. She knew she deserved that slap. What had possessed her to say such a thing? It wasn't as though the thought hadn't crossed her mind, it had—more than once as she watched her parents drift apart while the bond between her and her father grew stronger. But she never meant to actually say those words. They'd just popped out and at what cost? Would her mother ever forgive her? Would things ever be the same again?

It was true she was closer to her dad than her mother. Now that she thought about it, it had been that way for as long as she could remember. Did her mom feel left out? If that was the case, she'd never let on; just acted like their endless forays on Lake Okeechobee was fine with her. That she didn't notice them giggling over something she "wouldn't understand."

Suddenly Annie became aware of the chasm that existed between her mother and them. Only now did she realize the pain she must have endured all those years. And she never complained, not once, not a single time. Acted happy her husband and her only child got on so well: How lucky she was that her man was there for the family, as she put it, in this day and age when so many shirked their responsibilities. Annie, who was herself contemplating marriage, was horrified. What had she done?

Oh my God, what have I done?

Chapter 5

As Lisa stared out the window, she scarcely glanced at the palm trees swaying in the wind or the snowy egret that had been hanging around the yard. She thought instead about the day she first met Craig, more than twenty years ago.

She'd been crabby that morning. Her boss, Rosa Menendez, had called before seven asking her to fill in for Larry who called in sick. Yeah right, sick, more like hungover. That meant instead of an easy day at the Cultural Center, Lisa would have to take a group of stuck-up college students on tour. To make matters worse, she'd been out late the night before, celebrating with friends. Celebrating what? Who knew? Just being away from the Pueblo and their parents was cause enough for celebration.

At nineteen, Lisa was more than ready to be on her own. Working in close proximity with tribal elders who watched her every move, wasn't conducive to independence.

She didn't look forward to ferrying college students around all day, answering ignorant questions about Native Americans. It wouldn't be that bad if they weren't so condescending. In her opinion, all they had going for them was being white and part of a family who could send them to college. Then, of course, they'd get the good jobs. They didn't have the deck stacked against them from the get-go. What did she have to look forward to? Waiting on gringos at the Center while they bought souvenirs of a day spent with real "Injuns." Then, eventually she'd marry Tomas and have babies. That was it. She felt suffocated.

"Lisa, your group just pulled in," Rosa called out. "Better get moving."

She groaned and went outside to the bus. Greeting the driver, she picked up the microphone, and said, "Good morning." She pasted a smile across her face, trying to project pleasure she didn't feel. "Welcome to Acoma. Before we go to Sky City, I thought you'd like to hear a little about my people and our history."

"I'd like to know a lot more about you," a male from the back of the bus called out. The group exploded in laughter.

Lisa was thrown off balance. She glanced down the aisle. There were about thirty students. Many wore expensive fashions from labels she admired but could never afford, such as Liz Claiborne and Ralph Lauren. The girls with their ultra-teased hair and beauty moles laughed and whispered to each other. Several boys sported long curly hair and Crocodile Dundee hats.

Must be nice.

As the bus exited the parking lot, she adjusted the pages of her script, cleared her throat and began again.

"Acoma Pueblo is the oldest continuously inhabited community in North America. A federally recognized Indian tribe, Acoma covers four hundred and thirty-one thousand, six hundred and sixty-four acres and is home to four thousand eight hundred tribal members. In 1629, construction began on the massive San Esteban del Rey Mission, which we'll visit today."

"Why is the tribe called a 'pueblo?' Doesn't that refer to a building?" one student called out.

Lisa was glad that at least one person in the group was listening and interested enough to ask a question. She smiled at the young woman.

"The word 'pueblo' is used to describe Native American communities who live in the Southwest. The first Spanish explorers used the term to describe structures made from stone, adobe mud, and other material. They were usually multistoried, surrounded by an open plaza and occupied by hundreds of thousands of Native Americans. But the term also refers to members of a tribe. I can see how it might be confusing." She paused to see if the girl had another question—hearing none, she said, "Anyone else?" She looked around and then resumed her narrative.

"Today, Acoma Pueblo comprises several villages including Acomita Lake, McCartys, Anzac and the newer subdivision of Sky Line. Sky City, which is our first stop, is built on top of a three hundred and sixty-seven-foot sandstone bluff in a valley studded with huge rocks. It's been continuously occupied since around 1150 A.D." She gave an inaudible sigh. It was going to be a very long day.

The bus stopped to let a cow meander across the road. For a moment she just stood there, staring at the bus and chewing her cud. Then as if bored, she continued on her way.

Lisa resumed her narrative and tried to ignore the couple necking several rows back. To say they were a distraction would be to put it mildly. "Some people believe the name 'Acoma' comes from the Keresan words for 'People of the White Rock.' While others think it means 'to prepare,' reflecting the tribe's defensive posture against raiders. The mesa's sheer drops make access difficult.

"In the late 1500s, invading Spaniards attacked Native Americans in what is New Mexico today. During one battle, they fired small cannons into the village. Attack dogs, believed to be fed on human flesh and trained to eat humans alive, also were used."

To Lisa's surprise the group's laughing and murmuring dialed back as she described in gruesome detail what happened. "Acoma lost the battle, and the Pueblo's population of approximately two thousand, was reduced to around two hundred and fifty. Surviving children were taken from their parents and handed over to Spanish missionaries. Most of them, along with other survivors, were sold into slavery."

Lisa paused and glanced up at her audience. She could tell by their somber expressions the brutality of what took place touched them. She let a sad smile play across her face and then continued.

"Today members of the Pueblo trace their ancestry back to the inhabitants of the twelfth century ruins and carry on many of their traditions. For hundreds of years, my people have traded with neighboring tribes, including the Aztecs and Mayans. Traditional alliances between the various pueblos continue to exist today. In 2006, Acoma was named a National Trust Historic Site."

As the bus approached Sky City Lisa cleared her throat and said, "Welcome to Sky City. If you wish to take photographs, you need to buy a permit at the visitors' center. Please note that videotaping and sketching are strictly prohibited. Enjoy your visit."

She added, "We'll meet back here in two hours,"

Lisa stood aside to let the students off. She was exiting the bus when the heel of her shoe caught on the bottom step and she pitched forward. Just then someone reached out and broke her fall. That someone was Craig Whitaker.

At six feet tall with a full head of thick brown hair, Craig had a square jaw and athletic build. Thrown literally into his arms, Lisa was immediately taken by his dimples, cornflower-blue eyes and infectious laugh.

For the balance of the day, whenever she glanced around he was next to her: at the visitors' center, Sky City, the mission church, even when they stopped for lunch. By the end of the day, she realized this gringo had captured her heart.

When they exited the bus for the final time, he asked for her phone number. Lisa didn't really think the handsome white boy would call, but to her astonishment the very next night he did exactly that.

It started innocently enough: There were phone calls followed by lunch dates since he was "going to be nearby visiting friends." Next came invitations to dinner and the movies. An embrace. A lingering kiss. And then, so much more.

Each time he came around, Lisa's feelings for him deepened. To her surprise, her parents didn't object. Perhaps they thought this college boy from Boston would provide their daughter with a brighter future than the tribe could offer. They even grew to like him, that is, until the day they learned what his father did for a living. That's when the trouble started.

Lisa sighed, her eyes misted over at thoughts of her family and ancestral home. She recalled how each evening at sunset vivid gold, red and purple splashed across the sky making the Pueblo's adobe structures glow.

Then there was her family: her dad, Larry Sanchez; her mom, Marie and her younger sisters, Vera and Claire. They lived in a small house in Acomita Lake. By now Vera and Claire had most likely moved out and were married with families of their own. Did they ever think about her? It had been over twenty years now, and her dad's words still echoed in her mind, *You marry that boy and you're no longer part of this family, you hear me? You'll be dead to us so don't bother coming back.*

Native Americans have a profound love and respect for nature. There was no way they could accept a man whose father made a living poisoning the environment. If it had just been his father who was involved with the chemical industry, they might have felt differently. After all, a child has no power over how his parents earn their money. But it wasn't only Mr. Whitaker who made his living by defiling nature. His son, the man Lisa loved more than life, was being groomed to follow in his dad's footsteps.

The devastated look on her mother's face as Lisa walked out the door still haunted her. She'd tried to make them understand how much she loved Craig, but it was to no avail. Her father's mind was made up; there would be no changing it.

Craig and Lisa headed across the country to Boston to meet his parents. They were so full of love for each other and anticipation of their life together; it never occurred to them the elder Whitakers wouldn't share their joy.

Lisa took a deep breath as she remembered the terrible scene. They had driven up to a magnificent brick house on Boston's north side. She'd never been inside such a place. Before they had a chance to ring the bell, the door flew open and Craig's mother, father and older sister, Tammy, greeted them with squeals and hugs. More precisely that's how they greeted Craig.

When he drew back and introduced Lisa, their reaction became frosty and formal, especially when Craig said they were engaged. It was as though someone had turned off the sound. Their attempts at civility were muted, their expressions pained. Finally, Craig's mother said, "Well. My goodness. You must be starving. Why don't we have something to eat?"

Lisa shuddered recalling that awful luncheon. First there was the effort at small talk all around. How was their trip? Anything interesting happening in Albuquerque? When was school out? On and on. She was the elephant in the room around which everyone tiptoed. Finally, with a pinched look, Tammy asked Lisa where she lived and about her family. As Lisa eagerly rattled off the information, Craig's sister nodded, trying to act like she gave a damn. It finally dawned on Lisa that the woman wasn't at all interested in what she had to say; she was simply waiting for her to finish speaking.

When the meal mercifully came to an end, Mrs. Whitaker turned to Lisa and asked where she planned to spend the night. Then she suggested a motel over by the expressway. Those words were seared into Lisa's memory. She remembered thinking at the time that despite the tiny house she'd grown up in, visitors were never turned away. Her family always found room, no matter what. And these wealthy people with their enormous house couldn't find it in their hearts to allow one Indian girl to spend a night under their splendid roof?

As the meaning of his mother's words sank in, Craig stood and asked Lisa to wait in the living room while he spoke to his parents. Fifteen minutes later, his face flushed with emotion, he said, "Let's get out of this fucking place."

Lisa dabbed a tear from her cheek recalling what Craig explained to her as they left town. When he'd told his parents he met someone and would be bringing her home, he'd neglected to reveal that she was a Native American. He loved Lisa and assumed they would too. Looking back on it, Lisa realized that was a big mistake. They should have known better.

The Whitakers were wealthy members of Boston's high society. They expected their children to make them proud. Then Craig brought home a nobody, and not just a nobody—a Native American of all things. He assumed they'd welcome her into the family. Well it wasn't going to happen. After all, how would they explain to their friends that their daughter-in-law was an uneducated Indian? How would that look? She'd never be accepted.

No, his father told Craig, he had to marry someone more like them: wealthy was what he meant, although he hadn't come right out and said it. If he wanted to keep Lisa on the side, that was his business, but he was not bringing that girl into their family and that was all there was to it.

Craig told Lisa not to worry. Their parents would come around eventually. "Just you wait and see," he'd reassured her with a hug. Twenty years later they hadn't "come around" and now her darling Craig was dead.

Lisa was startled from her reverie by the scrape of a shoe on the hardwood floor. She turned to see Annie in the doorway, tears streaming down her face.

"Mom, I'm so sorry," she said. "It was a stupid thing to say. Please forgive me. I know you loved Dad as much—no more—than I did."

Lisa opened her arms and her heart, hugging Annie in a tight embrace. "We both loved him," she said and let it go at that.

Chapter 6

Annie was at loose ends. There was only so much painting and yard work a body could do. Nathan had just left after spending the week in Moore Haven with her and had to get back to Tampa.

She hid her feelings until he drove away, then broke down and sobbed. It was all so hard. This summer was supposed to be wonderful: Getting engaged to the man she was crazy about; going to work with her dad. Then poof, it all disappeared and she was left with nothing. Had she known her father was going to die, she would have taken a job in Tampa to be near her fiancé. She grinned wryly. How stupid. Had she known her dad was about to die, she would've moved heaven and earth to prevent him from getting in that boat in the first place. Then he'd be alive and they'd be on Lake Okeechobee right now.

She knew her mother needed her, but she was so bored. It would be a very long summer. Annie headed into the house for some lemonade. It was a sweltering hundred and five degrees according to the outdoor thermometer. That was hot even for Florida. Although she wasn't crazy about air conditioning, Annie welcomed the cool air that slapped her face as she went inside.

"Annie," her mother called out. "Someone from Dad's job called. They want to know if you're still interested in that internship. I told them you'd call back. The number's by the phone."

Surprised at the unexpected message, Annie didn't know whether to take the job or not. On the one hand, her reason for staying in Moore Haven had been to support her mom. And on the other, the internship was why she'd come home to begin with. She didn't know what to do.

"Mom, what should I tell them?"

"It's up to you, dear. Do you want to spend the summer working over there?"

As usual, Annie's mother asked the right question. Did she really want to spend the next three months working on the lake?

"I'm not sure." Annie hesitated. "Don't you need me here?"

"Honey, I love having you around and appreciate all the work you've done. But you'll be here if I need you. Still if you prefer pulling weeds and scraping paint, I won't object." When Annie didn't say anything, she laughed. "I'm teasing. Look, it's time you get back to doing what you came home for in the first place. We both know that's what Dad would want."

With that last comment, her mom had her. She was right. Dad wouldn't want her moping around in a place where pig hunting was the highlight of the week. She reached for the phone.

* * * *

The first day on any job is difficult, but for Annie it was especially so. Echoes of her father and their time together were everywhere. Several times she had to stop, swallow hard, blink back tears and promise herself things would get better.

She quickly learned there was more to being a waterkeeper than riding around in a boat checking for pollution. There were organizing and fundraising aspects of which Annie hadn't been aware. Attending community meetings to attract volunteers was time-consuming. Plus there were efforts to get violators into compliance with the law, first by persuasion and when that didn't work, by hauling them into court. Annie's respect for her father grew along with her understanding of the work.

When her dad had expressed concern for the condition of the nation's drinking water, she thought he exaggerated. That changed the day he took her down the Caloosahatchee and pointed out a pipe protruding from the ground spewing waste into the river. From then on, Annie made no secret of the fact she wanted to follow in her father's footsteps. Her subsequent decision to major in environmental science surprised virtually no one.

It had been nearly a week since she started her internship, and Annie sat in the office reading a book on Lake Okeechobee, one of the largest freshwater lakes in the country. Seminole Indians, who populated the area, had come up with the name which means "big water."

She remembered learning in a middle-school history class that back in the nineteen-twenties, a hurricane blew through south Florida creating a storm surge in the lake. The surrounding area was flooded killing nearly three thousand. Annie was familiar with the tragedy as some victims were from Moore Haven and she'd gone to school with their relatives. Every Memorial Day she went with her mom and dad to the Port Mayaca Memorial Gardens north of Pahokee to honor the approximately sixteen hundred storm victims buried there.

To prevent a recurrence of the disaster, the Army Corps of Engineers built a system of locks connecting the Caloosahatchee on the Gulf with the St. Lucie River on the Atlantic side. Annie and her dad had often passed through the Moore Haven Lock on their way to the Caloosahatchee from Lake O., as she was fond of calling it. The Corp subsequently built an earthen levee, the Herbert Hoover Dike, completely surrounding the lake for additional protection.

"What're you reading?" Philip Buckley, the acting waterkeeper, came in the room.

Annie jumped at the interruption. "You startled me," she said.

"Sorry about that." He glanced over her shoulder at the book cover. "*Lake Okeechobee, Wellspring of the Everglades*. That book's ancient." Philip was Italian in that dark, handsome kind of way that made girls swoon when he flashed his dazzling smile or gave them a look with his jet-black eyes. His thick wavy hair and well-developed pecs didn't hurt either.

Embarrassed to be caught reading when she was supposed to be on the phone soliciting donations, Annie set the book aside. "I know it's old, but the history of the lake is fascinating."

"If you say so. Look, I'm heading out to take samples. Want to come along and see how it's done?"

"Sure," she said, trying to hide her eagerness to get out of making any more calls.

As they made their way around the lake, Philip suddenly pointed as a stingray jumped from the water not far from the boat. "You have to be careful. Hitting one of those babies can put you in a world of hurt."

Annie knew stingrays can weigh as much as five hundred pounds. Not long ago a Florida woman died after colliding with one. Is that what happened to her dad? It didn't seem likely. Besides he was an excellent swimmer. In the past few weeks she'd begun to wonder if his death really had been an accident. But if it wasn't, then what happened? Who'd want a man like her father dead?

"Philip," she said hesitantly. Did she really want to open this can of worms? "Did you know my dad?" If he did, he hadn't broached the topic in the few days she'd been there. Maybe, like most everyone else, he didn't want to cause her pain.

"Know him? Of course I knew him. We worked together for several years. He was a great guy, your father." He leaned over the side with an empty vial and scooped up some water. "See, slap on a label with the date, location and your name; that's all there is to it." He gave her a look. "Just be careful." He hesitated. "Well, you know."

Yes, she knew. He didn't have to say it. She didn't want to meet the same fate as her father had either.

"So, what have you learned about the lake's water quality since you've been with us?" He leaned back and steered the boat with one hand.

Annie couldn't help but notice how handsome Philip looked in the early afternoon sun. She realized he was off-limits. She was engaged and not only that, he was ten years older than she. Besides even if she was available, getting involved with her supervisor was a bad idea. He looked at her, awaiting an answer.

"The farms and ranches around here have polluted Lake O. for years with fertilizers and animal waste, clouding the water, causing algae blooms and decreasing the oxygen level fish need to stay alive."

"Excellent," Philip said. "I see you've done your homework. I don't know if anyone told you, but according to the EPA, phosphorus levels in the lake doubled over the past decade. Did you know there's a three hundred square mile 'muck zone' on the bottom of the lake containing one hundred tons of phosphorus? To make matters worse, there's no clean-up plan."

Annie was speechless. She knew the lake had problems but had no idea it was this bad.

Oblivious to her horrified look, he continued, "A series of federal court decisions have taken the EPA to task for failing to enforce the Clean Water Act in Florida.

"Whenever lake water's diverted to the Caloosahatchee and St. Lucie, it devastates local fishing and tourism. So, you can see how important our work is." He flashed her that dazzling smile. "Okay, I'll get off my soapbox. That's enough for today."

"How did you get involved in all this?" Annie said. "It's not like you'll get rich. My dad certainly didn't."

"Boy have you ever got that right. I became interested in water purity when I heard Bobby Kennedy, Jr. speak. He started the Waterkeeper Alliance out East thirty years ago. Like his father, he's someone you can't simply dismiss. I started looking into it and decided to get involved. That's when I met your dad. He was struggling to start an organization here so we worked on it together and eventually got it up and running."

When they reached the pier, Philip cajoled her, "Time to make some more phone calls. I know how much you love doing that."

When Annie winced, he added, "I hate it too, but without donors, we'd be toast. They're the lifeblood of any grassroots organization."

Back at the office Annie adjusted her chair, picked up the list and dialed a number. When someone answered, she began to read from a prepared script trying to sound natural: "Hello. Mrs. Donahue? My name is Annie Whitaker. I'm calling on behalf of the Okeechobee Waterkeeper. We're part of the national Waterkeeper Alliance which provides a way for communities to stand up for their right to clean water …"

As she continued, it was an effort to hide the boredom she felt at repeating the same information over and over: "The vision of the Waterkeeper movement is for fishable, swimmable and drinkable waterways worldwide. Our belief is that the best way to achieve this is through grassroots advocacy …

"From the Great Lakes to the Gulf of Mexico, the Amazon to the Ganges, the Waterkeeper Alliance has become a powerful voice for the world's waters." In her head Annie could almost hear background music reach a crescendo as she concluded, "Would you like to get involved by making a cash donation or by doing some volunteer work with us?"

She braced herself for the inevitable question: "Say, are you related to the man who drowned a few weeks ago?"

When she responded in the affirmative, condolences were usually expressed, after which a cash donation was the frequent result. Sometimes she felt used. Philip knew what he was doing when he'd asked her to make those calls. At first she was angry, but after thinking about it, she realized how desperately the organization needed money. Besides it wasn't his fault if people recognized her name. The window of opportunity was open and he was taking full advantage of it. Annie bit her lip, dialed back her emotions and punched in the next number.

Chapter 7

A few days later, Annie was hard at work in the office when the door opened and a rough-looking man walked in. Balding and overweight, with an ample gut that spilled over his belt, he had a salt and pepper beard and an angry expression.

Before she could give him a proper greeting, he said, “This where I can find that waterkeeper feller?”

“You mean Mr. Buckley?” The man looked like he meant business. He scared her.

“If that’s his name. So where’s he at? I need to talk to him pronto.”

Annie looked at the clock. “Sir, he’s not in at the moment. If you leave your name and number, I’ll see that he gets it.” She picked up a pen and message pad.

After scanning the office again as if to confirm that he wasn’t hiding under a desk or behind a door, he said, “Listen Missy, you tell him T. J. Conroy wants to speak to him ASAP, and underline the ASAP, you hear?” He raised his voice and sped up the pace of his speech toward the end of the sentence. Then he provided his cellphone number.

"I'll see he gets this as soon as he comes back," Annie assured him, making an effort to keep the tremors out of her voice.

"Make sure you do. You tell him I expect to hear from him the minute he gets in, got that?"

"Yes, Mr. Conroy, yes I do. I'll be sure and tell him. Thank you for dropping by." She pasted a smile on her face and breathed a sigh of relief as he left the building.

Two hours later, Philip walked in with a bag containing hamburgers, fries and soft drinks. "Thought you might be hungry," he said.

"You thought right," Annie said. It was past one and she'd only had a piece of toast and some coffee for breakfast. Her stomach let her know more than once that it was time for a refill.

As she dug in, she remembered her hostile visitor. "By the way, a T. J. Conroy was here looking for you. He asked me to have you call the minute you return."

Philip gave her a look between bites.

"I think it can wait till after lunch," she said.

"I think so too."

"He looked upset. Who is he?"

"Only one of the biggest polluters around here. He has a big farm over on the Caloosahatchee and lets his animal waste drain directly into the river. When your dad was alive, we went over there several times to ask him to put in a system to prevent that. At first he ignored us and then offered a bribe. When that didn't work, he set his rottweilers on us. Your dad got a nasty bite on his leg from that. You were probably away at school at the time.

"Anyway, we've been fighting him ever since. About two weeks ago, I decided to take him to court; that's probably what has him so riled up."

"Does that sort of thing happen very often?" Annie dipped a french fry in catsup and took a bite.

"Often enough," Philip said.

"Is Conroy dangerous?"

"Anytime you mess with someone's livelihood, cost them a bunch of money or take them to court, you'd best be careful, especially if the person has a temper." He wiped a dab of catsup off the table.

Annie started to take a sip from her soft drink, then set it down. "Do you think he had something to do with my dad's death?" There, she'd put into words what she'd been thinking. Her father's death hadn't been an accident, Annie knew it, could feel it in her bones.

Finished with his burger, Philip balled the wrapper and tossed it in the wastebasket. "What do you mean? You think Conroy murdered your father? Do you have any proof?" His expression had gone from casual to deadly serious. "Annie, if you think the guy's angry now, spread word he murdered your dad and I can't imagine what he'll do."

Chagrined, Annie nodded. "You're right. It's just that no matter how hard I try, I can't help but think Dad's death was no accident."

Philip stood up. "Let me give you a word of advice: If you have evidence someone murdered your father, report it to the police. Till then keep your opinion to yourself. If you go around insinuating this person or that one's responsible for your father's death simply because they're angry at us, we're going to have an awful lot of suspects—and problems."

Annie was embarrassed by Philip's unexpected scolding. "I wasn't planning to go around accusing people of murdering Dad, but his death—that so-called accident—just doesn't make sense to me."

She had Philip's complete attention. It was unnerving how those dark eyes could drill right through her.

"You knew him. Does it make sense to you?"

Philip shrugged. "I don't know, Annie, but accidents do happen. I'm sorry you're still in so much pain over it, but from now on you need to be careful what you say, okay?"

Annie nodded and watched as Philip headed back to his office. Did he really think she was that stupid? She'd only let her guard down and confided in him because, well, why had she made such an outrageous statement? They'd been talking about Conroy and how angry he was. That's when she'd made the leap and wondered aloud if he could have been involved in her father's unfortunate "accident."

She went back to the computer to finish what she'd been working on. She didn't feel like talking right now, not to Philip and certainly not to anyone on that endless list of potential donors. No, she'd finish what she was doing, lick her wounds and call it a day.

Chapter 8

That night after supper, Annie was in her room reading. The window was open and a sudden breeze made the curtains dance. It felt good after the heat of the day, but the cool air on her sunburned arms gave her a chill. She went to the closet to find the "Go Gators" throw Nate had given her last Christmas. She'd stuck it on the top shelf along with some things she brought home at spring break. She remembered thinking at the time she had only so much room in her car and wanted to bring back as much as possible before the end of the year.

She and Nate planned to move in together when school started in the fall. They'd signed a lease on a place but couldn't get in until September, so they put what furniture they had in storage and took the small stuff home. Annie's room, with its unpacked boxes and overflowing closet, looked more like a warehouse than the attractive surroundings to which she was accustomed. She knew it was only temporary, but still the mess grated on her.

As she dug through the closet in search of the blanket, her elbow bumped a box scattering its contents on the floor. Puzzled, her first thought was that Nate must have tried to surprise her by tucking something in with her belongings. He was always doing cute little things like that, something Annie found charming. But a closer look told her this wasn't love tokens from her fiancé, unless he was rich. It was cash. Lots of it. For a few seconds she just stared at the bills as though they were something foreign.

Then she realized her mom must have done it. She'd always been distrustful of financial institutions, but this was plain silly. What if someone broke in and found it? She'd lose everything. As Annie stooped to collect the bills, she decided to speak to her mother about it as soon as she got home.

Two hours later, Lisa unlocked the front door to find her daughter sprawled across the sofa watching television.

"Hey Mom," Annie said. "Have a good time?"

"We really did, thanks. Ginny was right to insist. It's hard to adjust to going out without your father but it's something I'll just have to get used to doing."

"I'm available too, in case you need someone."

"I know sweetheart. It's kind of you to offer, but I'm going to have to get used to being on my own. Besides you're heading back to school in a few months so I might as well face it." She started to head down the hall to her room when Annie called after her, "Oh, Mom, by the way do you have a minute? There's something I need to talk to you about."

Lisa stopped and turned around. The look on her face said, *"What now? Will bad news never stop coming?"*

"Mom, you don't have to look so scared. It's just that I found the money you hid in my room. You need to put it in a bank so it won't get lost or stolen."

"What money? I didn't hide anything in your room."

"You don't have to be embarrassed. I know you don't like putting your money in banks. But, really Mom, stashing that much cash in my closet wasn't very smart."

When Lisa just stared at Annie, a dumbfounded look plastered across her face, the younger woman went to her room and came back with the box of cash. "See. It's all here. If you want to count it, be my guest."

Lisa looked from her daughter to the money and back. "Annie, what have you done? Where did you get that?"

"I told you it was in my closet."

"Look honey, it's true now that your father's gone, things will be tight around here until I can find a job. But that's no reason for you to do whatever it was you did to get your hands on that kind of money. Nate gave it to you, didn't he? Tell him I appreciate the thought, but we'll be just fine. Give it back to him, you hear?"

"Mom, Mom, stop. I'm telling the truth. That money was in my closet." Both women looked from the box overflowing with bills to each other and back again. Where on earth had it come from?

Annie's room and its contents were as familiar as her own name. This box couldn't have been more alien. If neither her mother nor she hid the money that left two possibilities: Either someone broke in while she was at school and stashed the box in her closet, or her father did it.

Worry lines creased Annie's forehead. She seriously doubted anyone would break in and hide money in her room. Besides no one she knew could spare that kind of cash. That left her father. Would he do something like that? Annie was afraid she knew the answer and it wasn't good. She recalled Philip's earlier comment about T.J. Conroy: *At first he ignored us and then offered a bribe.*

A sudden possibility crashed down on her like a blow to the back of the head. She felt faint with the realization that her beloved father—the man whose memory everyone cherished, the one person she most wanted to imitate—had taken bribes from the very people he was supposed to be fighting.

Lisa, who continued to puzzle over the matter, said, "What is it? Did you figure it out?"

"I'm not sure." Still stung by Philip's reprimand, Annie didn't want to accuse her dead father of accepting bribes or worse. Before destroying her father's good name, she at least had to have proof. A box filled with cash might be considered proof, but of what she didn't know.

Perhaps like her mother, he didn't trust banks and preferred to stash his money in the back of her closet. But where did he get it in the first place? There again, maybe there was a logical explanation. Perhaps it was donations for the Okeechobee Waterkeeper. Maybe he hid it in her closet for safekeeping until he was able to deposit it in the organization's bank account and died before he had a chance to take care of it. That must be it. Her dad wasn't a crook. As usual, she'd leapt to conclusions, the kind Philip warned her about. She really had to stop doing that before someone got hurt.

"So, Mom, what should we do with it?"

For a moment they stared at the box as if it were a malignant presence that needed to be purged from their lives. Then rolling her eyes to the ceiling, as if in search of an answer, Lisa replaced the lid and slid the box across the table. "Why don't we just put it back where you found it for the time being? Perhaps in a few days we'll figure it out."

As if relieved a decision had been made, they decided to go out to eat and maybe even stop by the Seminole Casino in Brighton. It wasn't that far and it would be a fun distraction. They didn't gamble very often, so what was the harm, especially if they put a limit on how much they spent—and stuck to it.

Chapter 9

"So, Mom, I met Dad's parents—er, my paternal grandparents, but you haven't told me much about yours. All I know is they're from New Mexico. Did you live in Albuquerque? That where you met Dad?"

Annie sat at the kitchen table, lingering over a late breakfast. It was Sunday morning and she had the whole day to herself. Why she chose this particular moment to quiz her mother about the facts of her birth, she didn't know for sure. It was just something that had been in the back of her mind since the funeral.

At first Lisa seemed to hesitate as if searching for an answer to her daughter's question, then she said, "No, dear. We didn't live in Albuquerque. We lived in Acomita Lake, about an hour from there."

"Acomita Lake? Never heard of it."

Still appearing to struggle for the right words, Lisa said, "It's not likely you would have. It's a small town." She sighed and took a deep breath. "It's part of the Acoma Pueblo." When Annie didn't react, she added, "That's an Indian reservation. Honey, I'm Native American. The

Acoma are my people. I met your father when he was with a group of college students visiting Sky City. It's a national tourist attraction."

She stopped talking and waited, as though fearing her only child's reaction upon learning she was half Indian.

"I always kinda wondered about that. I mean, we—you especially, but me too—have features that kinda remind me of Native Americans or at least some kind of nonwhite ethnic group."

Lisa looked surprised. "You wondered about it? Really? For how long?"

"As long as I can remember," Annie's eyes seemed to glaze over, as if going down some sort of memory lane that was none too pleasant.

"And yet you never said anything." It was more an observation than a question.

"I guess I thought the subject was off-limits. I mean, you never talked about your parents or siblings, never said a thing about growing up. I got the message. Personally, I thought you and Dad were in a witness protection program and didn't want anyone—including me—to know."

Lisa laughed. "Honey, we weren't in the witness protection program."

Annie put her coffee cup down. "So I'm part Indian." Then she said something that brought tears to Lisa's eyes. "How cool is that. Wait till Nate finds out. He'll be so impressed."

The balance of the conversation flowed as naturally as the bed of a creek through a forest.

"Why haven't your parents come to see us all this time? Are they poor? Why didn't we ever visit them or at least phone or write?" As the torrent of questions slowed to a trickle, the answers began to dawn on Annie. "They didn't approve of your marrying Dad any more than his parents approved of his marrying you. That's it, isn't it?"

Lisa, who had stood up to clear the table, leaned over and gave her daughter a hug. "Yes, that's exactly what happened." Then the smile on her face faded and she began to blink back tears.

"What is it, Mom?"

Lisa dabbed her face with a paper towel as tears made their way down her cheeks. "It's okay, honey; you had every right to know."

Now Annie understood why her mom had treasured that Indian pottery on the shelf in the kitchen all these years and why she was so upset when Annie broke one of them. And that book, *Somewhere Out There.* She remembered asking her mother why she loved reading it so much. Lisa had told her the author, Simon Ortiz, was from New Mexico and that her dad gave it to her when Annie was a baby. She hadn't told her that Ortiz was an Acoma Indian. It would have been the perfect time to impart that bit of information, but the opportunity slipped through her fingers and it hadn't come up again—until now.

Chapter 10

To say Harold Johnson was angry would be an understatement. Enraged and possessed of a simmering hatred would be more accurate. For the better part of his life, he'd lived with an intimate knowledge of the devastation the widespread spraying of pesticides can wreak. He'd seen it firsthand.

As a child, he lived with his parents and baby brother, Bobby, on a Michigan farm that had been in his family over a hundred years. They raised cattle, fruit and vegetables. All told, it was a wonderful life, at least for a five-year-old not tasked with the endless chores running a farm entailed. His memories before the spraying were of playing with the dog, feeding the chickens and watching the sun set and the stars come out with his parents at the end of the day.

Their idyllic existence came to a gradual but no less tragic end the day the crop duster flew over and sprayed deadly chemicals onto their property.

Harold was in kindergarten that day, learning his A-B-Cs and making a picture in art class, licking more paste off his fingers than he managed to get on the paper. Little did he realize the effect events taking place in the air over his home would have on the balance of his life.

While nothing seemed out of the ordinary, it didn't take long before strange things began to take place: The cows, horses, rabbits, pigs and chickens took sick and died despite Mr. Johnson's and the veterinarian's desperate attempts to save them. The vet said he didn't know why they died. Maybe it was something in the water or a virus of some kind. He said the state would have to run tests to find the cause and, in the meantime, the Johnsons should boil their water, to be on the safe side.

Next, the crops started to shrivel up. The fruit turned brown and fell from the trees. Harold remembered hearing his mother and father argue. His dad had shouted the name "Whitaker" over and over. "That damned Whitaker Company, that's who done it. They're gonna pay if it's the last thing I ever do," he said, waving a clenched fist over his head.

He was unused to hearing his parents fight, and his father's angry voice frightened young Harold. It left him feeling unsettled, as if the house might fall on top of him as he slept.

It wasn't long before Harold heard them argue about not having enough money to pay the bills. He wondered if it was somehow his fault, that maybe he ate too much or wore out his shoes too fast. Or perhaps it was the baby who was at fault. After all, before Bobby came along, everything was just fine.

When he was sure his mother wasn't looking, he bent into the playpen and gave the baby a good pinch. Bobby immediately set up a yowl that brought his mother running. It was hard to keep a straight face when she asked what happened. The baby was just fine one minute, he told her, and bawling his head off the next. Who understood babies anyhow?

One day not long after the pinching episode, a man showed up with some kind of papers. At the time, Harold didn't know what they were, only that, judging by the sour expressions on his parents' faces, it wasn't good. He learned later they were being kicked out of their house. Apparently if you don't pay, banks can do that.

"Well, Mr. Craig Whitaker, all your money, planes and fancy-ass friends didn't save your son, did it? Who's crying now?"

Harold went into the kitchen where Bobby was trying to guide a spoon into his mouth. The tremors made even the simplest task next to impossible. Who would have thought that at age fifty-seven he'd still be taking care of him? Harold sat down, took the spoon and dipped it in the bowl of soup. The younger man opened his mouth and waited.

Chapter 11

It was one of those days where you couldn't get much accomplished no matter how hard you tried. A hurricane had blown through over the weekend, knocking out electricity to Moore Haven and much of the surrounding area. Annie probably should have stayed home and slept late. In fact she'd been tempted to do exactly that, but then she remembered Philip had asked her to put together a press kit for a meeting being held at the end of the week, and some of the materials hadn't yet been written.

She was flattered Philip considered her sufficiently well informed on the issues that she could draft copy for a news release and position paper. "At some point, maybe you could draft my speeches as well," he'd told her. Philip's growing confidence in her was a welcome change from Nate's critical remarks that often eroded her self-esteem.

Rain drummed the gutters, distracting her as she tried to focus. The press release would announce Okeechobee Waterkeeper's lawsuit against the area's largest polluter.

Since the electricity was still out, she wrote by hand in the gloom. Despite good-sized windows, the overcast skies allowed for only limited illumination.

She sat there doodling, hoping those chicken scratches would spark a creative headline that would catch reporters' attention. New to writing press releases, Annie didn't quite know where to begin.

As she scribbled, to her chagrin she found herself writing Nathan's and Philip's names over and over. As soon as she realized what she was doing, she touched the small stone on her engagement ring as if in apology. Then ripping the sheet from the pad, she balled it up and tossed it toward the wastebasket, missing by a wide margin.

She'd just stooped to retrieve it and was getting up when the front door opened. Rushing wind and rain mixed with the tap of footsteps on the linoleum floor were accompanied by the voices of Philip and an unknown female.

"It's your own fault," Philip said. "I told you not to do it, now didn't I?"

"But it was your idea in the first place."

A trill of laughter rippled through the room. At that point, Philip stopped short. "Annie, you're here. I didn't expect to see you today," He shook his umbrella, sending water splashing across the floor. "What with the electricity out and all, I thought you'd stay home. My, my, such dedication, I'm impressed, I really am."

Annie forced a smile. "I considered staying home but remembered you needed those publicity materials," she said dryly.

For a second no one spoke as the two women took stock of each other. Then Philip said, "Oh, you haven't met Rebecca. She's going to be helping out around here. Becky, this is Annie. She's the intern I told you about."

For reasons Annie didn't understand, a dizzying array of emotions surged through her. They ranged from anger and hurt to disappointment, confusion and even jealousy. Rebecca, Becky. He probably calls her "the Beckster" when they're doing it.

"Annie, you okay?" Philip said—his face held an odd expression.

"What? I'm fine. Why?" Annie's cheeks warmed as blood rushed to her face.

"Becky asked how you like Gainesville. She graduated from there three years ago."

"Fine. I like it just fine." Her words were clipped; it was all she could think to say. Besides what did this woman with the skinny jeans, curly blond hair, green eyes, perky breasts and dimples care what she thought anyhow?

"Which sorority did you pledge?" Becky said.

Annie's mind drew a blank. Why didn't they leave her alone? It was obvious they were just making small talk to be polite.

"I, uh, I didn't join a sorority," she said and turned toward her desk. Maybe they'd take the hint.

Philip cleared his throat. "We should let Annie get back to work," he said. "Let me show you around." He touched Rebecca on the small of her back, nudging her in the direction of his office.

Annie picked up her pencil. Show the bitch around? Bet she'll show him around, if she isn't already doing it. Help? Really? Exactly who's she here to help? She drew jagged lines across the page till it was completely filled and the lead point worn down. Just then the lights came on. Enough of this nonsense, it was time to get something done.

Chapter 12

When Annie arrived at the office the following Monday, she found Becky sitting at the desk she herself had occupied since coming to work for the Waterkeepers. Aside from Philip's office, it was the only decent place to sit—and the only computer available to volunteers. For a few seconds, she stood there, her mouth agape.

Becky looked up, gave her a broad dimple-filled smile and said, "Hi Annie. Have a nice weekend?"

Anger that surged through Annie stopped her from saying anything except a mumbled, "Yes. You?"

If Becky noticed the rebuff, she didn't let it show. "I really did. Phil took me out on the lake to check on some reported pollution. Then we went through the locks and on to the Caloosahatchee."

Annie was still stuck on the image of Philip and Becky out on the lake. He'd never offered to spend time with her on the weekend. Becky was twittering away like a noisy bird. She finally seemed to notice Annie's lack of response because she added, "I'm sorry for going on like that. You've no doubt done it so many times, it's no big deal."

Annie nodded. "You're right. I've lived here my whole life. My dad and I used to..." An image of her on the lake enjoying a summer afternoon with her father flashed before her mind's eye. She swallowed and blinked, then turned away ostensibly to find a place to park her things.

"Oh, that's right. Phil told me what happened." Becky's face went from smiley and dimply to serious in the bat of a long mascara'd eyelash. "I am so, so very sorry for your loss."

The knot in Annie's throat precluded a response, so she simply nodded and sat down.

"Oh, by the way, Phil said he'd be late. He asked me to tell you to make some calls."

She crossed the room in her tight jean cut-offs, flip-flops and low-cut top and handed Annie the list. In less than five minutes, she'd managed to press every button that made Annie see red. She couldn't have done it more perfectly if she'd tried.

Both women were hard at work an hour later when Philip walked in. One look at his face told them that not only was something amiss, but that it was serious. In the brief time she'd known him, Annie had seen Philip express a variety of negative emotions from disappointment to anger bordering on rage, but she had never before seen this side of him. It made her want to run and hide.

"Hi Phil," Becky said.

Annie grabbed the phone and pretended to speak into it. Whatever was wrong, let Miss Perkyface deal with it.

Philip grunted a reply and growled, "Come into my office. Both of you."

Annie gave Becky a look that said, "Did we screw up?"

Becky shrugged. They followed Philip into his office. He waited until they were seated and then said, "Someone embezzled money from the Waterkeeper's bank account. I discovered ten thousand dollars missing last night as I was going over the books." He stopped talking and glanced from Becky to Annie and back. Then with a look on his face that would make an innocent person want to confess, he said, "Do either of you know anything about it?" Again he scrutinized them.

"No," Becky said.

Annie thought about the cash hidden in her closet. Had Dad been stealing from the organization and hiding it in her room? Surely not. There must be a logical explanation for what she'd found. Still, as much as she hated to even consider the possibility he'd done something like that, she had to admit it was the only logical explanation. She sighed. The sadness of his unexpected death was now compounded by her reluctant suspicion that her cherished father had engaged in something criminal. Annie was about to reveal her discovery when she remembered the agreement she'd made with her mother to say nothing about it.

Philip was looking at her, waiting for some kind of response.

"I don't know who took it either," she said and that was the truth. She didn't know who hid the money in her closet. What she did know was that she had to get it out of there.

"I didn't really think either of you had anything to do with it but I had to ask. Now the only thing left is to call the police."

Again he paused and looked from Becky to Annie and back. When neither one reacted, he said, "Well, I guess that's it then. You can get back to work."

Before they had a chance to get up, Philip added, "The thing is if I call the police the board will blame me. They'll say it's my fault for not keeping a handle on things. So girls, if you know anything—anything at all about this, speak up, I'm begging you."

Annie's heart was caught in a vise. On the one hand if she said anything her father's good name would be destroyed. Plus she'd be breaking the agreement she'd made with her mother. Who knew if the money in her closet was the missing money anyway? On the other hand it would be wrong to let Philip take the blame for something he didn't do. Feeling torn, her resolve began to crumble. As the two women rose to leave the office, Annie turned and said, "Philip, do you have a minute?"

Chapter 13

"So, Annie, what's on your mind?"

Philip still wore that serious expression that had put the fear of God into her earlier. It made Annie want to change her mind about saying anything. What would he think when she told him? Would he believe her? The whole thing was so bizarre.

She hesitated, unsure whether to go through with this or not. Would it get her and her mother in trouble? She'd not only be going back on her promise to her mom, but cast aspersions on her father's reputation. What was the right thing to do?

"Yes?" Philip said. "Is there something you want to tell me?"

Reluctantly Annie sat back down. "Yes, no, I mean I don't know."

Philip's stone face cracked with the hint of a smile. "Well, which is it?"

Annie's stomach suddenly cramped up. She felt nauseous. Clearing her throat and giving a little cough, she said, "I don't know if this has anything to do with the missing money but the other night I found a box of cash in my room. When I asked my mom about it, she said she didn't know where it came from. As silly as it sounds, we decided to put it back in the closet till we could figure out what to do. So now I'm wondering if it's the money missing from the Waterkeeper's account." She spoke rapidly and was almost out of breath as she added, "Don't ask me how it landed in a box in my closet because I haven't the slightest clue."

There she'd said it all. The ball was in Philip's court. He could call the police and have her arrested, fire her, yell at her—do whatever he wanted. She looked up from her lap where her hands were clasped together so tightly her knuckles had turned white.

Philip had leaned back in his swivel chair. Silence filled the office as he decided her fate. Annie held her breath. Finally he began to speak.

"I don't know how the money ended up in your closet either and there's no point in speculating." He leaned in, his voice softened along with the expression in his dark eyes. "How much was it?"

If Annie ever felt more stupid she couldn't remember when. In a voice scarcely above a whisper she said, "I don't really know. We didn't count it but there was a lot."

"Could it be as much as ten thousand?"

Visualizing the bills scattered on her bedroom floor, Annie reluctantly nodded.

Philip tapped his pen on the desktop and then said, "Here's what we'll do. You go home and get the money and we'll put it back in the account. Nothing more need be said. How's that sound?"

Relieved to have the matter settled, Annie rushed home to fulfill her end of the bargain. As she drove the few miles between the office and her house, she reflected on Philip's reaction to her revelation. He'd been surprised and yet sympathetic. After all, she wasn't the one who took the money, and if her father had, he must have had a good reason. They would never know now, so Philip said the best thing would be to put the ugly affair behind them.

Annie felt her heart quicken recalling Philip's compassion at her distress. *Whoa there girl, slow down,* she admonished herself to remember she was engaged. Wriggling the third finger on her left hand, the stone sparkled, reflecting the morning sun. Besides it was obvious he and the Beckster had a thing going on. Annie got it but really, did they have to flaunt it like that? She sighed remembering how much fun it had been working there before Becky arrived. Sometimes life sucked big time.

Oh well, the summer would be over soon enough and she'd be back in Gainesville with Nathan. Until then, she'd just have to hang in there. Some summer this was turning out to be—more like the summer from Hell.

She pulled up to the house and went straight to her room, not bothering to respond to her mother's call, "Hi honey, you're home early."

She opened the closet door and reached up to where she'd carefully placed the box—between a stack of last year's textbooks and a box of CDs. But what she found was a whole lot of nothing. What? Where was that box? She was certain she'd placed it in that exact spot. She remembered because she'd had to make room for it and given the amount of stuff on the shelf, it hadn't been easy.

Her heart beat faster; heat rushed to her face; perspiration ran down her cheeks and made her armpits wet. She dragged a chair from her desk and standing on it, frantically pulled boxes off the shelf, spilling the contents willy-nilly across the floor.

Puzzled by the racket, Lisa appeared in Annie's doorway and for a moment watched her daughter search through the closet with the urgency of a house on fire. Finally as if she could stand it no longer, she said, "What're you looking for? You're making quite a mess."

Annie stopped and looked at her mother; she was so upset that for a few seconds she couldn't speak.

"Ma, where's that box of money? I can't find it anywhere."

A puzzled look planted itself on Lisa's face. "The money? I don't know. Didn't we agree to put it back where you found it?"

"Yes," Annie said, "Did you move it?" Although she didn't come right out and say so, Annie recalled that her mother hadn't been especially worried when she was losing money at the casino a week ago.

Lisa took in a deep breath then said, slowly and deliberately as though trying to maintain control over her emotions. "No, I didn't take that money. What would make you think I did?"

By this time Annie was in full panic mode. "Because, because Philip said someone took ten thousand dollars from the Waterkeeper's bank account. He said the board would blame him for it and wanted to know if me or Becky knew anything about it." Her eyes brimmed with tears. "Mom, he looked so worried. I felt sorry for him. I just couldn't let him take the blame for something he didn't do, so I told him about finding it. He said just to return it and nothing more would be said, that the board needn't be told." She threw her arms out in a futile gesture in the direction of the closet and the room that had the appearance of a hurricane's aftermath. "I can't find it anywhere. I've looked and looked. Are you sure you didn't take it to the bank?"

Lisa hugged her daughter. "I'm sorry honey, but I didn't touch that money. I don't know where it could be." She pulled back. "Do you think that whoever put it there, came back and got it?"

They looked at each other and considered the possibility, then Annie said, "Ma, what'm I going to do? Philip's waiting for me to return that money." Annie trembled at the thought of facing the man's wrath.

"Honey, calm down," Lisa said in a soothing voice. "We don't know for sure the money you found came from the Waterkeeper's account. Perhaps your dad had been saving it from his salary."

"Sure Mom and we're not positive Santa Claus and the Easter Bunny aren't real either, but I wouldn't bank on it." She slumped to the floor and put her head in her hands. Then she looked up, and asked gently, "You've been kinda flaky since Dad died, you sure you didn't hide it somewhere and forget all about it?"

If Annie's question offended Lisa, she didn't let it show. "I'm sure, sweetheart," she said, adding softly, "After we agreed to put it back, I didn't think any more about it."

Annie was grateful her mother hadn't mentioned their agreement not to say anything about their discovery—an agreement she broke by telling Philip.

"So you think I've been flaky?" Lisa said, a wistful look on her face. "I'll have to do something about that." Then she gave her daughter an affectionate pat on the back and left the room.

As Annie sat there trying to summon the courage to go back and tell Philip what she'd found—or to be more accurate, what she'd failed to find—she was distracted by a fly at the screen that repeatedly crawled up in a failed attempt to find a way out. It would go three-quarters of the way up, fall and then start over. This summer it seemed as though Annie was that fly, repeatedly beginning and failing. No matter what she did or how hard she tried, everything turned to dust. As the fly once again started its trek upward, she decided to go back to the office and face Philip with the bad news, but first she opened the screen and let the fly escape.

Chapter 14

"What do you mean the money's not there?" Philip's face turned a brilliant red, his eyes blazed. His very countenance frightened Annie to the core.

"It's gone, the money's gone," she said. She was so afraid that her voice was reduced to a near whisper. "It's not in my closet where I put it. I asked my mom if she took it, but she said no." As he continued to stare at her with steely eyes, she added, "I don't know what else to say. Besides we aren't absolutely sure the money I found belonged to the Waterkeepers. Maybe Dad was saving up for something. Or maybe he earned money working on the side."

Philip gave her a look that was a repeat of her own reaction when her mother had suggested as much.

"I admit it looks bad, but Philip, I simply don't know how the money got there or where it went. That's all I can tell you. What else can I do?"

"You're right, there's nothing you can do, but you weren't the only one in the house."

"What? You think my mother had something to do with it?"

"Well, it *is* her house."

"So it's her house? What's that got to do with it?"

"Think about it Annie. If stolen money is found in your car, isn't it reasonable to suspect you had something to do with it?"

Annie felt short of breath. What was he saying? That her mother was somehow involved? That's exactly what he was saying. The heat of anger began a slow burn in her chest and morphed into a firestorm.

She stood up, leaned across the desk and pressed her face inches from Philip's. "How dare you! After all she's been through; I can't believe you'd suggest such a thing." She bashed her fist on the desk, making Philip's papers jump; then walked out of the office and slammed the door behind her.

Chapter 15

Lisa was in the back of the house doing laundry when she heard the doorbell, then pounding, accompanied by a man's loud voice, "Police. Open up."

Her recent encounter with law enforcement on the occasion of Craig's death immediately came to mind. Oh my good lord, something happened to Annie. She rushed through the house and threw the door open.

Far from the gentle, soft-spoken policeman who had guided her through those early hours of determining whether her husband was dead or alive, the person standing before her wore an official demeanor.

She started to ask what he wanted, but he interrupted. "Are you Lisa Whitaker?"

"Yes," Lisa said, her heart sank at the conviction something awful had happened to her only child.

"You need to accompany me to the police station to answer questions in connection with the theft of funds from the Okeechobee Waterkeeper's bank account. You may have a lawyer present if you wish."

"Theft of funds? What funds?" Then she remembered

the cash Annie found. "Is this about that money my daughter found?"

"Ma'am, I'm only here to escort you to the police station. The detective assigned to the case will clear up any questions you have."

Realizing she had no choice, Lisa locked the house and got in the back of the squad car. She noticed the neighbor's curtain move slightly. They were, no doubt, wondering what new disaster had befallen the Whitakers.

* * * *

The police station looked nothing like Lisa imagined it would. Instead of a crowded bullpen teaming with officers grilling perps as depicted on television, the building she entered was small, modern and quiet. It even had a somewhat cheery ambience with cream-colored walls and a few plants here and there.

The police officer escorted Lisa past the desk sergeant and down the hall to a small office. "Detective Johns will be with you in a few minutes. Can I get you some water or a soft drink?"

Lisa's mouth was so dry she could scarcely respond. "Yes, some water would be nice."

As she waited, her gaze roamed the interrogation room. Again it was nothing like she envisioned. The walls were a soothing pale blue; the chairs padded and comfortable. Even the table looked more like it belonged in the conference room of some upscale business rather than the setting for questioning lawbreakers. It bore no evidence of graffiti or scratches of any kind. She was impressed, well as impressed as you could be when you're about to be grilled by a hardboiled law enforcement officer.

Detective Johns turned out to be a slight-built man with tired eyes. He wore a navy blue suit with a burgundy tie whose knot was pulled a few inches from his collar. Lisa thought he looked more like a businessman than a member of the police force. She was almost disappointed. The TV mystery shows had it all wrong.

"So, Mrs. Whitaker, Lisa. May I call you Lisa?"

"Yes, of course."

"I'm Detective Jonathon Johns. Yes, I know." He chuckled. "My parents had a bizarre sense of humor. People call me JJ." He paused, cleared his throat and said, "I understand ten thousand dollars was stolen from the Waterkeepers."

His dark eyes caught hers. "What do you know about the missing money?"

"The Waterkeepers' money?"

"Yes. That's why we're here." He leaned in toward the table; all hint of congeniality had evaporated.

"I don't know anything about what happened to their money. Perhaps you should talk to the Waterkeepers. Maybe one of them took it—or misplaced it. How would I know?"

"Well, that's the thing, Mrs. Whitaker; they're the ones who called us. They seem to think you or your daughter took it."

"Really? What makes them think a thing like that?"

Detective Johns gave her a soul-searching stare that seemed to drill into her very soul. While it lasted only seconds, to Lisa it seemed to go on for hours, making her feel guilty—she didn't know exactly why. All she knew was that she had to paste on the most innocent expression she could muster. As he continued to scrutinize her, she had to fight the urge to confess; that's how good he was. Finally the silence in the room was more than Lisa could bear.

"Detective the only thing I know about money is that my daughter, Annie, who's home from college for the summer, discovered a box full of cash in her closet. Neither of us know how it got there."

"Did you call the police and report it?"

"No. We probably should have, but at the time we were so baffled, we thought perhaps my husband had been saving up for something and stashed it there."

"Your husband? He the one who drowned on Lake Okeechobee a few weeks ago?"

Tears welled up in Lisa's eyes. With a sudden knot in her throat she could only nod. She swallowed hard then took a sip of water.

"I didn't connect your name with the accident. I'm sorry for your loss."

He let a few seconds pass so Lisa could regain her composure, then started in again. "So you put the money back, then what? You decided possession was two-thirds of the law and decided to spend it?"

"What? No. We just left it there."

"You left ten thousand dollars sitting in a box in your daughter's closet?"

"Yes."

"Didn't have the urge to go on a shopping spree, maybe buy a new dress, get your hair done, spend some time at the casino?"

"No, I didn't do any of those things."

"Seriously? You didn't go to Brighton with your daughter last week?

Lisa was stunned. How did he know that? Were they under surveillance? "No, I mean, yes, we went to dinner and dropped by the casino after, but it had nothing to do with that money. We just went out to have a little fun and get away from all the, you know, problems we've been having. Besides, we put a strict limit of fifty dollars apiece on what we bet."

"And did you stick to your limit?"

"We did."

"You come out ahead?"

Lisa shook her head. "I never do. Seems like when I win, a little voice urges me to play again, that I could win even more. Eventually I lose it all and either break even or go home poorer than before."

"Make a habit of gambling, do you?"

"No, of course not. Craig and I enjoy, I mean, enjoyed stopping by there from time to time for a night out, that's all."

"Mrs. Whitaker, Lisa, what do you do for a living?"

"I'm a housewife. Craig never wanted me to work. He said it was important for me to make a comfortable home for Lisa and him. So that's what I did."

"And now?"

"Now?"

"Your daughter's grown and off to college. Your husband's dead. What do you do for money?" His blunt question cut Lisa to the quick.

"I'm still trying to figure that out," she said, her voice barely above a whisper.

"What's that? You have to speak up. I didn't hear you." Johns' face took on a hard, almost hostile aspect.

"I said I'm trying to figure it out. Craig's death was unexpected. It's not something a person plans for, you know." The heat of anger began to burn inside.

Instead of backing off, the detective continued his drive for information. "I see, but plan or no plan a person still has to buy groceries, put gas in the car and pay the water bill. How're you managing to do all those things without an income?"

"We had money saved, you know, for a rainy day. I'm using that for now, but you're right, I have to find a job and soon or we'll be in trouble."

"And with, as you say, with trouble looming, it didn't enter your mind to take that money and squirrel it away for safekeeping?"

"No, it didn't. Annie and I agreed we'd put it back and try to figure out where it came from. It was only when she discovered it missing that I thought any more about it. Detective Johns I honestly don't know what happened to it. I don't."

He looked directly into her eyes and held them for a few seconds. Then he said, "Okay Mrs. Whitaker. That'll be all for now. I'll have an officer drive you home."

There was no apology for her inconvenience, no suggestion they'd made a mistake, not even a hint as to whether he believed her. Lisa noticed he hadn't said not to leave town or that this had all been a bad joke. If it was, she failed to see the humor in it and began to wonder if she should contact a lawyer.

As the squad car pulled into her drive, she decided to wait and see if they tried to question her again. If they did, she'd refuse to speak to them without a lawyer. That's probably what she should have done in the first place, but she'd never been interrogated before and like everything else lately, it was a new experience; one she ardently hoped would not be repeated.

Chapter 16

Annie burst through the front door, slamming it so forcefully it rattled knickknacks on shelves in the living room.

Startled from her nap, Lisa let out a yelp. "Oh, Annie, it's you. What is it, dear? What's wrong?"

Gritting her teeth, both hands balled into fists, Annie muttered, "I'm so mad I could spit."

Lisa started to laugh, but stopped when Annie didn't join her. "What's wrong?" she repeated.

Sinking into an overstuffed rocker-recliner and grasping the arms so tightly a keen observer might think she feared it was about to take flight, Annie said, "It's that damned money. I told Philip what happened and the SOB didn't believe me. He actually had the gall to suggest you took it or at the very least was in on it with Dad. I got so mad I walked out."

Lisa gave her daughter a sympathetic look. "So that's why the police brought me in for questioning."

"The police did what?" Annie was incredulous. "You were arrested?"

"Not arrested, questioned. They wanted to find out what I knew. Philip must've given them my name and suggested I had something to do with it. I answered their questions and that was that."

"Mom, you need to be careful. Next time—"

"I know, I know. If they contact me again, I'll refuse to talk without an attorney present. I should've done that today, but I wasn't thinking straight."

"So, did they say it was okay? That they knew you were innocent?"

"Not really. They just said that was all the questions they had and I could go home. They didn't thank me; tell me not to leave town or anything. Just 'go home.' At least they provided a ride, I'll give them that."

Annie felt like crying. See where her honesty had gotten her. She was so concerned about Philip getting in trouble with the board, it never occurred to her she might be putting her mother in jeopardy. She curled up in an attempt at comfort. This chair always made her feel as though she was rocking in someone's arms.

"So, darling girl, why don't you go back to the office and apologize for overreacting? Philip had no choice but to call the police, you know."

Annie nodded and continued to rock, letting the back and forth motion soothe her. What to do. What to do? The problem was far from solved: The money was still gone. What the hell happened to it? The thought of someone coming in the house, planting cash in her closet and then retrieving it, gave her the creeps. What would they do next?

"Mom, we've got to be more careful; keep the windows and doors locked, maybe get a burglar alarm—or a dog."

"You're right, we really should do something. With all the publicity about your dad, everyone knows we're alone." Lisa gave her daughter a long penetrating look. "Somehow I think you have more on your mind than that money. Are you and Nathan having problems?"

Annie hesitated, then shook her head no. "Nathan's a sweetheart. It's not him, it's me."

"You? What about you?"

"It's just that, I just," Annie danced around the answer trying to find words to express emotions not yet fully formed. "I just don't know how I feel anymore," she said at last.

"How you feel about Nathan—or how you feel about Philip?"

"Philip? What do you mean?"

"I'm not blind. I see the look on your face whenever Philip's name comes up. Isn't that what this is really about? You have feelings for him and don't know what to do about it. You feel torn between your pledge to marry Nathan and your attraction to Philip. That's what it looks like to me."

Annie put her head in her hands and began to cry.

"Honey, I didn't mean to upset you. Forget what I said. Besides what do I know? I should just mind my own business." She went across the room and began to pat Annie on the back.

Annie scrubbed her eyes, breathed in and said, "No, Mom, you're right. I don't know how you do it, but you always know when something's wrong."

"I do?" Lisa smiled. "So you want to talk about it?"

"No. I don't know. Maybe." Annie stumbled over the words. "It's just that I'm so confused. I love Nathan, I do." She held out her left hand and admired her ring. "But sometimes I'm just not sure I'm ready to get married. Know what I mean?"

Lisa sat back down. "I know exactly what you're saying. Annie, the decision to get married is huge, life-altering. It's something you shouldn't do unless you're absolutely positive."

"That's the thing. When Nate asked me, I was sure I loved him more than anything. But now, now…" her voice faltered.

"Now that you've been apart for a month, you're attracted to another man. Right?"

Annie nodded.

"And that man is Philip?" It was more a statement than a question.

Again, Annie's head moved up and down in agreement. "So, Mom, what am I going to do? Besides, I don't think Philip has feelings for me anyway. It looks like he and Becky have something going."

"That's beside the point, isn't it? I mean would you go ahead and marry Nathan simply because Philip's not available?"

"No, of course not. It's just that I'm not ready to, you know, break it off. I mean, he'll be so hurt. He doesn't deserve that."

"Don't you think it'll hurt worse if he marries someone who doesn't love him?"

"Mo-o-m," Annie said in exasperation. "I didn't say I didn't love him, now did I?"

"Not in so many words, but wouldn't you say you're headed in that direction?"

* * * *

The following morning Annie woke up to the persistent ringing of the telephone. She'd spent the night on the living room sofa, a baseball bat beside her.

By the time Lisa came in from the patio, Annie had already slammed down the receiver.

"Damned marketing people. Can't they at least wait for a decent hour to start calling?"

As if waiting for her to continue ranting, Lisa said nothing. When it became apparent she was finished, she said, "Did you fall asleep watching TV?"

"No, why?" Annie looked pointedly at the television set which was obviously not on.

"No reason. I just wondered why you slept out here instead of in your room."

Annie stood up, stretched, then sat back down and tucked her feet under her. "Would you like to sleep in a room where someone took stuff in and out of your closet? How do I know when they'll be back—or what they'll do? You think I can sleep when I'm afraid they might crawl through my window any minute?"

With a furrowed brow, Lisa shook her head from side to side. "I'm sorry honey. I should have thought of that. You want to trade rooms?"

"Aren't you afraid?"

"Not really. If whoever did this was out to hurt us, don't you suppose they would've done it by now?"

Annie could see the logic of her mother's reasoning although it didn't assuage her fear. The thought of a stranger going in and out of her room whenever they felt like it made her feel violated, despite the fact they had neither harmed her nor disturbed her belongings. Still it was the principle of the thing. She just couldn't go into that room without the urge to check under the bed.

It reminded her of when she was little and scared of the dark. Every night before she went to sleep, one of her parents—usually her dad, had to check beneath the bed, in her closet and behind the door to make certain the boogeyman wasn't there waiting to grab her.

Now the boogeyman was back and no longer a figment of her imagination; he was real.

Before she had a chance to respond to her mother's generous offer, the phone rang. This time Lisa picked it up. While her mother alternately listened and spoke, Annie wandered into the kitchen and poured herself some coffee. She was sitting at the table leafing through the newspaper when Lisa came in, a peculiar look on her face.

"What is it now?" Annie said.

"That was Philip. He said the bank called; that it was all a mistake, some kind of accounting error. No money was missing after all."

Annie was at once relieved and perplexed. She was thankful at having the burden of the missing money and the accusation of theft removed from her mother and her, but at the same time the question of the appearance and disappearance of that money confounded her.

Lisa stood in front of her, a questioning look on her face. "So what should I tell him?"

"Him? Who? What're you talking about?"

"Philip. He's on the phone. He wants to know when you're coming back."

Chapter 17

Harold Johnson put down the phone and let out a belly laugh so loud it startled Bobby who was snoozing in an easy chair across the room. To his quizzical look, Harold said, "It's working. The plan's on track. Those damned Whitakers will be in a world of hurt before I get through with them. You just wait and see."

Carefully wrapping his lips around words he was unable to clearly enunciate, Bobby gave him a slurred response of affirmation, and added, "Tell me again. Why're we mad at them?"

Harold, who by this time could easily decipher Bobby's speech, said, "They're the SOBs responsible for us losing the farm, for Mom's cancer and Dad's suicide."

When Bobby continued to stare at him as if waiting for more information, he added, "It's their fault you came down with the Parkinson's."

Bobby's eyes fell. He nodded in agreement then said, "Why'd they do that? They mad at us or something?"

"No, it wasn't like that. They owned the company that flew over farms spraying chemicals to get rid of

Japanese beetles and other insects that destroy crops."

Bobby looked puzzled. "But that's a good thing, isn't it? Get rid of bugs that kill plants? How could that make me and Mom sick?"

Harold sighed. He'd explained it to Bobby so many times over the years, it felt like he was repeating words from a monologue. He didn't know why the younger man failed to remember things, if it was part of the Parkinson's or if he'd suffered some kind of brain damage too. But really, what difference did it make? Considering the extent of his disabilities, whether he remembered things or not was of little consequence. The man would be dependent on him for the rest of his life.

Harold rubbed his hand through his thinning hair, remembering the early years when Bobby was a pesky little brother and Mom and Dad doting parents. Those were the happy days. His biggest concern back then was avoiding detection for making Bobby cry. Sometimes he'd steal his bottle and drink all the milk, causing his mom to be amazed at how fast the baby drank and surprised he was still hungry. He grinned and blinked his eyes.

Over the years, Harold had painstakingly researched the situation. He'd learned that there was a link between pesticides and Parkinson's, and that people who lived near sprayed fields were at higher risk of developing the disease.

"So how could killing a few bugs make me and Momma sick?" Bobby repeated.

His persistent attempt to make sense of his life stabbed Harold in the heart. No matter how many times he explained it, Bobby would never fully understand it. What was the point in going over it yet again?

There was no point. Now was the time for action. He'd get revenge for what those people did. They'd remember the Johnson name for the rest of their miserable lives. He'd make sure of that.

Chapter 18

Annie got out of the boat, balancing a box of sample vials on one arm and a clipboard crammed tightly with pages of data on the other. All she had to do now was trip and drop them in the water and the morning's work would be out the window. She didn't know why she took risks like this; she could easily have made two trips, but no, she had to do it the hard way, like everything else she did anymore.

In the past week, Annie and Philip had come to a tentative truce, but so far neither had much to say to the other. Annie still smarted over his not so subtle suggestion that her mom had taken cash from the Waterkeeper's bank account. Then, when the matter was cleared up, the man didn't have the class to apologize. He just acted like nothing happened.

Well, it wasn't that easy for Annie. She remained highly irritated and wanted him not only to know it; she wanted to rub his nose in it. She had to fight the urge to take this whole box of vials and smash it over his head of thick, wavy hair. That gorgeous smile wouldn't flash so broadly at Becky then, would it?

Annie was at her desk finishing a baloney sandwich, chips and a coke, when Philip came in, trailed by the blonde bitch.

"Hey," Philip said with all the enthusiasm of someone who just saw his best friend after a long absence. Becky echoed his greeting and tossed a neon-lit smile her way. Annie, who had grabbed the phone upon hearing their imminent approach, lifted her index finger and continued a fake phone conversation: "Yes, the Waterkeeper organization accepts donations in any amount." She gave them a less than sincere smile, lowered her head and continued speaking, "You can drop it off or mail it, whichever's more convenient." She concluded by supplying the street address, speaking slowly in the hope that by the time she finished Philip would be ensconced in his office with the door closed. No such luck.

When she put the receiver back in its cradle, she felt a light tap on her shoulder and glanced up.

Rats.

Philip was standing next to her chair waiting for her to finish.

"Making millions for us, are you?" Philip said, a jovial tone dripping from his voice.

Annie wanted to gag.

What a fucking phony.

She forced a smile. "Hey," she managed to spit out.

"Any messages?"

"I put them on your desk." Her hand moved toward the phone.

Philip clamped his hand over hers. "That can wait. Come into my office."

Annie's heart sank. He was going to fire her; he'd

had enough of her snotty attitude. She couldn't blame him. If she was in his shoes, she'd do the same thing.

Reluctantly, Annie pushed back from the desk and followed her boss across the room, past Becky-with-the-electric-smile who sat at the desk she'd appropriated, relegating Annie to the battered desk in the corner. That still bugged her.

Oh well, what did it matter now? Annie was about to lose her internship. She wouldn't care so much if it wasn't for the fact that she'd lose the credits she was supposed to earn spending the summer working here. And to be honest, as angry as she was at Philip, she still had a crush on him that just wouldn't quit. It had gotten so bad Nathan had begun to notice. It wasn't so much what she said as her lack of enthusiasm that he questioned when they spoke on the phone the other night. She'd covered nicely when he asked if something was wrong; said she was tired, that she hadn't been getting enough sleep, which was actually the truth what with being worried that someone might break in again. He seemed to accept her explanation, or at any rate dropped the matter and went back to talking about himself.

Philip settled into his aging swivel chair. It always squeaked when he turned a certain way. Annie felt the urge to buy some oil and give that baby a good dose. Maybe she'd do precisely that—assuming she wasn't fired.

Philip leaned back; his dark eyes meandered from Annie's well-defined cleavage to her shoulders, resting when their gaze intersected.

"So, Annie, how're you doing?" he said, his mouth expanded into that electrifying smile that sent her heart into spasms.

She was expecting to be fired or at the very least given a stern dressing down, and Philip's pleasant demeanor caught Annie off guard. What should she say? That she was furious with him and not only that but she was crazy about him at the same time? That she was so confused she didn't know which way was up?

"F-fine. I'm just fine," she managed to say.

"Really?" Again Philip's eyes drilled her. "Because lately you don't seem like yourself. Is your father's death bothering you? I know it takes a long time to get over something like that. If you need time off or there's anything I can do, let me know."

Philip's unexpected kindness brought tears to Annie's eyes. She looked down at her hands, tightly clenched in her lap. Seriously, the guy had no clue. First he parades his girlfriend around when he must know she had feelings for him—really, how could he not know? Then he trashes her mother and offers no apology when he's proven wrong. Now he's all solicitous, wanting to know what's wrong. The whole situation left Annie floundering; unable to gain purchase on solid ground. She felt as though she was falling from a great height and couldn't catch her breath.

Philip watched her, awaiting an answer.

"I'm fine, really," she said.

"You sure?" he leaned in, his arms extended across his desk, his long, slender fingers intertwined.

"I'm sure."

"Well, that's a relief. Losing both of you at the same time would put a real crimp in the operation."

"Lose both of us?" Annie's forehead rippled. "What're you talking about?"

"Didn't she tell you? Becky's leaving at the end of

the week. She's taken a job in Miami." He sighed. "We knew all along her stay was temporary, but she fit in so quickly I'd hoped she'd be here at least till the end of the summer. Oh well," his face brightened, "It's back to being just the two of us, unless you can get someone on that endless list of yours to come and help out."

All Annie heard was that Becky, the bane of her existence, would soon be gone for good. Oh my God, the woman was leaving; she could have her desk—and her self-respect back. She could have Philip all to herself. God does answer prayers.

For the first time in days, a smile played at the edges of Annie's mouth. "I'm so sorry," she heard herself say as fireworks went off in her head and an imaginary chorus sang, "Hallelujah."

Chapter 19

It was getting late and Lisa's losses were mounting. She knew she should stop playing and leave the casino, but a niggling little voice kept saying, "One more game. Just one more and you'll win big." And so it went hour after hour. But she didn't hit it "big" and the few wins she made were quickly wiped out by subsequent losses until her debt began to mount and she wondered how it had come to this.

When Craig was alive they rarely gambled. Oh, there was the occasional night out with friends, but they always limited the amount they wagered. At the time, Lisa couldn't see the attraction it held for so many people. To be honest, it had bored her silly.

With Craig gone and Annie out at meetings or with friends most nights, she'd grown increasingly lonely, finding the empty house almost intolerable. The casino provided an instant party atmosphere and pseudo companionship even if it did end when she walked out the door. Still it lifted her spirits, providing some relief from her overwhelming grief.

Now, however, she'd begun to dig a hole of addiction so deep that if she didn't get it under control, she'd lose everything.

She went to the cashier and pulled out her credit card. Just a few more games and she'd go home. Maybe this would be the big score she'd been hoping for all evening. When she got to the window, the woman swiped her card and then frowned.

"You've reached your limit," she said. "Have another card?"

Lisa unzipped her purse and began to root around as a line of gamblers formed behind her.

"C'mon lady, we don't got all night," a man with a raspy, smoker's voice called out.

"Move it or lose it," another said.

"Step aside while I wait on these customers," the cashier said.

With increasing embarrassment, Lisa moved to the empty spot on her right. She knew that other card was in her purse but for some reason simply couldn't find it. As her fingers continued to roam the contents of her handbag, she heard a voice say, "Miss, come with me please."

She glanced up to find a man about six feet tall with Seminole Indian features stamped on his face. He was dressed in the shirt, vest and tie that identified him as a casino employee. The name embroidered on his vest read, "Raoul Tucker, Manager."

Lisa was puzzled. Why did he want to speak to her? She hesitated and he again said, "Follow me." The expression on his face said he wasn't taking no for an answer.

Raoul led Lisa down a hallway to the back of the casino. He stopped at a closed door with his name and title on it, then he opened it and stood aside for her to enter. When they were both ensconced in reasonably comfortable chairs, he reached in his top desk drawer and pulled out a small black notebook.

Lisa grew increasingly puzzled. What did that man want with her? As far as she knew she'd done nothing wrong.

"Lisa Whitaker, right?"

How does he know my name?

"Yes. Is something wrong?" Lisa realized her voice had begun to close up. She spoke in a near whisper.

"Not yet, but it's heading in that direction," he said. His dark eyes reflected a kindness and concern Lisa had rarely seen before.

"I'm afraid I don't understand," she said. "What're you talking about?"

"Your gambling. It seems to be getting out of control." He waited as his words sank in. "Don't get me wrong. We're happy to take your money, but we're not here to destroy lives." He cleared his throat and leaned in. "You've been here several times a week lately and you're losing so much you've begun to put it on a credit card. Tonight you maxed that out and were looking for another one when I stopped you." He gave her a gentle smile. "Mrs. Whitaker, I think you might have a problem."

At first Lisa just looked at the stranger and wondered how he could possibly know how many times she'd visited the casino let alone that she had a gambling problem. Then a rush of emotion swept over her. She was at once mortified and ridden with guilt. The little money Craig had carefully put aside for the day he could no longer provide for her was gone.

Tears flooded her eyes and fell like a rushing stream down her cheeks. She covered her face and sobbed.

Raoul watched quietly for a moment and then said

gently, "You don't have to be embarrassed, Mrs. Whitaker. You're not the only one that got bit by the gambling bug. That's why we keep an eye out for the signs."

He shifted in the desk chair and flicked a fly off his arm. "You've had it especially hard lately what with the death of your husband and all. It's understandable that you'd try to find some kind of escape."

Raoul's words gave Lisa a start. How did he know so much about her?

"It's been all over the news, you know. I didn't recognize your face, but the name's familiar to everyone around here. It was such a tragedy. Your husband did so much for the area."

Lisa nodded. Of course, that's how he knew. Everyone did. Whenever she told someone her name they immediately connected her to Craig's untimely death.

"I'll stop," she promised him. "Thank you for your concern." She rose to leave.

"You're welcome," he said, then added. "Mrs. Whitaker, are you by any chance a Native American?"

Once again the man startled her. In all the years she'd been away from Acoma, no one had ever asked her that question.

"Yes," she said. "I belong to the Acoma Pueblo out in New Mexico. Have you ever heard of them?"

"Indeed I have," Raoul replied. "In fact I visited Sky City some years ago." He paused and cleared his throat. "Do you need a job by any chance? We have some openings and you'd fit right in."

Those words represented the first glimmer of hope she'd had since the accident.

"I really do," she said and sat back down.

Chapter 20

Annie sat at a card table in the entrance to the American Legion hall, encouraging people to sign in. She'd stacked a pile of informational brochures to one side and handed them to each one along with a generous smile.

By now she'd been to enough of these meetings that she knew what to expect. Philip would dazzle them with a warm welcome and tell them coffee was available. He'd say to feel free to get a cup whenever they felt the need. The murmur of voices would gradually fade along with his smile as the business of the meeting was explained in excruciating detail.

Annie could recite this part by heart, and why not? She'd written the script herself. As she sat alone at the back of the hall signing in stragglers, she thought about her dad and the times he'd taken her to similar gatherings over the years. At the time, she'd found them mind-numbingly boring. No matter how often he explained how important it was to raise awareness of pollution and water purity issues, she would eventually tune him out and let her mind focus on things that were important to her such as boys, dates, the latest pop stars, which movies were coming out and what fashions were currently "in."

Now, however, watching Philip charm the crowd with his good looks and charisma, she wished she'd paid closer attention when it was her dad who was up there on stage. Well, it was too late now.

Annie was so deep in thought of days long past that she failed to notice a burly man blow through the door and head down the aisle toward the stage, until it was too late.

"You fucking son of a bitch," he shouted. "I warned you what would happen if you didn't back off."

Before she could react, a shot rang out. People screamed and dove for cover. Several men leapt into the aisle and tried to tackle the gunman before he could get off another shot.

Annie's eyes frantically scanned the stage for any sign of Philip. Had the shot found its mark? Was he dead? If he was, it was her fault for not seeing the man come in.

She pushed through the small crowd to the stage where she found Philip sprawled out, blood spilling down his shirt making a crimson path to a growing puddle on the floor. His normally pleasant features were pinched in a grimace of pain.

"Annie," he said in a breathless gasp. "You're okay. Thank God."

The scream of sirens grew louder with the approach of emergency vehicles. Before long, Philip was loaded into an ambulance and Annie was left with a gaggle of stunned volunteers to clean up and head home.

Her heart thumping wildly, she did her best to maintain a semblance of self-control as she picked up discarded cups, folded card tables and gathered leftover fliers. However, her body refused to cooperate, and trembled uncontrollably as the sound of gunshots reverberated inside her brain.

Had the bullet done serious damage? Would Philip be okay? There'd been so much blood. She recalled how even as he lay there wounded, he'd expressed concern for her. He was thinking of her. Not Becky. Her.

As she fumbled with the fistful of keys to lock the back door, the tiniest grin tickled the edges of her mouth. As Philip lay there, bleeding, possibly fighting for his life, he'd thought of her.

Annie raced to the Hendry Regional Medical Center. Lucky this particular meeting had been held in Clewiston, a stone's throw from the hospital. When she arrived, Philip was being prepped for surgery. All she could do was join the dazed group in the waiting room—and hope for the best.

Chapter 21

Annie sat at Philip's bedside reading a magazine and waiting for him to wake up. The previous night, doctors had assured the anxious group of well wishers that Philip's wounds were not life threatening and that they should go home; he'd be out for hours.

Now, as she glanced up from her reading, the mere look at his face sent an electric jolt through Annie. Tears welled in her eyes as she reflected on how close she'd come to losing him. The bullet had traveled through his body missing vital organs by mere inches. Lying there, his dark curly hair made a sharp contrast against the pastel-colored pillowcase.

Annie went to the window and looked out at the cloudless sky. Palm trees on the hospital grounds waved their fronds in the wind. A pelican flew past. With its outsized bill, it reminded Annie of a prehistoric bird.

"Hey," a weak male voice behind her said.

"Philip, you're awake. How do you feel?"

"Okay," he said, "They must of pumped me full of painkillers. I don't feel a thing." A frail smile crossed his face. "That's some good stuff; I'll have to get a supply before they let me go."

Annie laughed.

"So, how bad is it, do you know?" Philip said, his grin quickly fading.

"All I know is you were lucky. The doctor will give you the details when he comes by. Philip," she started to say how she felt. It couldn't wait any longer. Her heart fairly burst with love for him.

"Yes, Annie, what is it?"

Just then the door opened and Becky walked in, her arms filled with an enormous bouquet of flowers and a giant teddy bear.

"Phil, you're awake. Thank God. I was so, so worried. I hardly slept a wink," she gushed. Then placing the toy on his bed, she leaned over and kissed him—right on the mouth.

Watching the tender scene, Annie wanted more than anything to simply disappear. She turned to leave, but Philip stopped her. "Hey, wait, where're you going?"

"I have to get to the office," she said, her voice tight with emotion. "People'll be calling to find out how you are."

"Oh, hi, Annie," Becky said, belatedly acknowledging her co-worker. "I'm afraid I didn't notice you there. Guess I was just so happy to see that Phil's going to be okay." Turning back to him, she added, "You are, aren't you?" Her sentence ended in a flirty trill.

Annie quickly left the room before "Phil" could see the devastated expression on her face. Although she couldn't see it for herself, she was all too aware of how she looked when her feelings were hurt. So, her heart in tatters, Annie departed with Becky and Philip's mingled laughter ringing in her ears.

Chapter 22

Waitressing in the Josiah Restaurant and Lounge wasn't as easy as Lisa had anticipated. For one thing, she wasn't used to being on her feet eight hours a day. With only two fifteen minute breaks and thirty minutes for lunch, for the first two weeks her body had been one mass of pain. Although she was beginning to get used to it, most nights she still came home and soaked her feet.

When he offered her the job, Raoul warned her about gambling. He said the casino was off-limits and that if she violated this rule, she'd be fired. Lisa knew it was for her own good. Working in such close proximity to a casino provided a source of temptation few gamblers could resist. So she'd accepted the job along with the restrictions and had so far kept her end of the bargain.

In between working, she tried to absorb as much Seminole history as she could. It enabled her to answer tourists' endless questions about the tribe. A hand-painted mural depicting Seminole culture covered one entire wall of the restaurant. Lisa enjoyed looking at it during the course of her shift each day. It reminded her of her own tribal connections, something she'd buried during the two decades she and Craig were married. Funny how the past reasserts itself. Her daily trek to the reservation was a constant reminder of who she was and how much she'd lost.

So far, she'd learned that, like her people, the Seminoles were a federally recognized tribe, but had the distinction of being the only one that never signed a peace treaty with the U.S. government. To this day they referred to themselves as "The Unconquered Ones."

Learning the tribe's history, she realized that, like her ancestors, Seminoles had been on the receiving end of brutal treatment by the U.S. government. Lisa reflected on Native Americans' justifiable anger and briefly wondered how government officials must feel having conquered people living as sovereign nations within their borders.

She read somewhere that America was the shining city on a hill. Seriously? The United States actually was built on the murder of Native Americans, the theft of their land and countless broken treaties.

Lisa sighed and tried to put the ugly matter out of her mind. Still she couldn't help but think about her own people and wonder how they were doing. Were her parents still alive? And her sisters, did they still live on the rez or had they, like her, found a life elsewhere? Did she have nieces and nephews now too?

She shook her head as if to free herself from thoughts too painful to pursue. Perhaps a good soaking in the tub would help. Grabbing her purse from the top shelf of her locker, she headed for home.

Chapter 23

Annie sat in the office answering one call after another, each had the same questions: "How's he doing? Will he be all right? Isn't what happened a disgrace?"

She responded to each with the same cheerfulness as though it was the first. "Thank you so much for inquiring. Mr. Buckley will be fine. He should be out of the hospital in a few days. Yes, I'll be sure to let him know you called." She'd made that last part up since she really didn't know when he'd be released. The callers had all been women. *Great.*

Between calls, Annie tried to expunge the lingering sound of Philip and Becky's laughter. No matter how hard she tried, the echo remained, sour like the aftertaste of a pickle.

As before, she felt a mix of guilt and longing. Nathan would be devastated if he found out what had been going through her mind the last few weeks.

She shook her head slowly back and forth. What was wrong with her? She was engaged to the sweetest, most kind and loving man in the world. They were perfect for each other—everyone who knew them said so. What more could she possibly want? Even her mother and dad liked him—well, of course, before, when Dad was alive. They had no objection to them dating and most likely knew where it was headed.

And now, just look at her: Mooning over a man she scarcely knew; livid over his obvious affection for another woman, who was thankfully leaving soon anyway.

She slammed her hand on the desk. The loud thump echoed through the quiet room. The phone rang again, startling Annie from her thoughts. She reassured the female caller that he'd "be all right" repeating the same information she'd relayed all morning long. She wrote down the caller's information and added the message to the growing stack. Imagine that. All those women were probably infatuated with him too. How ridiculous. She had to stop obsessing over him before everything was ruined.

Gathering up the pile of messages and morning mail, she went into Philip's office and was about to deposit them on his desk when her gaze fell on what appeared to be a bank statement. Philip had probably been scrutinizing it to make certain the accounting error they'd made was corrected.

That whole matter remained something of a mystery to Annie. Where had the money in her closet come from and where had it gone? It was as though she and her mother imagined the whole thing; that it never happened in the first place.

Curious to see how the bank reported the error, Annie sat down in Philip's swivel chair and began to peruse the statement. To her surprise, the ten thousand dollar withdrawal wasn't listed. There was no line item indicating any kind of accounting error on the part of the bank either.

Annie checked the dates on the statement against the time frame Philip claimed the fraudulent activity took place. There was nothing resembling such activity anywhere on the document. She was baffled. How could that be?

She was so intent on trying to understand the situation, she didn't hear the click of the outside door being opened and the sound of footsteps crossing the room.

"There you are," Becky's bigger-than-life voice called out. Her perky smile lit up her face as she gave her hair a little flounce. She wore a low-cut tank top and pink shorts that set off her dark tan and blond hair—which made a stark contrast to the dark roots that had begun to sprout. As Annie suspected, she wasn't a natural blonde. Her hair was fake—just like the rest of her.

"So, watcha doin?" Becky's gaze fell from Annie's face to the desk top and the bank statement.

Annie shrugged and let a worried expression overtake her face. "Hey Becky. How's Philip?" She held Becky's eyes with her own as her hands deftly shifted to the stack of mail and phone messages.

"He's doing fine. You know Phil." She wrinkled her nose in an almost flirty manner. "He's not about to let a little bullet keep him down." Her eyes seemed to actually sparkle when she said his name. "You should see how the nurses fuss over him," Becky continued. "And the flowers he's been getting, well, they practically fill the room. You'd think he was a rock star or something."

Annie smiled and nodded. Just what the doctor ordered—more women. "He's something all right," she said.

"Oh, yeah and you needn't worry. I told Philip I'd be happy to stay on till he came back. He said I could use his office while he's gone." She smiled and inclined her head toward the desk. "So, if you don't mind..." She stepped aside as Annie got up and left the room.

Chapter 24

Annie spent the balance of the morning on the water, ostensibly taking samples from spots where earlier pollution had been detected. Actually it was just an excuse to get away from "bubbly Becky." She couldn't stand the woman. Stupid bitch calls him "Phil." Wonder what she calls him in bed. Angrily slapping the water with her hand, she gunned the motor and startled a blue heron fishing nearby.

Taking over the office like that, Becky had deliberately humiliated her. Annie turned the boat sharply to the left, nearly capsizing it and making her realize what she'd almost done. She had to get hold of herself. Destroying the Waterkeeper's boat and drowning wasn't the answer.

Annie turned off the motor and let the boat drift. Her stomach growled. She was glad she'd remembered to grab her lunch on her way out the door. She reached inside the cooler and withdrew a ham sandwich, some chips and a Pepsi. Leaning back, she took a bite of the whole-wheat bread complete with lettuce, mayo, onion and tomato. In her rush to find out how Philip was doing, she'd neglected to eat breakfast. Now she consumed the sandwich with the gusto of someone on the verge of starvation. Wishing she had another, Annie wiped her mouth, balled up the baggie and tossed it in the cooler alongside the empty pop can.

She knew she should go back to the office and work on a press release letting the Okeechobee community know their handsome waterkeeper—she corrected herself—"acting" waterkeeper, would be all right. First she'd have to check with the police to find out if they'd arrested the shooter.

Looking at the cloudless sky, a gentle breeze caressed her face. If it wasn't for the relentless anger simmering inside, Annie could kick back and enjoy a beautiful summer day like anybody else. But, of course, she wasn't like anybody else now, not ever again.

She started the motor, then remembered what she'd discovered just before Becky interrupted her. She'd been scrutinizing the bank statement but hadn't found anything about the accounting snafu.

Could Philip have fabricated it? At the time, he'd seemed genuinely concerned, had even gone so far as to call the police and have her mother hauled in for questioning. Annie didn't understand why he'd do something like that if he was the one behind it in the first place. She shook her head. None of it made sense. There must be something she was missing, but what it might be, she hadn't a clue.

Then it occurred to her: since the bank made the error, they should be able to provide some answers. There was most likely a good reason it hadn't been included on the statement. Perhaps, since the matter had been resolved, it was deemed unnecessary. That didn't seem right to Annie, but if so, at least she'd stop wondering if Philip was behind it all. Deciding to stop by the bank on her way home, Annie headed back to the office and little Miss Perkyface.

Chapter 25

Lisa could feel Raoul watch as she went about her job, making her more than a little self-conscious. She gave customers a generous smile as she placed menus in front of them. Her uniform was spotless. What could be wrong? She'd stayed away from the casino as she promised; arrived on time, never took more than half an hour for lunch, often when they were busy, she even skipped breaks. Had she somehow offended a customer or co-worker?

She mentally flipped through conversations she'd participated in over the past few days. Had she made a derogatory remark about politics or religion? She knew expressing her opinion on such topics could offend and tried to limit her comments to the weather or other innocuous subjects. So, why was he scrutinizing her?

When she finished clearing the last of the tables in her section, he approached. "Come with me, we need to chat." Glancing over his shoulder, he added, "Jena'll cover for you."

As she followed her boss to his office, Lisa's heart beat double-time; her mouth suddenly went dry; the palms of her hands were wet with perspiration. He was going to fire her for sure. She bit her lower lip, sat down and braced herself.

"Lisa," Raoul began.

She felt herself stiffen.

Here it comes.

Lisa had never been fired before.

"I'm impressed with the job you've been doing. Everyone likes you—the customers, even the other waitresses, and getting along with co-workers isn't easy. Anyway, I believe in recognizing a job well done, so I wanted to let you know how pleased I am. In fact, if you continue the way you're going, you'll be getting a raise at the end of the month. How does that suit you?"

Lisa was momentarily speechless. "I-I- Thank you so much," she stammered.

Raoul grinned. "You're welcome. You looked so scared. Did you think I was going to fire you or something?"

For the first time, Lisa noticed his gentle expression and the look of amusement in his dark eyes. "Fire me?" she said, trying to cover her earlier fear. "No, of course not. Why would you do that?"

"Why indeed." Raoul chuckled. "Better get back to work before I change my mind."

Lisa rose to leave, then stopped. "Raoul, thanks so much for giving me a job. I really appreciate it."

"You're welcome. You're a good, reliable worker, Lisa, and believe me that's hard to find these days." He paused as if debating whether or not to continue, then said, "By the way, would you like to go to a powwow next Wednesday night?"

Chapter 26

From the moment she watched the Grand Entry and heard the Native Indian National Anthem, the rhythmic drumming and chant of the powwow drew Lisa in, not only calling to her spirit but pulling her back more than twenty years to Acoma.

She recalled the Buffalo Dance she'd participated in with Tomas. To her sixteen-year-old mind, he was the most handsome boy in the Pueblo. That night he'd looked mysterious with the buffalo skin over his head and much of his face. Dancing beside him, she was almost giddy, but managed to cover it up. Her outfit had been simple compared with the brilliantly colored regalia worn by tonight's dancers.

The intricate designs, multicolored feathers, long fringes swaying in time with the drumbeat, and shrill cries and guttural chants all combined to provide a display of sight and sound that swept her away.

She was especially impressed by the Jingle Dance. Seven rows of metal cones had been sewed onto the dancers' outfits. As they moved in time to the beat, the tinkling sound was hypnotic.

It had been such a long time since Lisa attended a powwow. When she and Craig were first married, they often went, but over time, as he became more heavily invested in the Waterkeeper movement, they went less often and finally stopped altogether.

She glanced up as the Two Step was announced. Raoul stood in front of her, his hand outstretched. "Be my partner?"

"I don't know how," Lisa said, embarrassed. She had dug her traditional Indian dress out of the trunk where it had been stored for years and was pleased to discover it was still in fairly good shape. Trying the garment on, Lisa was amazed to see that it fit. A bit snug in several places, she solved that problem by letting out a few stitches here and there.

"Nonsense," Raoul said. "It's a simple dance; besides who cares if you miss a step?"

Realizing he wouldn't take no for an answer, Lisa reluctantly joined him and was surprised when the drumming and chanting swept her up. All too soon the evening came to an end.

"Raoul, I had a wonderful time. Thanks so much for inviting me," Annie said as he walked her to her car. "I haven't been to a powwow in years. I'd almost forgotten how much it meant to me."

"I'm glad you enjoyed it. I thought you would," he said. "Say, you want to get a bite to eat?"

Lisa hesitated. For some reason she felt guilty, as if spending an evening with Raoul, or any other man, would be cheating on her husband. It made no sense. She realized Craig was gone and that she was free to do as she pleased. Still, it didn't feel right.

As if he'd noticed her reticence, Raoul's expression changed from anticipation to empathy. "Lisa, I'm sorry. I should've realized it was too soon." He opened the car door and gave her a wistful smile. "Maybe next time."

With a little wave and slight tap on the horn, drumming and chanting still echoing inside, Lisa drove away.

Chapter 27

It was after four in the afternoon and Annie was on her way to the bank, proud she'd made it through the afternoon without taking Becky's head off. The stupid bitch had continually interrupted her with the most inane questions: What should she do about the mail? Open it or wait till "Phil" returned? What if it was something that needed immediate attention?

Then there were the phone calls. She'd insisted on picking up the phone and identifying herself, all puffed up with her own importance. But then she couldn't answer any questions except those having to do with Philip's condition. She obviously knew the answers to those, as evidenced by her gushing response. Annie was glad to get away from her, even if it was only temporary. Now she needed to figure out what was going on at the bank.

Five minutes later, she pulled into the parking lot, relieved to see it was nearly empty. Maybe this would be a quick "in-out and all her questions answered" visit. She could only hope. It had been a long day and she was tired. The thought of dropping the matter and going home crossed her mind, tempted her actually. Instead of confronting some hostile bank officer, she could be chilling out in front of the TV, eating supper or sitting on the patio watching the pesky egret that had taken up residence in their yard.

She shrugged her shoulders.

Just do it, she thought and smiled.

That had been Dad's motto. Whenever there were chores she didn't want to do, he always said, "Just do it. It'll be done before you know it. Procrastinating only makes things worse. It doesn't solve anything." She knew he was right and often got through onerous tasks making use of that mantra. "Just do it," she muttered under her breath and got out of the car into the late afternoon sun.

As the mostly deserted parking lot forecast, there were only a few people lined up at tellers' windows. At first Annie dithered as to whether to get in a teller's line or see a manager for a private consultation. She chose the latter.

The woman was probably one of the strangest people Annie had ever encountered. Aside from being overweight to the point of obesity and wearing an outfit that looked like a circus clown reject, her voice was a combination slur and shout, making her next to impossible to understand.

"I work for the Okeechobee Waterkeeper's organization and have a question about our last bank statement."

"Yes?" the woman screamed. "Do you have a copy of your statement?"

"I'm sorry but I didn't bring it with me."

A look of disapproval crossed the woman's face making Annie feel like she was in the process of holding up the bank.

"I'm sorry," she said, "I didn't think I'd need it. I just have a quick question."

The woman sighed and looked at her watch. "What do you need to know? We close in fifteen minutes so..."

She didn't have to finish her sentence. Annie knew she wasn't about to stay past five, just to answer a customer's question, especially since this particular customer wasn't a big depositor. Her blank stare told Annie she'd best get on with it while she had the chance.

"Several weeks ago, ten thousand dollars was withdrawn from our account. The bank subsequently reported that it made an accounting error. When I checked our most recent statement covering that period, none of that activity was reported. I wondered why, I mean, if an error is made and reversed, shouldn't it be included in a statement?" There, Annie got it all out despite the consternation on the bank official's face.

"Of course, all account activity is reported on monthly statements."

"Even if it's an error on the part of the bank?"

"Even then."

The woman's shouting had begun to give Annie a headache.

Turning to her computer, the woman rapidly tapped several keys. "What's your account number?"

Having scribbled it on a scrap of paper just before the Beckster interrupted her, Annie was able to provide the loudmouthed banker with that bit of information.

"So, let's see now. You said there was a withdrawal in the amount of ten thousand dollars two weeks ago and then a reversal indicating the bank made some kind of accounting mistake, correct?"

"Yes," Annie said.

Again the woman tap-tap-tapped the computer keyboard. Then she stopped and gave Annie a look that said *what're you trying to pull?*

"Are you sure you have the right information?"

"I'm sure; at least that's what I was told."

"Look, lady, I don't know what your game is, but there's no record of either a ten thousand dollar withdrawal or any kind of error on the part of the bank." She stopped talking and gave Annie the same stern look she used to get in school when she was sent to the principal's office. After a few seconds, she said, "Anything else I can help you with?"

Annie was momentarily stunned. "Are you, like, sure?" she said. Perhaps the woman had looked at someone else's account.

The banker sighed and looked back at the computer screen. "Waterkeeper's account? Your most recent statement? Yes, I'm sure. Now, if there's nothing more, another customer's waiting."

Annie glanced over her shoulder. A man sat in the lobby, nervously checking his watch. The bank would close in five minutes and Miss Screamer didn't seem like the kind to sacrifice her personal time for a mere customer.

"No, you've answered all my questions. Thank you," Annie said and left the bank no wiser than when she'd come in.

Chapter 28

Harold Johnson zipped up his brother's pants and held out his arm to steady him as they exited the bathroom. This was a snapshot of the future to which he had to look forward as Bobby's Parkinson's progressed. He shuddered.

Bobby was first diagnosed ten years ago. His kids were only twenty-one and fifteen at the time. Harold remembered it like it was yesterday. Bobby's wife had come over on the verge of hysteria. She always was on the emotional side anyhow, making more of a situation than it demanded.

At first he'd dismissed her yawling as being her time of the month, but later on when they were alone and his wife, Shelly, explained what Parkinson's was, he'd felt bad that he'd given her so little sympathy.

Now, Shelly was in the grave and Bobby's wife had run off with some guy. The pressure of watching him deteriorate day after day, month after month had been too much for her.

That left him to care for his brother. Bobby's kids, well, they were stepping up to the plate, but the brunt of it fell on him. They were still young, after all, and had their own lives to live. His was all behind him.

Harold gritted his teeth as he thought again about how it had all come to pass. It was exhausting living and reliving the sad circumstances of his ruined life. He should just let the molten anger inside him go, but he couldn't. Instead of dissipating, it grew until it consumed him.

Those damned Whitakers; they'd destroyed his life and hadn't given it a second thought. No one held them accountable for the death and destruction they'd caused spraying those pesticides. They'd lost their farm; their father killed himself; their mom got cancer and died; and Bobby might as well be dead for the kind of life he was forced to live.

And the Whitakers? They're on Boston's social register with their names in the paper all the time, attending fancy balls and stuff. Harold's face went sour as he recalled the last time he'd read Whitaker's name in the paper.

"Harry," Bobby said in his hard-to-understand combination slur and stutter. "What's wrong? You got a cramp?"

Harold snorted. "Yeah, a cramp in my gut, that's what."

"You ought to take some Milk of Magnesia. That'll clear it up right away. That's what I take when my stomach acts up."

Harold patted his brother's hand. "Thanks but it's not that kind of pain."

"What kinda pain is it? Maybe some of my other medicine'll help."

The look of concern on Bobby's face tore at Harold's heart. Bobby was such a sweet soul, ready to do anything he could for anyone. The trouble was, of course, there was nothing he could do for anyone anymore. Everything had to be done for him. He was gracious about it, but Harold knew it ate at Bobby's soul.

"The kind of medicine I need isn't in a bottle."

When his brother gave him a puzzled look, Harold said, "Don't worry about it, the pain's nearly gone" Or it soon would be. He tripped on a smelly bag of garbage he meant to take out more than a week ago. A mouse skittered across the floor.

Part of the pain had gone with the death of Craig Whitaker. It was so satisfying to see the distraught expression on the bastard's face as he laid his only son to rest. Doesn't the Bible say something about the father's sins being visited upon the son? Well, Whitaker's boy had paid with his life for what his father did. So very satisfying, but he wasn't finished yet, not by a long shot.

Chapter 29

It was after ten on Saturday morning. Annie, who'd been up late watching an old movie starring Humphrey Bogart, was still in her pj's—blue and orange-flowered silky shorts topped by a matching tank top. Her long curly hair was a tangled mass. She'd just finished a breakfast of raisin bran and orange juice and lingered with coffee over the paper, when the doorbell rang.

Puzzled at the unexpected intrusion, she glanced toward the front of the house thinking she may have imagined it. Then it rang three more times. Thinking it might be her mother home from shopping with her arms full, Annie reluctantly unfolded herself and went down the hall. The bell sounded yet again.

"All right, all right, I'm coming. Don't get your panties in a bunch," Annie muttered. She twisted the knob, yanked the door back and gasped in surprise.

"Nathan," she said to her grinning fiancé, whose arms spread in anticipation of a hug. "What're you doing here? I forget you were coming?"

Nathan's arms drooped along with his mouth. "No, I

thought I'd surprise you." He eyed her unkempt appearance, and added, "Looks like I succeeded."

Suddenly realizing she wasn't dressed, Annie said, "C'mon in. There's coffee in the kitchen." Before he had a chance to respond, she turned and dashed down the hall.

Alone in her room, Annie's emotions yoyo'd from elation and joy to annoyance and anger. The bottom line was that Nathan's sudden appearance confused her. She hadn't had a chance to plan her weekend and here he expected her to drop everything and spend it with him. She still smarted from her discovery at the bank and had been trying to figure out what to say to Philip about it, so hanging out with Nathan all weekend would be a major distraction. Besides, her feelings about him had become increasingly ambivalent. She needed time to sort things out. The whole Philip-Becky thing had thrown her for a major loop too.

She threw on a clean pair of shorts and an orange T-shirt with a Florida Gators' logo. Then she ran a comb through her hair and applied a touch of makeup. Donning her flip-flops, she pronounced herself good enough to face Nathan. If he didn't like what he saw, too bad. Maybe next time he'd let her know before just showing up. Her feet made snicking sounds on the hardwood floor as she went back to the kitchen.

"Hey, babe," Nathan looked up from the newspaper. He stood and kissed her, then pulled back, his hands still resting on her shoulders. "Watcha want to do today?"

Annie didn't have a ready answer. "Well, truthfully, I hadn't given it much thought." Gesturing at the countertops cluttered with dirty dishes, she added, "I thought I'd do some chores around here and run a few errands."

"Oh," was all Nathan said, letting the disappointment on his face complete his thought. When Annie didn't respond, he added, "I thought we'd rent a boat and spend the afternoon on the lake. What do you think?" His eyes sparkled in anticipation, irritating her even more.

"I think if that's what you want to do, you should do it," she said, her words clipped, almost staccato.

Nathan looked confused. "No, I mean, I want you to go with me. It won't be any fun to go alone." The pleading in his voice reminded Annie of a five year old.

"I'm sorry, but since I spend half my time on the lake during the week, it wouldn't be much of a treat." She sat and folded her arms across her chest. He wasn't getting his way for a change. She realized he'd driven all the way from Tampa, but taking her for granted like this wasn't going to work. She had things she wanted to do too. It wasn't all about him.

For a moment, neither one spoke. The only sound in the room was the buzzing of a fly at the window. Sun filtered through the palm trees, splashing shadows across the floor.

"So..." Nathan said. "Is there anything you want to do?"

"Not really. Maybe tonight we could go to a movie or out to dinner?"

"And I'll spend the night?" There was a hopeful glint in his eyes.

"I don't think so. My room's all torn up and with mom in the house, it's not a good idea."

"What do you mean? You let me stay here last time? What's changed?"

"Lots of things have changed. For one thing, I haven't been sleeping in my room since..." She realized she hadn't told Nathan about the break-ins. She didn't know why she hadn't told him, she just hadn't. The truth of the matter was they hadn't spoken very often in the past few weeks. She wasn't home when he called and by the time she got his messages, it was too late to call back. They texted back and forth but she hadn't wanted to burden him with the whole break-in thing.

"And why not?"

"Nathan, that's not the issue, okay?"

He paused as if to let her message sink in. "Is it that Philip guy? That why you don't want me around?"

"What're you talking about? Philip's my boss. Are you suggesting we're hooking up or something?"

Nathan's expression was so serious it scared Annie. She'd seen him angry before but never like this.

"Are you?"

"I'm not even going to dignify that with an answer. You know me better than that or at least I'd hope so." How Nathan had picked up on her conflicted feelings about Philip she didn't know, but this wasn't the time to go into it. She needed to sort things out first.

"I notice you're not wearing your engagement ring. Is that so you won't scare off the locals?"

Annie felt anger rise from the pit of her stomach to the back of her throat. "I think you'd better leave before we say things we'll regret."

Nathan's angry expression morphed into a blush of embarrassment. "Annie, I'm sorry, I didn't mean to suggest…"

"But that's the thing, Nathan, you suggested that I was—what's the word for it? A slut? Is that how you act when you don't get your way?"

When he didn't respond, Annie said, "Just go."

Nathan looked torn between giving her a hug and walking away. He chose the latter after mumbling something that sounded like "later."

Annie closed the door and burst into tears. If she was confused before, her encounter with Nathan made it that much worse. She stepped over to the window and watched through the curtain as he drove away. Would she ever see him again? Did she even want to? She simply didn't know.

Chapter 30

Lisa walked the aisle of the Save-A-Lot thinking about the powwow, and to be honest, about Raoul. As she filled up her cart with the cheapest food she could find, she tried to put him out of her mind.

It had been a wonderful evening, something she hadn't experienced in a long time. Even before Craig's death, nights out had almost become a thing of the past. She'd forgotten how much fun it could be to put her worries aside and enjoy herself. It was exhilarating. She smiled as she pulled a box of cookies from the shelf. She should save some money and make them from scratch. They'd taste better too. But now that she was working, time was so scarce. Besides, neither Annie nor she spent much time at home anymore.

She went through the checkout line, which miraculously was nearly empty, a fact for which she was more than a little grateful. After working all week and going to the powwow, she was tired and looked forward to sitting on the patio or—she glanced up—if it rained as it threatened to do, she'd spend the afternoon doing laundry and watching TV.

A little while later, she pulled into the drive, puzzled as she thought she recognized Nathan's car going the opposite direction. She must be mistaken. Annie hadn't planned to see him this weekend; at least she didn't think so. Besides if it was him, why would he be leaving so soon? She shrugged and parked the car, giving her horn a little tap. Annie's help unloading the groceries would be appreciated.

When her daughter failed to appear, she leaned on the bell. The least the girl could do was open the door so she wouldn't have to set the bags down to unlock it. When that didn't happen either, she sighed. Oh well, maybe she wasn't home, although her car was. Maybe she'd gone for a run. Never mind.

As she put her key in the lock, the door flew open. Annie stood there all puffy-eyed and red in the face. "I'm sorry, Mom, I didn't hear you drive up. Here let me get those." She reached for the overstuffed bags.

"That's okay, dear, there's more in the car. Why don't you… Are you all right?"

Annie didn't say anything, just nodded and quickly went over to the car. When she returned with her arms full, Lisa was stocking the shelves and refrigerator with provisions.

"That should hold us for a little while," she said, giving her daughter a furtive look. Although tempted to ask what was wrong, she held back; Annie might accuse her of prying. After all, she was a grown woman and had a right to her privacy.

Finally unable to keep still any longer, Lisa said, "Was that Nathan's car I saw as I drove up?"

With that Annie began to sob. "He just showed up, no call or nothing. I wasn't even dressed. He assumed I'd drop everything and spend the weekend with him without even asking. I mean, what if I had plans? He seems to think he owns me and that I'll do whatever he wants."

When Lisa didn't comment, she went on. "Mom, I don't know what to do. I really don't. We had a big fight and he left."

Lisa nodded sympathetically and proceeded to take out a jug of milk. Then she opened a package of chocolate chip cookies and put them on a plate. "Let's sit on the patio and sort this out," she said and, without waiting for an answer, headed for the door. Annie grabbed some glasses and followed. When they were settled comfortably, nibbling cookies and sipping cold milk, the afternoon heat seemed more tolerable.

Lisa put her glass down and leaned back. "Now, tell me again what happened?"

Annie went through the whole scenario, ending with, "Do you think I was wrong to be angry? I mean, isn't he taking an awful lot for granted? Just because we're engaged, does that mean I have to be at his beck and call?"

She looked so miserable, Lisa had to resist the urge to take her daughter in her arms like she used to when Annie was little. She wanted to assure her things would be all right.

"Annie," she began, "when couples are in a serious relationship, as you are, they begin to take certain things for granted. Nathan evidently decided to surprise you. He assumed you'd be thrilled. It probably didn't even occur to him that you had other plans. By the way, did you?"

Annie's face fell. "Not really."

"So what was the problem? I mean, you didn't have anything to do but hang around the house all weekend."

Annie stood up. "Go ahead, take his side, why don't you?"

"Annie, honey, calm down. I'm not taking anyone's side. I just don't understand why you're so upset. It seems like you're blowing this out of proportion."

"It's the principle of the thing that bothers me. He acts like he owns me; that whatever he wants to do, is what we're going to do. What I want doesn't count."

"I think you're overreacting. From what I've seen of him, Nathan adores you and would do anything to make you happy. You know what I think the real problem is?"

Annie reached for another cookie and looked uncertainly at her mother. "What?"

"Are you sure you want to hear my opinion? You might not like what I have to say."

Annie put the half-eaten cookie down, leaned back and folded her arms across her chest. "Go ahead."

"Philip has your head in a whirl and you don't know which way to turn, that's what I think and, frankly Annie, judging by the picture of him in the paper, it's easy to see why."

When Annie didn't respond, Lisa said, "You have to ask yourself if you're ready to settle down and be a married woman and if Nathan's the right man for you. We've talked about this before. Your reaction at Nathan's unexpected appearance tells me you have a lot of thinking to do before you plan a wedding."

Tears flowed freely down Annie's cheeks. She nodded and mouthed, "I know." Then she got up, gave her mom a hug, went into her cluttered bedroom and closed the door.

Chapter 31

Lisa sat in the living room looking through some family photographs she'd stashed away when she married Craig. At the time her feelings had run so high and hurt so deeply that she'd buried them in the bottom of the trunk along with everything else that reminded her of Acoma and home.

Now having gone to a powwow for the first time in nearly two decades, she was strong enough to take a backward look. There was her father in his ceremonial dress. He looked solemn next to her mother, who seemed unable to keep a straight face. She always did smile more often than she frowned and that was only to keep her children in line.

Lisa recalled with wicked pleasure some of the antics she and her younger sisters, Vera and Claire, had engaged in behind their parents' backs. How much they knew and chose to let them think they got away with, would forever remain a mystery.

Once again she thought fondly about her family and wondered how they were doing. Were her parents still alive and living in Acomita Lake? Perhaps it was time to swallow her pride and contact them. But what if they rejected her again? As she recalled, her father had been clear: *"Marry that boy and you're no longer part of this family, you hear me? You'll be dead to us so don't bother coming back."* Those words were etched in her heart. She'd never forget the cold dread that had gone down her spine as he spoke them.

Did he still feel that way after all these years? Wouldn't he welcome a granddaughter, especially now that Craig was gone?

Lisa didn't know if she was strong enough to deal with any more drama. The events of the past month had been more than enough to last her a lifetime.

As she sifted through the stack of pictures, her eyes fell upon the one of Tomas and her at the Buffalo Dance. Someone had snapped it and given her a copy. Although it was faded, she could still make out the details of their outfits and the fact that he held her hand. She teared up remembering exactly how she felt that night. She'd been so thrilled when he asked her to be his partner. They'd been something of a couple from that point forward. Everyone—including Lisa herself—assumed they'd eventually marry. Her life pattern had been set; at least that's what she'd thought. Then Craig Whitaker came along and everything changed.

Lisa leaned back in the rocker-recliner. Several photographs slid to the floor and remained there unnoticed as she closed her eyes and let the drumming and chanting of the previous evening wash over her. The sounds and colors remained so vivid there was no escaping the emotions they evoked. She could still feel the pressure of Raoul's hand on hers as they danced the

Two-Step. His appraising glance and the merriment in his eyes again warmed her heart.

Should she have said yes when he suggested they go out for a bite to eat? Was he offended when she refused? He appeared to understand, but did he really? Would he ask her a second time? Did she even want him to? Lisa wasn't sure. The man was her boss after all and if things didn't work out, then what?

She was so deep in thought that she didn't hear Annie come into the room.

"What're you looking at, Mom?"

Lisa opened her eyes with a start.

"I'm sorry. Were you asleep? I didn't mean to wake you."

Lisa laughed and began to stack the photos. "No dear, I wasn't asleep. I was just thinking about what a good time I had last night. You should come with me next time."

"Really? To a powwow? Don't you have to be a member of the tribe or something?"

"No, not at all. I'm not a Seminole and Raoul invited me."

"Yes, but you work at the casino and besides you belong to the Acoma tribe, so in a sense you're part of the club."

"Well, you are too. You're Acoma by birth."

"I'm a half-breed," Annie said, adding with a slight expression of disdain. "I'm a 'neither-nor.'"

"A 'neither-nor?' What's that?" Lisa leaned forward in her chair and retrieved the pictures on the floor.

"Someone who's neither white nor a full-fledged minority. At school they're called n-n's."

Lisa started to chuckle until her daughter, a wry look

on her face, said, "Now kids can say that about me too."

"Well, that's one way to look at it, but you could also think of yourself as a 'b-i-w'."

Annie's forehead wrinkled in puzzlement. "What's a 'b-i-w'?"

"That's when you're both Indian and white; b-i-w, get it?"

"Yeah, Ma, I get it. The whole thing's silly anyhow."

It was clear to Lisa they had exhausted the topic so she changed the subject.

"Are you feeling better about Nathan?"

"I guess." Annie leaned back in the sofa and folded her legs beneath her. "I decided to just let things be for now. Maybe it will eventually work itself out."

"That's a good idea," Lisa said. "Given enough time, they usually do."

"So, how was the powwow? You had a good time?"

"I really did," Lisa said, a faint smile played at the edges of her mouth. "It's been a long time since I enjoyed myself so much."

"Not even with Dad?" A pout began to spread across Annie's face.

"Of course, I had good times with your father. I didn't mean to suggest that..." Lisa let her sentence trail off.

"But this Raoul guy, he's a Seminole, right?

"Yes. So?"

"So, Dad was white. You couldn't possibly have felt the same way toward him as you would toward another Indian."

"Oh, Annie, where do you come up with this stuff? How could you know how much I loved your father, still love him, in fact? What does going to a powwow have to do with any of that?"

Subdued, Annie said, "Nothing, I guess. It's just that I miss Dad so very much and the thought of someone taking his place, well, it's more than I can bear."

Lisa stood up and went to her child, giving her a hug. "You don't have to worry about that, honey, I miss him too." And despite the chanting and drumming that continued to play inside her heart, she meant it with every fiber of her being.

Chapter 32

Near hurricane-force winds whipped palm-tree fronds into a frenzy, reminding Annie of her own storm-tossed emotions.

Ever since the summer began, she'd been whipsawed by one crisis after another beginning with the death of her father, through the silliness of that missing money, Philip getting shot and now this: a major blow-up with Nathan. Was she really prepared to return his ring? Did Philip mean that much to her? Even if she was in love with him—and she didn't know whether she was or not—how could she be sure he loved her back? Oh, she could come right out and tell him how she felt, but what if he just patted her on the head and said, "I love you too; you're doing a great job. Keep up the good work." How could she face him after something like that?

Then there were the odd things she was beginning to notice. Like, for instance, the fact that her mother said she'd never met him. Philip told her he'd worked with her dad for several years, knew him well. But her mom said she'd never set eyes on him and that her father never mentioned him either. While it was true her mom's involvement with the Waterkeepers had dropped off over the years, still, she'd be familiar with the people her dad worked with, or at least their names.

Then there was that whole thing about the missing and then not missing money which had showed up in her bedroom and then just as quickly disappeared.

Annie's head was about to explode. Was she making too much of all this? What if she just sat back and acted like nothing was wrong? She and Nathan were getting along just fine, thank you very much. Philip and Dad had been drinking buddies. Money moved in and out of the house—and the bank—all the time, what's the big deal? Like Mom said, let it all work itself out, then see what was what and go from there.

That was a tall order for someone like Annie. She was used to being in control of her life, or at least actively participating in it. She'd learned that much from her dad. Now it seemed she had no say in anything—even the most significant things in her life were beyond her grasp.

As the wind died down, Annie came to a decision: She'd confront Philip with what she'd discovered at the bank and concerning his tenure with the Waterkeepers. Then, if they were still speaking—she'd tell him she loved him.

Chapter 33

Annie sat at her desk trying to work up the energy to make some of those dratted donor calls. Suddenly a high-pitched shriek emanating from Becky caught her attention. She looked up and immediately understood the source of her co-worker's delight: Philip had just driven up and was getting out of the car.

Without waiting for Annie to join her, Becky sprinted to the door and threw it open. "Phil," she shouted, "you're back." Then she hurried over to the car and, throwing her arms around him, kissed him—right on the lips.

Watching from the window, Annie did a slow burn.

Yeah. Right.

She was going to tell Philip she loved him: NOT. Taking her time, she moved toward the door to greet her boss. As far as she was concerned, Becky had done enough welcoming for them both.

She hadn't been to see Philip in the hospital since that first morning when Becky had so unceremoniously brushed her aside. Now, as Philip walked through the door, he gave her an odd look.

"Hey, stranger," he said.

"Hey yourself," Annie replied. "Welcome back."

"Thanks."

"So?" she said, for want of anything better to say.

"So? What?" He continued into the room and sat down on the first available chair, as if the effort of walking from the parking lot to the office fatigued him.

"So, how're you doing?" Annie realized her question was more than a little lame, but it was the best she could do at the moment.

"Better than, you know, before." He gave her a wry smile.

"Are you in a lot of pain?" Annie managed to squeak out. In spite of herself, she really did care. Besides it wasn't his fault Becky threw herself at him like that. Still, he didn't have to enjoy it quite so much.

"Not when I take these little babies." He took a vial of pills from his pocket. "It's not as bad as it was, and hey, it could have been worse. A couple inches to the right and I wouldn't even be here, so who's complaining? Not me, that's for sure."

Becky stood next to Philip looking very proprietary, as if she owned the man. Her hand rested on the back of his chair. "Phil, you want to go over your phone messages and mail? I have it all sorted out and waiting for you." She cleared her voice and glanced around the room as if surveying her kingdom. "You'll need some detailed explanations for some of them."

Philip looked at Annie. "I'll be there in a minute."

Becky looked from Philip to Annie and back. "Well, okay then," she said, and with a shake of her curly hair, flounced across the room into Philip's office and closed the door.

For a few seconds, silence more deafening to Annie than a sudden clap of thunder, filled the space as neither seemed to know what to say. Finally, Philip broke the ice.

"How are you anyway?" His voice was as soft as a gentle caress.

Annie tried to shrug off her sudden surge of affection. She fingered her engagement ring as though to form a barrier between them. She was in a committed relationship with Nathan. And besides, from what she could tell, Becky pretty much had her hooks into Philip.

"I'm fine," she said.

"You didn't come to see me in the hospital."

"Yes I did," Annie said a tad too fast, as though she cared what he thought.

"Really? When?" he challenged her.

"I was there the morning after you got, you know, shot." The word "shot" was hard, almost painful to say in reference to him.

"Really?"

"Yes."

"I don't remember." The expression on his face said he was trying to access that part of his brain but having no luck. "I'm sorry but I don't remember you being there. I thought maybe you were mad at me or something."

"Yeah, sure, you almost get yourself killed and I'm mad. Why on earth would I be mad at you?" Annie could think of several reasons but now wasn't the time to bring them up. "I guess I should have come back to see you again, but you seemed to have more than enough company and I didn't want to intrude."

Philip's eyes filled with puzzlement. "Intrude? You? Annie, how could think you'd be an intrusion? It's just not possible. Yes, you should have come. I missed seeing you."

At those words a thrill ran through Annie akin to an electric shock. She wanted to tell Philip right then and there how deeply she cared for him; how much she missed him; how she fantasized about him all the time. She didn't want to wait to tell him; wanted to say it right now, right here. This would be the perfect moment; she might never get another.

She opened her mouth, "Philip," she said. "I have something to tell you."

Just then the office door opened and Becky's grating voice boomed out, "Well, Philip are you coming or not? I don't have all day."

Chapter 34

Harold Johnson was tired of waiting. He wanted to lock and load. The fact that fate had intervened, putting his plans on hold was no one's fault, but that didn't make it any easier. The sooner he could make that bastard pay for getting rich by destroying lives and property, the happier he'd be. At least then he'd have a semblance of peace, something that had eluded him ever since he realized who caused his family's devastating misfortunes.

Bobby called from the bedroom, "Harry, need you. Fell down."

Harold turned off the flame from the pot of soup simmering on the stove. He never knew how long his brother's mishaps would take and didn't want to risk setting the place on fire. The other day Bobby managed to wedge himself in between the toilet and the vanity—something Harold still couldn't figure out. It had taken the better part of half an hour to get him out. At one point, he was about to give up and call the fire department when, for whatever reason, he managed to extricate him. Since then, he'd insisted Bobby call whenever he needed to go.

It was inconvenient for sure, but not nearly as bad as risking something worse.

Ten minutes later, Bobby was ensconced in an aging rocker in the cluttered living room, and Harold was back at the stove mulling over what to do next. His plans were in the rudimentary stage, despite his desire to get a move on, but exactly how they'd go about it remained up in the air.

The elder Whitaker would be made to understand it was no accident, that it was payback. It would be satisfying to see the pain on the old man's face at his realization that he was to blame. Now if he could only coordinate everything to make sure the man knew what was happening without giving so much away that police interfered.

He poured the soup into bowls slopping some over the side and, without bothering to wipe it up, put them on the table. "Bobby, dinner's ready," His younger brother, with excruciating effort, got up and made his way across the room.

Chapter 35

Water sloshed over the rim of the glass, making a dark stain down Lisa's carefully ironed uniform. Her hand trembled as she brushed it off and tried to ignore Raoul's smile as she approached his table.

"Hey there, pretty lady," he said.

Heat wormed its way up Lisa's neck and onto her cheeks. "Hey yourself, Mr. Tucker."

"My, my, aren't we formal today?" Although the smile faded, the sparkle in his eyes remained.

"Well, you are my boss, after all. You deserve my respect." Lisa was all too aware that his gaze had dropped and seemed to appraise her. Would he notice the damp spot on her skirt?

"So, do you respect me enough to have dinner with me tomorrow night?"

His question took Lisa by surprise. She thought after turning him down the other night that he'd been offended and wouldn't ask her again. Now, here he was, inviting her to join him. What should she do?

Craig seemed to materialize, inserting himself

between them. How could she possibly go out with another man and desecrate his memory? Before she could respond, tears pooled in her eyes, blurring the room and its occupants.

Lisa blinked rapidly, unsuccessfully trying to stem their flow. Her face was soon wet as she began to sob. She didn't understand what was happening to her. All this time—from the very first—she'd been in complete control, comforting everyone else. But now, overwhelmed with grief, she couldn't stop crying.

Raoul got up from his seat and quickly went to her side. "Lisa, I'm so sorry," he said gently and nudged her in the direction of his office.

* * * *

An hour later, Lisa awoke with a start, momentarily confused. Where was she? She glanced around. Now she remembered: She was in Raoul's office, lying on his sofa. He'd left her there to rest and get composed.

God, what a fool she'd made of herself. He'd just invited her out to dinner and she falls apart? He must think she was some kind of basket case. He wouldn't bother her again, that's for sure.

Tap, tap, tapping from the computer keyboard and the soft rustle of papers across the room called her attention to where Raoul sat quietly working. She sat up.

"You're awake," Raoul said. "Feel better?"

"I'm so sorry; I don't know what came over me. That's not like me at all. I don't go around bursting into tears." To say she was mortified would be an understatement. She hadn't been able to stop crying, in fact she'd continued to sob well after Raoul left the office, and then, emotionally exhausted, had fallen asleep on the overstuffed sofa which sat in the corner.

"Maybe that's exactly what you needed," Raoul said and put a sheet of paper on top of several others. He removed his glasses and went over to Lisa, motioning for her to remain seated. "Don't you see? You've probably been a rock for everyone around you during that whole ordeal and didn't have time to grieve. You were a pillar of strength—had to be for the sake of your daughter, right? Couldn't let her see how vulnerable you really were.

"Then I come along and like a jackass, start putting moves on you. Oh, it was subtle; at least I thought so: Ask you to a powwow, then suggest we go for coffee, invite you out to dinner. Even after you said it was too soon, I still get up in your face. God, what an idiot. Lisa, I'm so very sorry. Of course you're not ready. How could you be? You just lost your husband."

"Raoul, you didn't do anything wrong. You didn't know…" Lisa let her voice trail off, leaving the balance of her thought unsaid.

"But that's the whole point, isn't it? I should've known. It was just plain stupid. I won't do it again, I promise."

If Lisa wasn't ready to get involved with another man, she wasn't willing to just let this one go either. Despite her mixed emotions, she recognized that Raoul was special. "How about we start over as friends?" she said.

"Friends go out to coffee," Raoul said.

"They do," Lisa said and added with a twinkle in her eye. "Sometimes they even go out to dinner."

"Sometimes they do," Raoul agreed. "But for now, how about you go on home and get some rest? Your shift's nearly over anyway. Besides, unlike you, I have work to do." The smile on his face said he was only teasing and for that Lisa was grateful.

Chapter 36

"So, the other day you were about to tell me something when Becky interrupted," Philip said. "What was it you wanted to say?"

Philip and Annie were alone in the office for a change. Becky was off doing whatever she did when she wasn't hanging around. Annie frankly didn't care where she was.

Philip's question took her by surprise. She wasn't sure this was the right time to tell him how she felt. There were still those other issues to clear up. She scratched the spot behind her ear that always itched when she felt unsure of herself. He watched her and waited.

"I, uh, it's complicated," she said in a lame attempt to buy some time. She looked at the stack of papers cluttering her desk, "Besides, we've got a ton of work to catch up on before Friday's meeting."

Philip took the pen from Annie's hand. "Come into my office," he said. The expression in his dark eyes left no room for debate.

When she was settled in the chair across from his

desk, Annie took a deep breath. Where to begin?

Philip folded his hands and leaned back in the swivel desk chair. "Okay, spill it, Whitaker. What's on your mind?" Despite the near-harsh words, his expression was warm.

"Well, since you insist, there are a number of things I wanted to talk to you about." Again the spot behind her ear prickled and without a second thought, she rubbed her fingers back and forth across it in an attempt to soothe away the irritation.

Philip watched her delaying tactic in amusement. "Yes? What is it you wanted to discuss?"

"Well, for starters…" How could she ask him to explain why it was her mom never met him, wasn't even familiar with his name despite the fact he claimed to have worked with her father for several years.

He leaned in, dropping his feet on the floor as the chair tipped upright. "Yes, for starters?"

It was clear he wasn't going to let this go; where was Becky when she needed her? Why didn't the annoying bitch barge in like she usually did? Couldn't the phones at least start to ring? Nothing. No Becky. No calls. Just the silence of the office and Philip's eyes quietly scrutinizing her.

She cleared her throat. "Well, this is probably silly, but when I mentioned your name at home my mom didn't know who you were, said she'd never met you. I thought that was odd since you told me you'd worked with my dad for several years and knew him well."

An almost imperceptible shadow fell across Philip's face. He straightened up in the chair crossed his legs and folded his arms across his chest. Then he cleared his throat.

"You're right, it *is* silly, but since you asked there's a perfectly logical explanation. I worked with the Waterkeepers' Alliance out east and met your dad when he came to a meeting of the country's waterkeepers several years ago. We hit it off and stayed in touch. I came for a visit shortly before his unfortunate, uh, you know, accident and offered to help out till a permanent replacement could be found." He stopped talking then added, "That's why your mom never heard of me. That make sense?"

It was perfectly logical. Dad dies; someone familiar with the organization and its work happens to be visiting and is willing to take over.

"Yes, it really does," Annie said. "But I thought you said you'd worked with him here in Florida for several years; helped set up the organization…" she could have quoted him chapter and verse as to what he'd told her, but figured this would suffice.

"What can I say? I exaggerated to impress you." Philip shrugged his shoulders and gave her a guilty little-boy grin.

Annie's suspicions had been groundless. She could see that now. But what about the bank? Would he explain that away too?

"That it?"

Annie hesitated. The phone rang, startling her. She laughed. "I'll get it," she said. "The rest can wait till later."

* * * *

"What do you mean they haven't arrested anyone?" Becky was nearly shouting. Philip gestured for her to pipe down "How could they not know?" She continued, "For God's sake, he shot you in front of a room full of people."

As Becky warmed to her topic she became increasingly animated, gesturing wildly, barely missing Annie with her elbow. "Are the police around here so stupid they can't find a single person to identify him?"

Annie watched Philip's attempts to quiet the woman in growing amusement. It was the first time she'd seen the two clash over anything. Maybe a crack had finally developed in their relationship. If only it were so.

It was late afternoon as they sat in Philip's office catching up on what had transpired since the shooting. "The problem is the man's apparently new to the area and disappeared immediately afterward," Philip explained. "No one could identify him or his car. He seems to have vanished into thin air."

"How convenient," Becky harrumphed, crossing her arms tightly over her chest and leaning back in the chair.

"What else?" Philip looked at Annie as if anxious to change the subject.

"We lost our lawsuit against Hanidad Chemical."

"We did? When did that happen?"

"Two days after the shooting the decision came down. I'm sorry I didn't tell you sooner, but I didn't want to upset you. The lawyer called and said they'd appeal. He thinks the judge made some basic errors. And besides, he's got a record of siding with polluters. I thought the whole matter could wait till you got back."

Philip gave her one of his rare smiles, the kind that lit up the room. "You thought right. Thanks for that, Annie." He paused as if he was about to say something but thought better of it, then said, "Is that it?" When neither woman offered anything more, he said, "Okay, let's get back to work. Oh, Annie, could you stay a moment?"

Becky gave her a look that said she didn't much care for Philip singling her out.

Well, good. Now the bitch knows what it's like.

Annie smiled and crossed her legs.

After Becky left the room, Philip got up and closed the door. Then he settled himself in his swivel chair. "So, what's on your mind?" he said.

"On my mind?" Annie's brow crinkled. "I'm sorry but I don't know what you're talking about."

"This morning after you asked why your mother didn't know who I was, you said that would be all 'for now.' I wondered what else was bothering you."

Not prepared to address the issue, Annie stumbled over her words. "I, uh, well, I ..." she really didn't want to get into it with him, not now, not with Becky no doubt listening, her ear glued to the other side of the door.

"Yes, what is it? You can tell me," Philip's expression was one of concern.

"Oh, it was nothing, really," Annie prevaricated. "I had a problem, but it's all cleared up. It's nothing to be concerned about."

Philip's expression said he didn't believe her. "Are you sure?"

His dark piercing eyes had a direct line into her soul. Maybe she should come right out and ask. What was the use of waiting? It wouldn't change anything.

"Well, now that you mention it, there is something." She sat back down.

Philip leaned back and waited.

Annie took a deep breath.

Might as well get it over with.

"While you were in the hospital," she began, dragging the words out in an effort to buy some time. She glanced out the window. It had been a gloomy day. The unusually early darkness reflected her mood. What would be the outcome of her revelation about the bank? Would their friendly relationship ever be the same?

"Yes, while I was in the hospital…what?" Philip tapped a pencil on the desk. Annie knew he wasn't the most patient person she'd ever known. He was handsome, charming and smart but he had a temper, she could tell. He hid it fairly well, but there were times, like right now, that he seemed to be on the edge of exploding. It quite frankly frightened her. Then he'd turn on the charm and she'd forget all about that side of his personality.

"I, uh, well,"

"Oh, for heaven's sake, Whitaker, spit it out and be done with it. Whatever it is we'll deal with it."

Annie knew she couldn't dodge the question any longer. She couldn't think of something on the spur of the moment that would justify her hesitation.

"Okay, but promise you won't get mad."

"Get mad? Annie, what are we, little kids? For god's sake, I'm not going to jump down your throat no matter what it is. Trust me."

His eyes drilled her with their intensity. She could almost feel the heat of his emotion.

She gave him an uncertain smile. "I'm sorry. You're right." She crossed, then uncrossed her legs and fiddled with her engagement ring. "The thing is, I was in your office and happened to notice the bank statement on your desk. That reminded me of the problem we'd had with the bank's, uh, er, mistake—you know, when they reported a ten thousand dollar withdrawal and then said it was an error on their part."

Philip just gave her a blank stare and appeared to be

waiting for her to finish, so she continued. She wished she'd just let it go. What good would confronting Philip like this do? Unfortunately, it was too late now.

"Anyway, I was curious about how it would show up on the statement, so I looked, I mean I didn't see the harm, it wasn't as if I was snooping or anything. It was sitting right there spread out as if you'd been reading it."

"You're right. I opened it and was looking it over just before the meeting that night. So…"

"So, I couldn't find a reference to it on the statement anywhere. That started me to wondering why."

Philip sighed. "Whitaker, sometimes you're too nosy for your own good."

Annie giggled. Anything to lighten the mood even if it did sound a little forced.

"Then what?" Philip wasn't laughing. His expression was stone-cold serious.

"Well, then I decided to go to the bank and ask them why they hadn't included it on the statement. I mean, if they're messing with our funds, taking money in and out and causing problems, they need to know we're watching, don't they? I mean, Philip, my mom was taken to the police station and questioned. They all but accused her of stealing the money." She knew the pace of her speech had sped up. She just wanted to get this unpleasantness over with.

Philip nodded. "So you went to the bank and confronted them. What did they say?"

"That's the thing. They denied knowing anything about it. Said there was no accounting error, that they'd never called you and reported one." There, she'd gotten it out. Annie stopped.

"So?"

"So, I got to wondering what happened. Could you explain it to me?"

"Well, not that it's any of your business, but it turns out the mistake was on my part. I panicked and claimed the bank called. You're right, they hadn't, I was just covering my tracks. Then when I discovered the mistake, I was embarrassed by what I'd put you and your mother through, so I blamed it on the bank. That's all there was to it. No harm, no foul. All right?" He gave her a pained smile. "Are we good?"

"You're not mad?"

"Mad? Why would I be mad? You're a bit too curious for your own good, but since I involved your mother, I can see where it would concern you. No," his eyes softened, "it would take a lot more than that to make me angry with you."

It was well after five and the dusk was growing deeper. Rain drummed softly on the gutters. The office was downright cozy. Now that the whole bank matter was cleared up, Annie felt relieved.

"Anything else?"

There was still the matter of that money found in her bedroom and where it came from. Neither one raised the issue or suggested the possibility that her father had somehow been involved.

"Not really," she said and stood up. That would have to wait for another day—along with telling him about her growing attraction for him. Another day, or maybe never—she hadn't decided which.

Chapter 37

It was well after supper. The dishes done and put away, Lisa decided to put her feet up and read a few pages from her latest murder mystery. With Annie working late, she had the place to herself. It was times like this that she missed Craig the most—not that he'd been there every night either. During those final months, he'd been at community meetings four or five times a week. It had been a growing source of irritation between them.

Lisa sighed. She should have accompanied him more often, but it had become such a bore. The issues were always the same: how to stop the pollution of their waterways; how to expose miscreants who acted without regard for the common good; how to get the Environmental Protection Agency to actually do their job; who to take to court; how to attract more people—and money to the cause.

At first Lisa had been as enthusiastic about the work as her husband. Then Annie came along and the pull of motherhood took precedence over everything else. Little did she realize she'd eventually lose them both: Craig to death and Annie to growing up. It would only be a matter of time and every night would be like this.

She settled back into her favorite chair, the battered old rocker-recliner. A floor lamp illuminated the area around her. She removed the bookmark and began to read. She'd just gotten to the part where the killer had broken into the house that held a sleeping woman and her children and was about to do the unthinkable, when the doorbell rang and startled Lisa back to reality.

Who would be coming to call at this hour? She glanced at the clock on the opposite wall. It was only seven, not late at all really. But to Lisa, who seldom had company anymore, it seemed late. She hoped it wasn't bad news, hoped that Annie, wherever she was, was safe. Her mind always seemed to go there whenever an unexpected phone call or doorbell summoned her. She opened the door to find Raoul standing there.

"Hey, Lisa," he began. "I was in the neighborhood and wondered if you'd like to go out for a drink."

Lisa looked at him. "You just happened to be in my neighborhood? Seriously?"

"It was the best I could come up with at the moment." Raoul gave her a shit-eating grin. "So, what do you think? Want to go out for a drink—with a friend?"

"What am I going to do with you?" Lisa laughed.

He shrugged. "What do you say? I could really use the company."

Lisa hesitated. "As it happens so could I. I'll get my purse."

Chapter 38

It had been a long day for Annie, starting with accompanying Philip and the Waterkeeper's attorney to court. In her opinion, it had been a big waste of time since the case was continued—yet again. Her time would've been better spent making donor calls. But Philip thought otherwise and being her boss, she kept her opinion to herself.

The one good thing was that Becky nowhere to be seen. Philip probably knew her whereabouts, although he didn't acknowledge it; just grunted and insisted Annie lock the office and go to court with him. He claimed it'd broaden her intern experience.

Now back at the office, working on a handout for their next community meeting, she was disgruntled. After writing informational pieces for the past few weeks, it became routine. She knew most of the issues and the players, had heard Philip state the Waterkeeper's position ad nauseam. She hated to admit it, but the whole thing started to bore her. It wasn't like this before her dad died, but then she hadn't been involved in the day-to-day running of the organization. She never realized how mind-numbing the job could be—until now.

She seriously considered resigning and taking the rest of the summer off, but remembered as an intern, she had to complete the full eight weeks in order to receive course credit. That, and the stipend she received, pushed all thought of quitting from her mind.

Then, of course, there was Philip. And Nathan? Whatever should she do? She fingered her engagement ring realizing she couldn't put off a decision indefinitely. Nathan hadn't so much as called since their blowup. Perhaps he'd made his own decision. If Philip hadn't been in the picture, would she have these doubts? Annie heaved a deep sigh. But he was very much in the picture and her feelings for him grew stronger every day.

Then there was Becky. For all she knew they were sleeping—maybe even living together. She'd never asked him about his personal situation. What if he was married? Surely not. He didn't wear a ring, but then lots of married men don't.

Annie leaned on her fist as she scribbled idly on a legal pad, so intent on her dilemma, she didn't hear the door open and footsteps make their way across the room.

"Now that's what I like to see," Philip said. "Staff working so hard they don't know what's going on around them. For all you knew, I could have been that gunman coming back to take a shot at the beautiful young intern."

Startled, Annie looked up to see Philip smile down at her with those gorgeous dark eyes and perfectly straight teeth. He touched her shoulder softly and said, "Where would I be without you?"

Annie's heart began to pound. Blood rushed to her face. "You'd do just fine. Better, actually, without me making dumb mistakes all the time."

"What dumb mistakes? As far as I can tell, you've done amazingly well for someone who came in without knowing the ins and outs of the organization. I'm proud of you." He patted her hand and left it there.

Annie thought she'd pass out from the surge of emotion flowing through her. She couldn't put it off any longer. She had to tell him how she felt. If he didn't share those feelings, then that was that; at least she'd know where she stood.

Philip gave her hand a pat and said, "Well, enough of this. I've got work to do."

Annie managed a tentative smile and said, "Do you have a minute? There's something you need to know."

"Of course, what is it?" Philip's forehead crinkled.

Annie looked around the empty bullpen. What if Becky walked smack dab in the middle of it? Wouldn't that be just like her?

"Could we talk in your office?" Her voice wavered, reflecting her uncertainty.

"Well sure. No problem." Philip looked puzzled.

Could she actually go through with this? She was stupid for thinking he returned her feelings. How could he? He was so much older than she, more mature, had more life experience. Besides, he had Becky, damn her. How could Annie compete with that?

"Uh, Philip, forget it. We don't need to talk after all."

Philip squinted in her direction. "Why not? Something change in the last few seconds?"

Annie shook her head no.

"Then it seems to me you have something to tell me. Let's talk."

The determination in his voice and serious expression on his face told Annie she had no choice. Unless she could make up something between the time her feet hit the floor beside her desk and landed in his office, she'd have to say what she'd been dying to for the past month. She stood up. Her knees trembled. Her eyes clouded up with tears. She tried to blink them back but they had a mind of their own and the drizzle turned into a flood.

"Annie, what's the matter?" Philip put his arm around her shoulder, walked her into his office and closed the door.

She could feel the warmth of his body next to hers; didn't want him to release her.

After settling her into a chair, he said, "Can I get you some water or coffee?"

Annie shook her head no.

"Okay then, tell me what's eating you."

That only started Annie to crying again. How could she possibly make such a fool of herself before this man? Dear God, what should she do?

Philip handed her some tissues and sat down behind his desk. Then he picked up some papers and began rifling through them. After a few moments, thinking he'd forgotten her, Annie stood to leave.

"Not so fast," he said. "If you're feeling better now, we have some talking to do." He leaned back in the desk chair. "Now, spill it, Whitaker. You're not leaving till I know what the hell's going on."

Annie took a deep breath. "I'll have that water after all." She drank slowly, trying to stretch out the time between swallows and when she'd have to speak.

Philip, his arms folded across his chest, watched—and waited. "Okay, that's enough water. What's on your mind? Whatever it is can't be all that bad. You're not the one who shot me, are you?"

The incongruity of her feelings for him juxtaposed against the hatred the gunman had displayed made her laugh.

"Of course not."

"Then I don't see what could be so terrible you can't tell me without crying." His voice softened; the gentleness reflected in his eyes melted her. "Annie, no matter what it is, I'll understand." He stood up, walked around the desk and stooped till he was eye level with her. "Tell me now," he said. "It'll be all right."

"That's just it," she said, "If I tell you, things'll never be the same again."

"I highly doubt that," Philip countered.

It was getting late and dusk had fallen after yet another rainy day. Annie and Philip had been so engrossed in their conversation they hadn't noticed. He stood up, leaned across the desk, and switched on a lamp.

Philip turned back to her. "Now what is it you wanted to say?"

All right, this was it. She couldn't put it off any longer. "It's just that I…" she twisted and re-twisted her engagement ring. It sparkled in the dim light. Cold chills made her shiver. At the same time, a rush of blood to her cheeks felt hot. "I'm sorry Philip, this is just so hard to say."

"Are you pregnant?"

The question was so far off the mark if felt as though he'd slapped her. "*Pregnant?* Of course not."

"You're not quitting, I hope?"

"No."

"Then whatever it is can't be much of a problem. Spit it out and get it over with." He looked at his watch.

The pressure building up inside Annie was almost at the breaking point. If she didn't get this over with soon, she'd explode.

"I love you." The words burst out of her mouth almost of their own accord. She hadn't planned on saying them, not like that. It would've been better to ease her way into it. Say something like, "Philip, I'm attracted to you." Or "I find myself drawn to you." Anything but blurting out "I love you." My God, he must think she was a silly little girl—just one of the many who were always throwing themselves at him.

"I'm sorry," she added quickly, "that's not what I meant to say. It's just that…"

Philip put his index finger over her lips. "Shush," he said. Then, enfolding her in his arms he kissed her.

Chapter 39

Annie unlocked the front door. With the exception of a lone lamp shining in the window, the place was dark.

"Mom?" she called out. When there was no response, she shrugged. "Must've gone out with her girlfriends. Well, good. She needs to have fun once in awhile."

Talking to herself in a half-dark and deserted room? After what she'd just done, it seemed about right. She was losing her mind, that's for sure. Where was her mother when she needed her? She wanted to tell her what happened and get her perspective.

Philip had kissed her; held her. Said he was "fond" of her too. Fond. Not in love with. Just fond. What did that mean? At least he hadn't laughed at her or patted her head and said, "I like you too." No, he'd kissed her.

She could still feel his lips press against hers, his arms holding her. It felt so good, so right. Then the phone rang and dang it all, the front door opened and who but that damned Becky walked in.

Fortunately, she'd called out, giving them time to separate, still it ruined the moment. What more could have happened had they not been interrupted? And when could they pick up from where they'd left off? Or would they? Would Philip start avoiding her? If nothing more was said, should she bring it up again or was this as far as it would go? At this point should she break things off with Nathan?

Annie curled up in the old rocker-recliner and rubbed her forehead. She was so confused, she was almost sick. She needed the advice of someone more experienced and more mature than she was. She needed her mom.

* * * *

Several hours later, Annie was dozing when she heard laughing. It was the entwined trill of male and female voices. She thought it was the neighbors coming home from a night of drinking when the sound of a key in the lock and the front door being opened startled her. Still half asleep, she wondered if whoever broke into the house before had returned.

The baseball bat was still under the sofa where she'd left it. She sprinted over and grabbed it, then stooped down and hid from view as the door opened. What she saw next surprised her more than any burglar could have.

There silhouetted in the doorway was her mother with some man. They were talking and laughing then they stopped and he kissed her. Oh, it was what most would consider a friendly peck on the cheek, but it was a kiss all the same, and wasn't that how it usually started? A touch, a friendly kiss, then another and then? What about Dad? Had she forgotten him already? Was she really moving on so soon?

The man disappeared, the door closed and Lisa called out to her. "Annie? You home?"

Too embarrassed to reveal she'd been eavesdropping, Annie scrunched down further, hoping not to be discovered.

When there was no response, Lisa shrugged and, leaving the lamp on, she walked down the hall and went to bed.

For what seemed a very long time, Annie didn't move. She was pinned to the spot not only for fear her mother would come out of her room and find her there, but also by an overwhelming anger at what she'd just witnessed: her mother kissing another man. How could she? It had been less than three months since her father died and here she was carrying on with some guy, laughing and giggling like a teenager.

She fought the urge to burst into her mother's room and confront her. In fact, she returned the bat to its hiding place and stood up, prepared to give her mother a good piece of her mind, when something held her back. Whoa, it seemed to say. Let it go until tomorrow and give her a chance to explain. You don't know who that guy was. For all you know, he's a long lost cousin. It might not be what it looked like at all.

Having worked it out in her mind and resolving to discuss her own dilemma with her, Annie turned out the lamp and went to bed.

Chapter 40

The following morning, having tossed and turned all night, Annie got up early. She'd fixed a pot of coffee and was on her second cup when her mom came into the room.

"Well, look who's up already," she said and gave Annie a warm smile. "The coffee smells wonderful."

"Morning, Mom," Annie said. "Hope it's not too strong."

Lisa poured herself a cup and took a sip. "It's just right." She sat down across from her daughter. Sun streamed through the window. A pelican flew past on its way to the lake. "So, what did you do last night? Something fun I hope."

Annie shrugged. "Had to work late. How 'bout you?"

"Same. Guess the two of us need to get a life."

"Yes, we really do." So her mother wasn't going to say anything about her "date."

That must mean she's ashamed to admit she'd gone out with some guy.

How could she broach the topic without revealing

what she'd seen? Annie was trying to decide what to say, when her mother seemed to notice her hesitation.

"What's up with you this morning? You don't seem quite yourself. Are you all right?" She stood up and placed her palm on Annie's forehead. "You feel a little warm. Want me to get the thermometer?"

The contrast between her mother's solicitation and her treacherous betrayal of her dead father was too much for Annie. She leaped from the chair. "I'm not the one who's sick," she said, her words galloped out of her mouth before her brain had a chance to catch up.

Her mother took a quick step back. "Are you talking about me? I'm not sick. In fact, I feel better than I have in quite a while."

"Really Mom? And exactly why is that?" Annie knew the tone in her voice was snappish, but couldn't help herself. What her mother did wasn't right. Sure, Dad was dead and all, but shouldn't she be honoring his memory instead of going out with some guy a few months after he was gone? Yes, she was angry, anyone would be, well anyone who really cared about their dad like she did.

"Annie, what's gotten into you?"

"Nothing, just forget it," Annie snorted. She got up from the table, went to her room and slammed the door. She pushed a pile of dirty clothes off the bed and planted herself face down on the spread.

Well, that solved absolutely nothing. When would she learn that stomping out of a room, while dramatic, served no real purpose? Eventually she'd have to come back out. She knew her mother wasn't the kind to run after her and beg forgiveness, especially this time; she didn't know why Annie was upset; didn't realize she'd seen her come home last night with that man.

The longer she stayed in her room, the longer it would be before she could seek advice about Philip. Not only that but she hadn't had any breakfast—only the two cups of coffee. And now, she had to pee.

After using the bathroom, Annie went back to the kitchen where she found her mother eating a breakfast of toast and scrambled eggs.

"Hi, honey. Want some?"

"Yeah, I'm starving."

The two women ate in silence for several minutes. Annie wanted to apologize for her outburst, but didn't quite know where to begin. She cleared her throat and took a long sip of juice.

"So, Mom, I'm sorry for, you know, earlier."

"That's all right, dear, everybody gets cranky now and then." She stood and began to clear the breakfast dishes.

"The thing is, I heard you come home last night."

"Really? I thought you were out. Where were you?"

"Doesn't matter. It's just that I saw you with that guy; heard you laughing and talking. Mom, all I could think about was Dad and how it would've made him feel to see you with another man."

Her mother stopped stacking dishes and sat down across from her daughter. "Are you saying I can't have friends?"

Annie was taken aback by the disapproving look on her mother's face. "No, not at all. But you have plenty of girlfriends. Why did you have to go out with a man, especially so soon after Dad died? It just doesn't look right. Besides, from what I heard, he sounded like a lot more than just a friend."

"Pardon me? Were you spying on me?"

"No, I just happened to be there when you got home."

"Where exactly?"

"That's not important. The point is I heard the two of you and it sure didn't sound like he was only a friend."

"Oh, really? And how would you know that? Besides who made you my keeper? Last time I looked, I was *your* mother, not the other way around. I don't answer to you concerning what I do—or with whom."

Annie's anger level rose rapidly, she felt heat from a flush in her face, heard her heartbeat drum in her ears. Her fists were tightly clenched. She stood up.

"Where're you going?"

"Out."

"Out where?"

"Anywhere but here." Annie dashed down the hall to her room and retrieved her purse. Then she headed for the front door. If she thought her mother was going to try and stop her, she was sadly mistaken.

Chapter 41

Almost immediately after storming from the house, Annie regretted what she'd done. Why the hell did her emotions always take over like that? It almost never worked out the way she thought it would; then she had to backtrack and apologize, making an even bigger fool of herself.

For the better part of an hour, she'd been driving around and finally decided to drive over to Pahokee where there was lake access from atop the twenty-foot dike. Today Lake Okeechobee sparkled in the sun, soothing her troubled spirit. The peaceful scene afforded her an opportunity to calm down and take stock of the situation.

It was the first time she'd been there since before the accident and she found it oddly comforting, as though her dad was again at her side giving her much needed advice. They'd come here often. If only he was still alive. She and Mom wouldn't be at each other's throats all the time. She'd be happily in love with Nate. Philip wouldn't even be in the picture and her persistent doubts wouldn't exist.

Annie sighed and pushed a lock of hair from her eyes.

On the one hand, her mother was right. What business was it of hers who Mom spent time with? On the other hand, her father had been dead less than three months. Wasn't it customary for a widow to wait at least a year before seeing someone? Annie didn't have experience with anything like that; she'd only read about it in romance novels. But to her, it seemed disrespectful for her mother to start dating so soon. Of course, she didn't know for sure that was the case. Perhaps she had jumped to the wrong conclusion. It wouldn't be the first time.

An hour later, Annie was back home and prepared to express regret for her outburst. From the looks of it, her mother was about to go to work. She had on her waitress uniform, her car keys and purse in hand.

"Mom, wait. Do you have a minute?" She wouldn't have blamed her one bit if she brushed by without saying a word. She deserved to be ignored.

"As long as you keep it short." Her mother glanced at the wall clock. The expression on her face said their hurtful exchange still carried a sting.

Annie didn't quite know where to begin, so she just plunged in. "Mom, I'm sorry for what I said. It's just tough seeing you with someone else. I'm still having a hard time getting used to Dad not being here. When I heard you last night, I guess I jumped to the wrong conclusion."

Lisa gave Annie a long hug. "It's all right, I understand, really I do. I miss him too, all the time. But difficult as it is, we have to go on living. Eventually there may be another man in my life, that's something you're going to have to come to terms with whether you want to or not. But now isn't the time to worry about it." She released her daughter. "Okay?"

By this time tears were streaming down Annie's face and all she could do was nod.

"Annie, darling, I didn't mean to cause you pain. The man I was with is Raoul Tucker, my boss. He happened to be nearby and invited me out for a drink." She took her daughter's face in her hands and said, "If Dad was here, he wouldn't have had a problem with it."

Her mother's kindness in the face of Annie's earlier behavior calmed her heart. Of course she had a right to have friends, even gentlemen friends. Who was Annie to judge? She was engaged, and yet she and Nathan both had friends of the opposite sex and neither objected; there was nothing wrong with it, at least there hadn't been—until now.

"So we're good?"

Annie nodded again. Then she said, "Mom, there's something I need to talk to you about."

Chapter 42

Annie drove her car into the vacant lot next to the Waterkeeper's office, leaned back and rubbed her temples. It was nine in the morning and already a headache had begun to make its appearance. She shuddered, not wanting to face a day of pain.

Not only that, but she hadn't resolved the situation with Philip. Should she call Nathan and tell him what was going on, or just let it be for now? After all, he hadn't exactly been the picture of the devoted fiancé lately either. Ever since their big fight, he'd been distant. She'd reciprocated by being "unavailable" whenever he called. They were behaving like immature teenagers, but she couldn't bring herself to be the first to break the cycle of anger and hurt they'd been riding. Her growing attraction to Philip certainly didn't help matters either. She simply didn't know which way to turn.

Talking with her mom hadn't been any help at all; she'd just frowned and said, "Be careful. Don't do anything you might regret."

She'd been sympathetic enough but couldn't—or wouldn't—tell her what to do. She pointed out that Annie had dated Nathan a long time; that they had a lot in common and only three months ago she'd been gung-ho to marry him.

But Philip was so intelligent, handsome and charming. She knew she was, if not in love with him, at least infatuated and until those feelings were resolved, she couldn't move ahead with her plans to marry Nathan. What to do? What to do?

A tap on the car window startled Annie from her reverie. She opened her eyes to see Philip standing there, a puzzled look on his face.

"So, ya gonna spend the morning napping in your car or what?" he said. The dazzling smile Annie loved spread itself across his face.

"Of course not. I was just thinking, that's all," she said, grabbing her purse and car keys.

"Thinking? You? Seriously?" Philip teased.

Annie rapped him on the shoulder. "Yes, me."

"So what were all those thoughts about?"

She looked into his dark eyes and said, "Oh, just some things I have to work out."

"Want to tell me?"

Philip's expression said he was sincerely interested in what was bothering her, but Annie knew she had to exercise control for a change.

"It's nothing, really. Thanks anyway." She gave him a wan smile and winced at a renewed stab of pain. "I have a monster headache." She rubbed her forehead.

"Is there anything I can do? Want to go home?"

"I'll be all right. I took something awhile ago. It should go away pretty soon."

Philip put his hand on her shoulder and left it there for several seconds. "Well, take it easy today, okay? We can't have you getting sick on us, now can we?"

"No, that would be unacceptable for sure." Annie returned Philip's smile and waited as he unlocked the front door. Her headache was beginning to subside, but the pain in her heart was worse than ever.

Chapter 43

Philip was surrounded by a group of volunteers. It was obvious to Annie, who sat across the room that the women, who composed the majority, were more interested in the handsome waterkeeper than in the mission they'd been recruited to perform. She had no doubt that if she was running the meeting, the room would be mostly empty.

Annie lowered her head and put her hands over her ears in an effort to shut out, not only Philip's instructions, but the near constant murmuring and giggling that ensued.

Oh come on, he isn't that funny, her mind proclaimed. *Y'all are just flirting with him. You don't give a fat fig about water pollution or the condition of the lake and you know it.*

Annie sighed and glanced up. Seven volunteers sat on folding chairs in a semi-circle around Philip. He leaned in, his tan arms resting on his thighs and spoke with animation about the importance of the Waterkeepers Alliance around the world and in Florida.

Annie noticed one woman who seemed especially

"interested." She wore impossibly skimpy shorts with an equally sparse top that revealed a shapely figure. In Annie's opinion her makeup had been applied with a heavy hand and did nothing to enhance her features.

After what seemed like hours, the meeting finally broke up. Although the rest departed promptly, the woman hung back asking "questions" about what she could do to help.

"So, you want to grab a bite?" Annie heard the woman asked Philip. "And you can tell me more about the important work you're doing," she gushed.

Annie deliberately lowered her head and tightened her hands against her ears. She didn't want to hear his response. When she looked up, the room was empty. Philip had, no doubt, accepted her invitation, and what man wouldn't? She was attractive; he was available. What was the problem?

Where was Becky when Annie needed her? If she had to lose Philip, and she realized she'd never really had him, she preferred losing him to someone like Becky who, for all her annoying ways, was preferable to someone like that.

Two hours later, Philip walked in, a satisfied expression on his face.

"Have a good lunch?" Annie said, trying without success to hide the annoyance she felt.

"I did. How about you?"

"Obviously not nearly as good as yours," Annie said.

Philip, who'd been heading toward his office, stopped cold and turned around. "What do you mean by that?"

"Oh, nothing," Annie said.

What do you suppose I mean, you big phony?

"No really, what're you talking about?" Philip went over to her desk and leaned in, his face a few inches from hers.

Annie leaned back, as much to regain her personal space as to avoid revealing how upset she was.

"It's nothing," she said, "I don't want to talk about it."

"You can't keep doing this, Annie," Philip said. "Starting something and then backing off. Either come out with what's on your mind or don't say anything at all, okay?"

"Okay."

"So, what's on your mind?"

Annie pushed her chair away from the desk and stood up. "All right, if you must know. That woman was obviously flirting with you. So what do you do? You go out to lunch with her, or maybe you did more than that, maybe had a little dessert to go with it? I might be wrong, but that's how it looked to me. Philip, I realize it's none of my business but I really wish you'd do your womanizing somewhere else. It's painful to sit and watch these women throw themselves at you like that, and you do nothing to stop them. In fact, from where I sit, it looks like you encourage them." Annie folded her arms across her chest. "There, you asked. I answered."

She started to walk away but felt his arms encircle her, his lips found hers. The kiss was long and deep.

"You silly girl," Philip said when he released her at last. "Don't you think I recognize a bimbo when I see one? Sure, I let her buy me lunch. We talked about the waterkeeper movement the whole time." He laughed. "Every time she tried to bring up something personal, I turned it right back to the organization and how desperate we are for money. The bitch's rolling in dough. I managed to get a five thousand dollar donation out of her. How's that for a good use of my time? And no, Miss Noseyface, there was no dessert."

By this time, Annie was mortified. "I'm so sorry," she began, "It's just that…"

Philip put his lips on hers and kissed her again. "You don't have to say anything," he said, "I feel the same way whenever I see you talking to some guy. Maybe it's time we did something about it. How about getting together tonight after work? What do you say?"

* * * *

That night after the office was closed, Annie got into Philip's black SUV, relieved that Becky hadn't shown up all day. For whatever reason, she'd taken the day off, but that was nothing unusual, she was always taking time off with no explanation. Regardless, Annie, who'd been nervously looking forward to her first date with Philip, was glad she didn't have to make small talk with the woman, much less hide the fact that she and Philip were finally getting together.

Philip slid into the driver's side and started the engine. "I know a little place where we can enjoy a good meal without being recognized."

At first Annie was offended. Was he ashamed to be seen with her? Then she realized that, like her father, he was known throughout the area. Like any public figure, he couldn't go anywhere without someone coming up to him and starting a conversation. She knew that firsthand. Whenever they went out to pick up supplies, people were always stopping him. Having dismissed her hurt feelings, Annie settled back to enjoy a lovely evening.

* * * *

Flora & Ella's Restaurant was around twenty-five miles west of Moore Haven, an area with which Annie was unfamiliar, making it that much more interesting. Philip had been right. Annie thoroughly enjoyed herself. The food was nothing short of spectacular. She had old-fashioned Southern fried chicken and dumplings. He had the fresh lump crab cakes with chipotle sauce. They shared a dessert of homemade pecan pie which was the best she'd ever eaten.

Afterwards, they returned to the parking lot. Philip leaned back and sat there a moment as if weighing a big decision, his arms folded over the steering wheel. Annie was about to say something when he leaned over, pulled her to him and gave her a passionate kiss. Then he began to slowly run his hands down her neck and back.

Annie started to reciprocate when her engagement ring scraped the back of her hand. She pulled back. "We'd better stop," she said, her breath husky with emotion.

"What? Why?" Philip stopped, then took her face in his hands. "You some kinda tease? Get a guy worked up, then change your mind?"

"No, that's not it at all," Annie twisted the ring on her finger. "It's just that..." Lights from the parking lot made her diamond sparkle, throwing little flashes around the car's interior. "I really like you Philip, I do. You know I do. But I just need time to figure things out."

"No problem." Philip removed his arm from Annie, straightened and without another word turned the ignition key. The SUV roared to life. As he drove, the road became increasingly rural and dark. Fields of dense sugarcane closed in on either side.

"Where're we going? This isn't the way home." Alarm

began to snake its way up from Annie's gut to her brain. Something didn't feel right. But what? This was Philip. Her friend, her boss, and perhaps one day soon, her lover. So why'd she have a sick feeling in the pit of her stomach?

"There's someone I want you to meet." He turned into a private road, lit only by the SUV's headlights.

"Who?" Annie said, unsure whether to be flattered or concerned.

"Hold on, we're nearly there."

Another five miles or so later, they came upon what appeared to be a farmhouse. He parked and they got out.

"What is this? Where are we?"

"We won't stay long." Philip gave her one of those heart-stopping smiles and helped her from the car.

They went up a wooden porch with sagging steps and into a room containing overstuffed furniture that had seen better days. The lone lamp had a torn shade and the area rug was cracked down the middle, bare floor peeked from below. The place reeked of rotten garbage, discarded cigarettes and, she couldn't be sure, but what smelled like urine.

"Hey," Philip called out. "Come down. She's here." He had an odd look on his face.

Annie didn't know what to think. Why had Philip brought her to this awful place? Was it his idea of a joke? And who was this person he was so anxious for her to meet?

The sound of heavy footsteps reverberated on the floor above and began to flow down the steps. A man's voice called out, "Philip, it's you. So I get to meet your friend at last."

"Yes, you surely do." Turning to Annie, he said, "Meet my uncle, Harold Johnson."

Chapter 44

Harold Johnson reached out and shook Annie's hand, then pulled her in for a hug. She could smell cigarette smoke on his red flannel shirt and whiskey on his breath.

"Welcome home," he said.

Welcome home? She must have misunderstood. He was a burly guy around five eight with greasy, thinning hair. His piercing dark eyes were similar to Philip's, and as far as she could tell, the only thing that reminded her of the younger man. If she hadn't been told, she would never guess they were related. Still, there was something about him that was oddly familiar. She just couldn't put her finger on it.

"Welcome home, Annie," Harold Johnson repeated. "We've been expecting you."

Again with the "welcome home?" There was no denying what he'd said this time. Welcome home? This wasn't her home. What was he talking about?

She threw a panicked look in Philip's direction, but he seemed oddly distracted. "Uh, why thank you for welcoming me to your home," she said in a feeble effort to clarify things. "I'm happy to meet you."

Harold returned her smile, revealing yellowing teeth and gaps where some were missing. "I'm glad to meet you too. I hope you'll be happy here."

What? Did he assume she'd come to stay? Surely she misunderstood. He was only trying to make her feel comfortable in their poor excuse of a home. God, this place was a sty; if she didn't get out of here soon she'd hurl. Wouldn't that make a great impression on old Uncle Harold? How welcome would she be then?

She was about to suggest that Philip take her home, when Harold said, "Show Annie to her room."

At that point, Annie was in full-fledge panic mode. Show her to her room? What the hell was going on? She wasn't about to stay in this dump; in fact she wanted to leave right now.

"Philip," she began.

Before she could say another word, Philip took her arm and began to hustle her toward the bare-wood steps. When she realized what he intended, she stiffened and said, "What do you think you're doing? I'm not staying here."

Harold Johnson's face lit up with what Annie thought was a wicked grin. "He's just trying to make you feel at home, darlin'. Be a good girl and don't cause trouble." His grin was replaced with a look of determination; the gleam in his eyes nothing short of evil.

A cold chill ran down Annie's back. "Philip, I want to go home. Please, take me home." She could hear the pathetic plea in her voice, but couldn't help it. The situation left her feeling helpless.

But Philip's expression said her entreaty fell on deaf ears. He tightened his grip on her arm. "Don't make this any harder than it has to be," he said.

"Why are you doing this?" Annie said. "I thought you cared about me." She looked into his eyes, trying to find a trace of the charming man she'd fallen in love with.

"I do care about you," he said. "Now, if you love me like you claim, do what you're told and things will work out. I promise." He edged her toward the stairs.

Annie grabbed onto the newel post with her free hand and tried to hold on. It didn't work. Philip simply yanked her aside and began nudging her up the steps.

"No," Annie shouted. "You let me go right now." When Philip didn't react to her demand, she said, "I mean it. Philip, stop kidding around. You're scaring me."

But Philip was deadly serious. As if he'd had enough of her resistance, he picked her up and began to walk up the creaky stairs.

Annie screamed, "Help. Somebody, help."

"Yell all you want," Philip said. "There's no one around to hear, so you might as well settle down."

By now Annie was more outraged than scared. What the hell did Philip think he was doing? If he thought for one minute that she was going to "settle" down and stay with this horrible man, he had another thought coming. She gave him a backward kick in the groin. As she hoped, it hit him in his most vulnerable spot. He dropped her and doubled over in pain.

She dashed down the steps, past Harold Johnson, who sat in the living room and out the front door. She didn't get far. Two rottweilers came bounding up, snarling and snapping as though they'd been expecting her and couldn't wait to get a taste.

Annie backed up and slammed the door, nearly hitting the dogs in the face. She could hear them growling and throwing their bodies against the door.

Harold Johnson looked up. "I see you've met the boys," he said pleasantly, as though remarking on the weather. "You might want to think twice before deciding to leave. They aren't fed very often. Besides they're very good hunters—'specially when they're hungry." He went back to watching a wrestling match on TV, leaving Annie to do as she liked.

Philip came downstairs. "If you're ready to behave now, I'll show you to your room."

Chapter 45

Philip nudged Annie none too gently in the back, propelling her up the stairs and into the dismal room. Before she had a chance to again demand what he thought he was doing, he closed the door. Just as she turned and reached for the knob, she heard the metallic click of a key turn in the lock.

She looked around. The space was a sad reflection of the rest of the house; reeking of body odor. Discarded clothing and old newspapers cluttered the floor; the lumpy mattress sported soiled sheets and a torn blanket.

A mix of anger, fear and despair boiled inside. Giving in to her initial instinct, she began to shout and throw the nearest object she could lay her hands on. It turned out to be a chamber pot, although she didn't know it at the time. Picking up the metal bowl, she hurled it across the room aiming squarely for the window. If the goal was to shatter the glass, she was sadly mistaken. It simply bounced back and crashed to the floor. It did, however make a loud, almost violent noise, which was somehow satisfying to Annie, although it accomplished nothing.

As the reality of her situation sank in, cold fingers of fear spiked their way up her spine and into her brain. Dear God, how had this happened? What did that horrible man want? Why had Philip brought her here when he knew what was about to happen? She trembled, then cried and pounded on the door with her fists.

"Let me out, please. Let me go. I won't tell anybody. Just let me out of here." Her voice, initially loud and strident quickly lost its volume and ended up in a soft plea. "Philip, Mr. Johnson, I'm begging you. I'll do whatever you want. Please, please, just let me go."

Silence, louder than any noise, was their response. They weren't going to let her go. In fact, all she heard was the sound of a car door slam. Oh my God, was Philip leaving? She ran to the window. In the dim light, she could see his SUV where it was parked in front of the house. The headlights suddenly came on and the vehicle roared to life. He was leaving her here with that monster.

Why? Why, Philip, why?

What had she done to so enrage him that he'd do something like this?

She pounded on the window, hoping to somehow get his attention. As she saw the red of the SUV's tail lights, she realized not only did it not work, but that the window was made of thick glass, the kind you install when you don't want anyone to get in—or out.

Annie began to wring her hands in despair, inadvertently brushing her fingers across her engagement ring. Nathan. If only he was here now. He'd give his life to save her, she knew he would. But he didn't know about Philip, or Johnson or any of it. And he knew nothing of how her feelings toward him had changed or about those kisses in the office and what had happened in the SUV several hours ago.

Suddenly Annie experienced a profound sense of shame at her betrayal of the man she professed to love. How could she have turned her back on him like that? Yes, Philip was attractive and charming; certainly he was smart and seemed to reciprocate her attraction to him. But look what happened? He'd seduced her and left her here for God only knew what purpose.

Sitting on the bare-wood floor, her back against the frame of the old iron bed, head in her hands sobbing, she didn't hear the key in the lock turn or the door open; and didn't see a man come inside.

Chapter 46

Lisa was dog tired; her feet hurt so bad she could scarcely walk; pain radiated from the bottom of her soles, up her calves and to her hips. A waitress had suddenly quit, leaving Josiah's Restaurant and Lounge shorthanded, so when Raoul asked if she'd be willing to pull an extra half-shift, she'd agreed without realizing how hard twelve straight hours of waitressing would be. Now she knew why the others turned him down. Next time, she would too.

She leaned back in the car seat and ran her hands over her forehead and down her neck. Relaxing had never felt so good. Well, now that it was over she could look forward to the extra money she'd earned. That, at least, made the ordeal worthwhile. Maybe she'd treat Annie to dinner—later, after a long soak in the tub and a nap. Better check to see if her daughter already had plans.

She pulled her cellphone from her purse and tapped the number one. That was the honored place Craig had held until—well, anyway, it was Annie's spot now.

The phone rang four times before it went to voice

mail. "Annie here. You know what to do—so do it already!" Her sassy voice rang in Lisa's ear. She'd have to talk to that girl about toning it down before she started applying for jobs next year. A prospective employer wouldn't be amused by a message like that.

"Uh, Annie, honey, it's Mom. If you don't have plans for dinner, want to join me? It'll be a late one 'cause I'm dead on my feet. Call me if you have plans, otherwise I'll see you at home."

Lisa glanced at the clock on her dashboard. It was nearly seven. Annie was probably home. When she pulled into the drive half an hour later, there was no sign of her daughter's car. She must have gone out after work with some friends, or maybe there was a community meeting she'd failed to mention. She'd call back and let her know if a late-night supper with her mom was something she wanted to do. Lisa hoped so. She was too tired to cook and didn't enjoy eating out alone.

Several hours later, after a nap and refreshed from a luxurious bath with her favorite scented oil, Lisa was completely recovered and looking forward to a good steak dinner. Annie would surely be home by now. She glanced at the clock on her bedside table. It was nine-thirty. She checked her cellphone. There were no messages.

Lisa opened her bedroom door and glanced down the hall. Light from the living room lamp made a small triangle across the floor.

"Annie," she called out. "You home?"

There was no answer. The house felt empty. Annie was no doubt out having a good time, but the girl could've at least called and let her mother know she couldn't make it. Sometimes her daughter's thoughtlessness was annoying. Lisa shrugged and headed toward the kitchen. She'd eat a bowl of soup in front of the TV and make an early night of it.

* * * *

The next morning when Lisa got up she expected to see her daughter poking around the kitchen for her version of breakfast. But the room was as empty as it had been the previous night. Thinking Annie was still in bed and sleeping late, she was extra quiet as she went about getting ready for work.

When it was time to leave and there was still no sign of her daughter, she glanced out the window and saw that Annie's car was gone. She must have left early to run some errands before work. Oh well, she'd see her tonight. Maybe they could go out for dinner then. She'd write her a note in case she got home first.

Lisa ripped a page from the notebook next to the phone. "Hey, sweetie. Missed you last night. Had to work an extra half-shift and was too tired to wait up. Want to go out to eat after work? Give me a call or meet me here around five. Love, Mom"

* * * *

In spite of brisk business at the casino as well as the restaurant—or perhaps because of it—the day went by quickly and Lisa found herself on her way home before she knew it. She glanced at her watch. It was a little after five. She hadn't heard from Annie so that must mean she was free to join Lisa for dinner. Now, where would be a good place to go that wouldn't require getting dressed up or driving too far? Annie would know. She was always up on the area's best places to eat.

As Lisa pulled in to the drive, she noticed the house was dark and Annie's car wasn't there. Damn. Where was that girl? She checked her cell for messages and when she saw there were none, Lisa had to resist the urge to call her daughter and leave a rude message. Besides, Annie was an adult. Just because Lisa was her mother, that didn't give her the right to demand an accounting of her whereabouts, did it? Maybe she was held up at work or something. She might not have even seen the note she'd left.

Entering the house, Lisa turned on a lamp and headed straight for the kitchen. Sure enough, the scrawled message remained on the table exactly as she'd left it.

Chapter 47

To Annie, the man who entered her room looked like something out of a horror movie. His clothes were ill-fitting and smelly; his hair matted and overgrown; his face marred by whisker stubble. He appeared to have difficulty walking as he clung to the door. His speech was a combination of stutter and slur. His mouth moved, but she couldn't make out what he said.

As he struggled to approach her, she shrank back and began to scream. Then she managed to get to her feet and began to throw things at him. That's what you do when a wild animal threatens, isn't it? She hurled the chamber pot, bed pillows, some kind of dead plant, even her shoe, all the while shouting, "Get out. Don't touch me. Leave me alone. Hel-l-p-p!"

If she'd stopped for even a few seconds, she would have seen the look of confusion on the man's face. Suddenly, a sound louder than her own came from outside the room and Harold Johnson's face appeared in the doorway.

"What the hell's going on up here?" He glanced from the man to Annie and back. An expression of amusement crossed his face. "Bobby, I see you've met our guest. Annie, this is Bobby. You needn't carry on like that. He's harmless. Just wanted to meet you."

Annie took aim and threw her other shoe at Harold. This time the missile made its mark, hitting him directly on the forehead. The high heel she'd worn the previous evening approximated a weapon as blood spurted from the wound it made.

"Ow." Harold's hand went to the spot where it landed. "Ow," he repeated. "What the hell? You little bitch."

He took two steps forward, swung his hand back and landed a slap on the girl's cheek. Annie screamed and cowered, as if trying to take shelter under the bed. Johnson hauled her to her feet.

"Now listen here. We can make this hard or we can make it easy. It all depends on you. Keep pulling crap like this and your stay with us will be very, very painful."

"I want to…"

Harold hit her again, knocking her off her feet. "I don't give a shit what you want, girlie. The only one who counts here is me. The sooner you get that through your head, the sooner I stop hitting you. Now, do you understand or do I gotta give you a good whippin'?" He started to take off his belt.

Bobby, who by now was halfway to the hallway, said, "Stop, Harry, stop. Why you hurting her?"

Harold turned around. "She's been very bad, Bobby. We got to teach her how to behave, don't we?"

Bobby nodded slowly. "Guess so, but she doesn't seem bad to me."

Harold turned back to Annie. "Now, you gonna stop all this racket or do I got to treat you like them dogs out there?"

Terrified, choking and gasping for air, her voice barely audible over the ringing in her ears, she said. "I'll behave."

"What's that you say?" Harold cupped his ear and inclined his head toward her.

"I said I'd behave." Annie's response, though shaky, was louder.

"Good. Now go downstairs and rustle us up something to eat."

"Get you something to eat? You want me to cook? I don't even…" she started to say "cook for myself" but Harold's arm went up. He obviously planned to deliver another blow across Annie's badly bruised face. Before he had the chance, she nodded, "Fine." The defeated tone in her voice said she realized this horrible man was in charge and she had no choice but to obey him. Trembling like a frightened puppy, she stood and headed for the hallway.

"That's more like it," Harold snorted and called after her, "You might want to do a little cleaning up down there while you're at it. Oh and by the way, I've had enough of your smart-lip. If I were you, I'd keep my fucking mouth shut from now on."

Chapter 48

Annie put both hands under her armpits trying to control the fear and trembling that overtook her. Why was she there? What did these men want? Was she going to be one of those women she'd read about: captive for years; routinely raped and bearing her captors' children? At the prospect of such a future, a new spasm overtook her, causing her to shake so violently, she was unable to open the kitchen cupboards.

"I don't hear any cooking being done," Harold Johnson bellowed from the second floor. "You better get to it if you know what's good for you." He appeared at the top of the stairs and glared down at her.

"Okay, okay," she said.

Harold barreled down, came up behind her and shouted in her ear, "What's that?"

Annie jumped. "Nothing."

He squeezed her upper arm. She could almost feel the bruise form. "Didn't I tell you to lose the attitude?" he shouted. "If anybody's going to be a wise ass around here, it'll be me. Got that?"

Annie nodded, trying to control the shudders that wracked her body.

"What? I didn't hear you."

Nodding rapidly, she said, "Yes, I got it." A tone of disgust crept into her voice in spite of herself.

Johnson struck her. "Let's try that again."

Annie rubbed her cheek and blinked back tears. She wasn't going to let the bastard see her cry anymore.

"Yes, Mr. Johnson, I understand. No more sarcasm."

"That's better. And call me Harold. Now get cracking. Me and Bobby're starving." With that he left the kitchen for the living room where he switched on the TV. The sound of a familiar sit-com reached Annie's ears, but there was nothing remotely funny in her circumstances. Stunned and confused, she began to open sticky cupboard doors one by one in hopes of finding something that, with her limited culinary skills, she could manage to cook.

The cupboards were filled with mismatched dishes, bowls and an assortment of canned fruits and vegetables. She also discovered boxes of dried pasta, cake mix and even some baking ingredients. It surprised her. Who knew that a bully like him and a slob to boot, would have the foresight to stock his pantry?

Then it occurred to her—he'd been planning this for a while. It wasn't that he was a cook, you could see from the empty TV dinner containers and pizza cartons it wasn't the case. He'd bought all this stuff knowing full well that she'd soon be his "guest" and, like it or not, she'd fill the role of housekeeper and cook.

A renewed bout of trembling overtook Annie. How was she going to get away from that horrible man? Would Philip ever come back for her? Could she even talk him into getting her out of here? After all, Harold Johnson was his uncle and apparently convinced him to kidnap her. But why? What was this all about?

Was she only a convenient victim or was there something more to it? If all Johnson wanted was a free housekeeper, she could manage to cooperate until an opportunity arose for her to escape. Considering those vicious dogs outside, the prospect seemed remote. Still, they had to sleep sometime. She'd just have to play along for now.

She checked the fridge: milk, eggs, even some lettuce, apples, oranges, hot dogs, lunchmeat and the usual condiments. The freezer held packages of frozen fish and meat, along with a stack of TV dinners, most likely for use in case his plan didn't work out.

She went to the sink and nearly gagged when she saw—and smelled—a stack of food-caked plates, pans and utensils. Grease ants swarmed over the mess, delighting in the gastronomic feast. Annie swatted at several that had started to include her arm in their territory.

Where to begin? The monster wanted food and if he didn't get it soon, he'd take it out on her. But she couldn't cook if there were no clean pans. Under the sink she found a half-empty bottle of dishwashing liquid. It was a place to begin.

An hour later, Harold Johnson pushed away from the table with what Annie took to be a pleased expression. "You can eat and clean up now. Me 'n Bobby're done." He wiped his mouth on his sleeve. He started to walk toward the living room, belched, then turned around and with a wicked gleam in his eyes said, "The longer you keep us fed, girlie, the longer you stay alive."

Chapter 49

It was Sunday night and Lisa hadn't seen her daughter all weekend. She sighed and switched the channel on the television set. On and off all evening long she had a sinking feeling, a kind of fluttering inside that told her something wasn't right. She couldn't put her finger on it and didn't know what to do, but knew with the certainty of a mother for her child that trouble was afoot and her daughter was somehow in the middle of it.

Finally, just before the news came on, she could stand it no longer and decided to make some calls. Annie was, no doubt, just fine. She was most likely out with friends and had lost track of the time. Yes, that's all it was. There was nothing to be concerned about.

Still, that sick feeling inside wouldn't go away and she knew to her very core something was amiss. So she began phoning the friends Annie had hung out with over the summer. There weren't that many, so it didn't take long. The results were not at all what she'd hoped:

"Jenna, I'm sorry to be calling so late but I was wondering if Annie's there?"

"Have you by any chance talked to her in the past couple of days?"

"Do you know if she had plans to go out of town or something like that?"

Lisa's heart fell a little more with each call. No one had seen her. No one knew where she was. Frightened and confused, she finally began to make the calls she dreaded: hospital emergency rooms, the police and finally, the morgue.

Once again all answers were negative:

"Nope, no one of that description has come in."

"No car of that make and model was in an accident."

No. No. No. Nothing. Where was that girl? The light of her life, her heart. Where was she? It wasn't like her to go off somewhere. She knew Lisa would worry. The only call she didn't make was to that Philip guy over at the Waterkeepers. She didn't have his home number and the office was closed. She'd have to wait till morning to get in touch with him. Maybe for whatever reason—well, she knew the reason—maybe they were together.

The thought that Annie was really all right, that she had just been preoccupied with her own life and unaware of the concern her absence had caused, occurred to Lisa and provided a small measure of comfort.

That was it. Annie had come and gone the last few days when Lisa herself was working or running errands; they'd managed to miss each other, that was all there was to it. It was that simple. Annie would be so annoyed when she found out how frightened Lisa had become. Her friends would, no doubt, tease her about her mommy looking for her. And then she'd get an earful. Oh well, as long as she was safe, that was all that mattered.

* * * *

The following morning, Lisa awoke early, hopeful she'd find Annie asleep in her bed, the weekend nightmare behind her. She rushed down the hall to her daughter's bedroom but saw the door was wide open and her bed made up as before, giving no evidence it had been slept in. The possibility that Annie actually was missing came crashing down on Lisa, causing her to feel faint.

She slumped onto the edge of the bed and prayed, "God, please, do what you want with me, but please, please, keep Annie safe and bring her home."

A little sob escaped her. She swallowed. It wouldn't do to break down. She had to be strong. She'd get dressed and have some breakfast. Then she'd go over to the Waterkeeper's office and see if Annie was there. It was possible, that all this time she'd been caught up with some weekend event and had simply neglected to inform her. Craig used to pull stunts like that all the time, to the point Lisa didn't worry too much when she didn't connect with him for a few days. Yes, and look where that had gotten her.

* * * *

It was a little past nine when Lisa pulled into the Okeechobee Waterkeeper's parking lot. Although several cars were there, Annie's was conspicuously absent. Still, Lisa held out hope. Maybe she was running an errand. She opened the car door and approached the building with a sad mix of hope and dread.

She hadn't been to the Waterkeepers' place since well before Craig drowned. As she went inside, she half expected to hear him call out from his office. An attractive blonde looked up from a computer screen as she approached.

"I'm looking for my daughter, Annie Whittaker," she said. "I'm her mother, Lisa." She'd never had to introduce herself around there before. Everyone knew she was Craig's wife. Now things had changed and Craig was a mere footnote in the organization's history.

"Uh, why, hello Mrs. Whitaker," the blonde said. "No, Annie hasn't been in yet today. In fact, I was about to call. She's usually here by now."

The cramp in Lisa's gut multiplied exponentially, bringing her almost to her knees.

"Mrs. Whitaker, are you all right?" the blonde said. "Phil," she called out. "You need to come out here. I think this lady's going to pass out."

She ran around the side of her desk and pulled out a chair. "Sit down and put your head between your knees." Gently pressing on Lisa's back, she managed to get her to follow her instructions.

"Becky, what's this all ab—" Philip said as he emerged from his office. "Who's this?"

Still a bit dizzy, Lisa sat up. "Are you Philip?" she said.

"Yes, and you are…"

"She's Annie's mom," Becky said. "She's looking for her and wondered if we'd seen her."

A look of confusion crossed Philip's face. "Seen her? You mean this morning? Why no, she hasn't been in yet. She sick or something?"

Lisa stayed seated, the weakness in her gut spread to her entire body. Cold chills ran up and down her back. Her legs trembled to the point she didn't think they'd support her should she choose to stand.

Instead of answering Philip's question, she countered with one of her own. "When was the last time you saw her?"

He rubbed his chin. "That would be Friday, right Becky? She was here all day."

"So you didn't see her over the weekend?"

"No, I'm sorry, Mrs. Whitaker, I didn't. Did you, Becky?"

The blonde shook her head rapidly. "No, Mrs. Whitaker, I didn't see her. I'm afraid we don't hang out after work. Sorry."

Lisa noticed perspiration on Philip's forehead and a slight trembling of his hand, but was so concerned about Annie, she didn't think much about it. For a moment no one said anything. Then with a sinking heart, Lisa said, "I think we'd better call the police."

Chapter 50

Lisa pulled into the police parking lot, leaned over the steering wheel, and rested her head in her hands. She was about to do something every parent dreaded: report her child missing. While it was true Annie was no longer a child, she would forever be Lisa's little girl, no matter how old she was.

Wiping away a few tears of fear and dread, she opened the car door and headed toward the same building where she'd so recently been questioned about that stupid missing money. Whatever had become of that whole matter anyhow? She shrugged and hoped this would also have a happy outcome.

"Yes? How can I help you?" The officer at the front desk had a pleasant, if somewhat distracted demeanor. He, no doubt, thought she was there to report a cat up a tree or neighbors who played their radio too loud; if only that were the case.

"I… I…" Lisa swallowed. Saying the words out loud would give them a reality she desperately didn't want to acknowledge. Maybe she was mistaken. Maybe Annie had gone to Tampa to spend the weekend with Nathan. That must be it. She shouldn't bother this busy man with her petty concern. Her daughter wasn't missing, she was just inconsiderate.

The officer looked at Lisa, an exasperated expression on his face. "Well?" he said. "What's the problem?"

"Nothing," she said and managed to smile. "Nothing at all. Sorry to bother you."

As she headed home, Lisa was relieved, as though a heavy weight had been lifted from her. She would give Annie a good talking-to when she got back home. It was one thing to come in late, but to take off without a word like that… Surely she realized how worried Lisa would be.

But that was the thing: young people don't think about how their actions affect others; the world revolves around them. No one else counts. She knew her daughter was a good person; she just had some growing up to do.

Lisa pulled in to the drive and raced to unlock the door. She was in such a rush to prove herself right about Annie's whereabouts, that she kept dropping her keys. When she finally made it inside, she looked up Nate's cellphone number.

God, how foolish of her. If she'd called him last night, it would have saved her hours of worry. She hadn't wanted to bother him; thought Annie'd be annoyed if she did, but now that she thought about it, it made perfect sense. Nathan and Annie had been on the outs lately and she was increasingly drawn to Philip. Perhaps she'd made an impulsive decision to drive to Tampa and either break up with him or get their relationship back on track. She would have been so focused on her decision, she wouldn't have thought about how her absence would be noticed.

It was a good thing Annie had given her Nate's number. At first she'd resisted, saying there was no reason for Lisa to have it. But Lisa had insisted; said she might need to get in touch. And since Annie spent so much time with him, it would be a good idea to have his number.

The phone rang three times before a male voice responded. His voice sounded foggy, like he might have just gotten up or was still in bed.

"Hi Nate. This is Lisa Whitaker, Annie's mom," she began.

"Oh, hi, Mrs. Whitaker. How are you?" The tone in his voice said, *and why are you calling?*

She provided the answer to his unspoken question. "I'm sorry to bother you, but I wondered if Annie's there."

There was a short pause on Nathan's end of the line as if he was processing the information.

"Excuse me?" he said. "Annie? Here? Why no, I haven't seen her since…" His voice trailed off and he cleared his throat. "We haven't been in touch for a while. Have you checked with Sam or Molly?"

Lisa's heart fell; she'd been so certain Annie was with Nate, that he'd say, "Why sure, she's here. You want to talk to her?" But that wasn't the case.

Sam was Samantha Stevens, her longtime girl friend. She was married and lived in Pahokee. Molly Jenkins had been her college roommate. She was from Boston.

"I called Sam last night, but she hasn't seen Annie. Do you have Molly's number?" Lisa sensed fear creep back inside.

Where's my daughter?

After providing Lisa with the information, Nathan

added, "Mrs. Whitaker, be sure to let me know if, er—when Annie shows up. Ask her to call me." His voice choked up as he added, "I miss her. Tell her that for me, will you?"

Lisa had met Annie's former roommate when she and Craig had attended special university events. She seemed like a nice enough girl. Annie never said much about her besides the fact that being an only child it was hard to adjust to living with another person, especially in the confines of a dorm room. Beyond that, she knew virtually nothing about her.

"Molly, this is Lisa Whitaker, Annie's mom. Is she, by any chance, with you? Oh, you're back home in Boston, I didn't realize..." she cleared her throat. "Have you heard from her in the last few days?"

Molly said she hadn't, then added something that made the hairs on the back of Lisa's neck stand on end. "I haven't talked to her lately, but she might've come up on her own. After her dad died and she found out she had grandparents in Boston, well, we talked about her coming to check them out. I told her not to worry about staying in a hotel, that she could stay with me."

"Really? She never mentioned it."

Molly hesitated. "Well, that's the thing. I, uh, I don't think she wanted you to know, said you'd just get, like, you know, upset or something."

Lisa was taken aback but managed to cover it up. "So, you think she might be with them?"

"I don't really know, Mrs. Whitaker, but if you're, like, worried, it might be worth a call."

Molly's suggestion made perfect sense. "If you hear from Annie, would you please ask her to call?" Then tamping down a mix of anger, hurt and confusion, Lisa thanked her and hung up.

Why hadn't Annie mentioned her desire to go to Boston and visit her grandparents? Seems like she didn't know her daughter as well as she thought.

Molly's suggestion to call the elder Whitakers echoed in her ear.

Call them? Again?

Last time she'd called was to inform them of Craig's death. It hadn't been pleasant and they hadn't been especially happy to hear from her.

Lisa wasn't surprised. Why should they be friendly? She'd stolen away their precious son; robbed them of their heir-apparent. Then, two decades later, she'd called to say he was dead. Now she had to contact them again to find out if her own precious daughter was with them. Dear God, what if they said, *"Yes, she's here and you'll never see her again."*?

Even in her panicked state Lisa knew how ridiculous that was. Annie wasn't helpless. She might be impressed by the Whitakers' wealth; they might even manage to charm her into wanting to stay; but Annie was a strong-willed, independent woman. She wouldn't be swayed by their beautiful mansion, or anything else they might throw her way.

Reluctantly, her stomach churning to the point of nausea, she flipped through the pages of her personal phone directory to the letter "W."

Each ring of the phone cut Lisa's heart. Her in-laws, if you could call them that, were the last people on earth she wanted to speak to. Still, if Annie was with them and safe, it would bring her some measure of peace.

"Whitaker residence. How may I direct your call?" The woman answering the phone was obviously a domestic of some sort or her father-in-law's secretary. Of course. He wouldn't answer the phone himself. Things like that were beneath such an important man.

Lisa could feel the heat of anger rise inside. She swallowed hard and said, "May I speak to Mr. or Mrs. Whitaker?" then added, "please" more for effect than out of courtesy.

"And whom may I say is calling?"

"Tell them it's their daughter-in-law, Lisa Whitaker, and that it's urgent."

Without a change in her tone of voice, the woman at the other end of the line said, "One minute please, I'll see if either is available to take your call."

Lisa wanted to throw up.

"Available?" Fuck them.

How good would it feel to say "fuck you" into their oh-so-expensive top-of-the-line phone? They'd probably go right out and buy a new one; wouldn't want their priceless possessions contaminated by the voice of a foul-mouthed Indian like her.

Lisa was so busy with her internal rant she almost missed hearing Mr. Whitaker's well-modulated voice. "This is Craig Whitaker. How are you, Lisa?"

For a minute she couldn't respond. His civilized tone took her off guard.

"Lisa? Are you there?"

"Yes, oh, hello Mr. Whitaker, thank you for taking my call."

"Not a problem. Call me Craig."

Craig? Really?

But that was her dead husband's name, not the bastard who'd driven them away so many years ago. She cleared her throat.

"Charlene said it was urgent. What's this all about?"

For a fleeting second, Lisa pictured a maid in a black dress and white apron relaying her message and handing him the phone. Or maybe Charlene was in a business suit with highly polished nails, behind a secretary's desk in his oh, so handsome office filled with expensive furniture, lamps, oriental rugs and shelf upon shelf of first editions.

"Mr. Whit… Craig, my daughter, Annie, your granddaughter," she emphasized "granddaughter" to remind him of the fact that she existed, "seems to have gone missing and I wondered if she was there with you?" It was the first time Lisa had come right out and said Annie was missing and the reality of it terrified her. She stifled a sob and took a deep breath.

"She's missing? Have you called the police?"

"No. I'm sure she just decided to go visit a friend—or relative and neglected to mention it, or if she did, I must have forgotten. You know how it is with kids these days. So anyway, I take it she's not there with you?" It was an effort to keep the emotion she felt out of her voice. It would do no good to give the impression she was a hysterical female. That's the conclusion this SOB most likely would jump to with the slightest shedding of a tear.

"No, I'm sorry, she's not here and we haven't heard from her." His voice softened. "Was she planning to visit us?" Lisa wasn't sure but thought he sounded hopeful.

"Actually I think she was. After meeting you and Noreen at the funeral, she wanted to get to know you. I mean, you are her grandparents, you know."

"Yes, I realize that. Listen, tell her when she gets back from wherever she is that she's welcome to come. We'd like to get to know her as well." He hesitated, cleared his throat, and then said, "Oh and Lisa, you're welcome too."

That last remark was bittersweet. It was the first time in over twenty years she'd been invited to visit her in-laws, if you could call that awkward statement an invitation. Still he hadn't refused to take her call or been rude and that was something.

"Thanks. I'll be sure to let her know."

Lisa hung up and just sat there for several long minutes trembling uncontrollably. She'd actually had a civilized conversation with the man. Well, despite the agony and fear her daughter's inconsiderate behavior had caused, she'd managed to accomplish something positive. After she got through yelling at Annie, Lisa would have to remember to thank her for that.

Having no other options and with a heavy heart, Lisa headed over to the police station.

* * * *

Reporting someone missing, especially one's own child, is nothing short of an ordeal. With each word, Lisa's heart objected that it wasn't true, that her daughter was just off somewhere having a good time. Her throat closed up, constricting her ability to speak; cold chills ran down her spine causing her to tremble; she blinked as her eyes welled up. The last thing she wanted the officer to think was that she was only an overprotective mother, refusing to cut the apron strings on a daughter long past childhood.

Eventually she got through it and the police said they'd put out a "BOLO" although they assured her Annie would be safely back home soon.

"I can't tell you how often mothers come in here totally distraught. They're positive something happened to their kid, then in a matter of hours, sometimes days, the kid shows up unaware of all the havoc they caused."

"But I haven't seen Annie since Friday," Lisa managed to say. "It's been three days without a word. That's just not like her."

The policeman nodded, a sympathetic look on his face. "Like I said, Mrs. Whitaker, we'll put out a "be on the lookout" notice for all area police. If she's not back soon, we'll find her. What I want you to do is go on home. That way if—when she comes home, you can give us a call with the news. Okay?"

Somewhat reassured by the cop's words, Lisa headed back to stand vigil in her empty house.

Chapter 51

It was shortly after noon and Lisa, having repeated her concern for Annie over and over, was exhausted. As she walked into the kitchen to fix a cup of tea, she noticed the phone's message light blinking. Hope surged through her. That would be Annie, apologizing for leaving without telling her where she was going. She was sure of it.

Her heart pounding, Lisa pressed the "play" button, but instead of hearing Annie's youthful voice, what she heard instead was Raoul, sounding more than a little annoyed. "Lisa, this is Raoul. You coming to work today or what? Soon as you get this message, call me."

A second message from Raoul was recorded half an hour later. This one made his aggravation clear. "Lisa, you'd better be in the hospital or dead, girl. I'm shorthanded and it's lunchtime. So if you still want a job I suggest you call immediately."

That had been fifteen minutes ago. Lisa reached for the phone. In the turmoil over Annie, she'd put work out of her mind and forgot she was due in at eleven. Her work schedule changed every month, and she wasn't used to the new hours. She was about to dial when the phone rang. The sound was loud and unexpected, causing her to jump.

"Hello?" she said, hoping against hope it was Annie.

"Lisa," Raoul's voice was stern. "What's going on? I've been trying to reach you. You do realize you're supposed to work today, right?"

"I'm afraid I forgot about the new schedule," Lisa began.

"Well, that's no excuse, but I guess it's the best you've got. So get your butt in here. We're busy and I don't like waiting tables. Besides," he chuckled, "your uniform's too small for me." That was apparently Raoul's feeble attempt at humor.

Go to work with Annie out there somewhere? It was out of the question. Lisa had to be here in case…

In case of what?

She flashed back to that fateful morning a few months ago when a knock on the door produced a policeman who asked her to accompany him to what turned out to be the worst day of her life. Could she even consider going to work when she didn't know how this would turn out?

"Lisa? You there?"

"Yes," she managed to say. The muscles in her neck tightened making speech difficult, as though someone had their hands around her neck and squeezed. Her voice came out in a strangled, croaking sound.

"Something wrong? You sick?"

"Uh, yes. No. Maybe. I don't know." Lisa wanted to tell him about Annie but had trouble getting the words out; she so desperately wanted it not to be true.

"So which is it, yes or no?" Raoul, who was generally patient, sounded frazzled. Then, as though a light suddenly went on, his voice softened, "What's the matter? You can tell me."

"It's Annie, I think she's gone missing," Lisa blurted out leaving almost no space between words. "I haven't seen her since Friday. I've looked everywhere and called everyone. Raoul, I just don't know where she is."

With that tears began to flow. Sobbing and taking deep breaths she added, "The police said I should stay here in case… when… That's why I didn't… can't…" Her words were scrambled; she couldn't seem to organize her thoughts.

Mercifully Raoul interrupted, "Of course you can't. Look, you stay there. I'm sure Annie'll show up. I'll check on you once things around here are under control. Okay?"

Lisa swallowed and nodded into the phone, then, realizing Raoul couldn't see her, she took a breath and said, just above a whisper, "All right."

"Talk to you later."

Trembling violently, tears streaming down her face, Lisa went over to the sofa and lay down.

Chapter 52

By Monday Annie had been captive for three days. Surely by now people had begun to notice her absence. Would she ever see her mother again? She'd been so snotty to her, snapping when she'd suggested Annie think twice before getting involved with Philip. And boy, had she ever been right. What an asshole he'd turned out to be—bringing her here under the pretense of meeting his uncle—if Harold Johnson really was his uncle.

"Girl, why you just standing there? Get busy and clean up this dump. You wanna keep breathin' you best do what yore told."

He grabbed her arm, twisted it and slammed her into the wall. She fell, her head exploding in pain. With trembling fingers, she touched her scalp. It was wet with blood which dripped onto the rug as she struggled to get up.

"Now look what you did. Clean that up afore it gets stained." He tossed an old rag at her.

As she stooped to pick it up, Annie's vision wavered, the blow to her head making her dizzy. She briefly wondered if she had a concussion and if she did—then what? Would Harold Johnson just let her die? Did a person even die of a concussion? Annie didn't know but guessed she'd find out if his treatment of her got much worse.

As she furiously scrubbed the bloody spot, Annie realized everything she did seemed to set the man off with a new round of shouts, punches, slaps, kicks and arm-twisting. The only time she got a break was when she slept—even then her repose was interrupted by nightmares. As the seriousness of her situation sank in, Annie experienced overwhelming terror.

"You finished cleanin' that up?"

Annie looked up and nodded, then remembered how much he disliked it when she failed to give a proper response. "Yes, Harold, I think I got it all."

"You think or you know? Which is it?"

Annie looked back to where the spot had been. Only the faintest outline showed. The problem now was that her scrubbing made the rest of the carpet look filthy, which it was.

"I know, Harold. The stain's gone."

"Real nice havin' a broad round," he said, as if to himself. "Been so long since the last one, almost forgot what it was like." Letting a malevolent smile crawl across his face, he added, "Too bad it won't last."

Annie wondered at that last remark. Had he realized this was a big mistake and decided to let her go? A tiny spark of optimism caught fire inside, making things a bit more hopeful. Maybe in a few days she'd be free and Philip'd take her home. Boy, would she ever give him an earful.

She almost smiled at the thought of how she'd tell him off. When she was safely home she'd unleash on him like nobody's business, punching him in the stomach, then kicking him in the groin like she'd done Friday night. She couldn't wait.

That afternoon Annie decided to tackle the living room. She started with a table in the corner upon which a plethora of garbage was stashed. Grabbing a trash bag, she removed layer upon layer of stinking, rotting garbage: half-filled beer bottles, the remnants of TV dinners and old newspapers. Near the bottom of the pile, she could see parts of a badly marred table top.

That's when a news clipping caught her eye. It was a photograph of her grandparents at a social function. The caption read, "Cancer Society honors Boston Whitakers." Seeing it, left Annie breathless. How had this found its way into Harold Johnson's house? What possible relationship was there between her grandparents and this vile man?

Harold Johnson must have clipped it from the newspaper. Then he had her kidnapped. Was this simply a coincidence? Yes, they had the same last name, but the name Whitaker wasn't all that unusual. There were probably loads of them around. Had he seen them at the funeral and put two and two together?

Her mom said the Whitakers were wealthy and that was why they'd disapproved of her marriage to their son. Is that what this was about? Was Johnson after ransom? If that was the case, she had news for him. Her grandparents hadn't shown a lick of interest while their son was alive, so why would they pony up a wad of cash now? The question in Annie's mind was how long it would be before Harold Johnson realized that. What would he do then?

"What the hell you think you're doing?" Harold Johnson bellowed, causing Annie to jump in alarm. Before she had a chance to respond, he struck her across the face, knocking her down. "Who gave you permission to snoop in my papers, you little bitch?" His hand was positioned to strike another blow, when Bobby intervened.

"Harry, stop," he said in his garbled manner of speaking. "Why you hurting her? She's nice: feeds us; cleans. Treat her good or she won't stay."

His disabled brother's voice stopped Harold Johnson cold; he dropped his upraised fist. Annie, who cowered at his feet, was equally surprised.

"She was going through my stuff. She'd no business doing that."

"Maybe she found it when she cleaned up. We're kina messy, ya know." He threw Annie his grotesque version of a grin.

Grateful to be spared another beating, Annie managed to give the strange man what she hoped was a smile.

"Well, okay then," Johnson snorted, "But I'm warning you—if I catch you nosing around, nothing Bobby says will save you. Understand?" He threw a meaningful look in his brother's direction. "And you, yes, I'm talking to you, Bobby, don't try telling me what to do. I'm the boss around here and what I say goes. Got it?" He looked from Annie to Bobby and back.

Annie shook so badly she was unable to speak so she nodded instead.

"What? I can't hear you, girlie? Speak up."

"Yes, Harold, I understand. I'll stay out of your things. But may I ask a question?"

"What?"

"How am I supposed to know where you keep your papers and if I should clean up that area?"

Bobby let out an odd mix of guffaw, giggle and snort. "She got you there," he said.

Harold cleared his throat and gave Bobby a look that said "knock it off." He harrumphed and then said, "Just leave my stuff alone. I'll put it in boxes when I get around to it, but in the meantime…" He stabbed his finger in her chest. "Next time not even Bobby'll stop me."

Annie didn't need to be told a second time. Harold Johnson had secrets and whatever they were, he was determined to keep them. Well, fine. She'd clean, cook their damned meals and try to win him over before he decided to get rid of her. In the back of her mind, she wondered how much—if anything—her grandparents would pay to save her

Chapter 53

Lisa was at loose ends: She couldn't leave the house in case Annie came back—an outcome she desperately hoped for; she was too exhausted to do anything useful and too revved up with fear to rest. So she just sat there, praying her darling daughter would walk through the door acting as though disappearing for three days was nothing out of the ordinary.

She stared out the sliding glass door to the patio, absently watching birds peck at something on the ground, when the doorbell rang. Her heart leapt. Maybe whoever's hand pressed it, had news of her daughter, and please God, let it be good.

Walking across the room barefoot, she stubbed her toe. "Ow! Damn!" The bell rang again. Limping to the door, she flung it open. The sight before her was not at all what she'd hoped.

A policeman stood there, a pained expression on his face. "Mrs. Whitaker?"

"Yes, I'm Lisa Whitaker. Have you found my daughter?"

"Annie Whitaker? You reported her missing?"

Lisa's heart plummeted as she awaited the news. Would it be a replay of the grim outcome several months ago?

"Yes, Officer." She steeled herself for the worst.

"Is there any reason she'd be going on an airplane trip?"

Crinkling her forehead, Lisa shook her head no.

"You sure?"

"Well, as far as I know, she had no plans like that. One of her friends said she was thinking about going to Boston to see her grandparents; but I called and they don't know anything about it. Why?"

"We found her car at the Pahokee Airport. Do you have any idea why it might be there?" When Lisa mutely stared at him, he added, "Anyone she know own a plane? Pahokee's a small airport used by private pilots. Could she have gone off with someone and didn't tell you?"

At this point Lisa didn't know what to think. It was becoming increasingly obvious that Annie kept things from her. Maybe this was one of them. The cop waited for her to respond.

"I really don't think so. She's never done anything like this, and it would be totally out of character for her to abandon a job she loves and take off without telling me."

"But it's possible, isn't it?"

"I guess anything's possible," Lisa reluctantly conceded.

"I can't tell you the number of times worried parents have reported their children missing only to find out they'd taken off with friends and failed to tell them. They usually return within a week or so. Look, Mrs. Whitaker, I can understand why you're worried. In your position I would be too. But try to relax. Annie'll show up, I promise."

"Does that mean you'll stop looking for her?"

"No, not at all, but unless we have some indication of foul play, there's not much we can do other than keep her on the BOLO list. She's an adult, free to come and go as she likes." He gave her a sympathetic grin, "When she gets back, you're free to let her have it, for all the worry she's caused."

Lisa tried to let herself be reassured by the man's somewhat lighthearted remark, but the news about Annie's car only deepened her conviction that something really awful happened, and now it appeared the police were convinced she'd run off somewhere and they weren't going to go to any great lengths to find her.

She thanked him, closed the door and sank to her knees.

Annie, honey, where are you? Please God, you've got to help me get her back.

* * * *

A few hours later, Lisa was in the kitchen trying to do some cleaning. Might as well make use of the unexpected free time she had on her hands while she continued to await Annie's return. She wiped down the countertops, stove and fridge, then got a mop and bucket and started on the floor.

The mindless activity served to skim off some of the fear that nearly paralyzed her. She was just finishing up when the bell rang. Knowing it couldn't be her daughter–Annie would use her key, walk in and yell, "Hey Mom, ya' there?"—or something to that effect—Lisa steeled herself.

Taking a deep breath, she opened the door and found Raoul standing there: the sleeves of his white starched shirt rolled up at the elbow, collar open, tie askew. His bushy brows furrowed atop eyes that bled concern.

"Hey," he began, "Just checking to see how you're doing."

The dam of Lisa's emotions broke and tears flooded her face. Raoul yanked open the screen door, put his arms around her and walked her over to the sofa. Then he just sat there, holding her and letting her cry.

"Where could she be?" Lisa said, finally getting control of herself.

Raoul shook his head. "I don't know." He glanced around the room. "I have an idea. Let's try to retrace her steps. When was the last time you saw or heard from her? Maybe something will pop out, something she told you and you forgot."

Lisa shrugged. "Okay, but I've been over and over it, and nothing seems out of the ordinary. She came home as usual Thursday. No, wait. That's not right. She was upset with me. We had a big fight and she left the house in a huff. She came back a few hours later and apologized. That's about it. The next morning she was back to her old self."

As Raoul listened, Lisa noticed how intently his eyes seemed to search hers. When she finished speaking, he said, "What was the fight about?"

Not wanting to tell him they'd fought over him taking her out, Lisa hesitated.

"Hey, I'm not being nosy; I thought if we looked at the reason for that fight, maybe we'd have a clue as to where she went." When Lisa didn't immediately respond, he added, "That's all right, you don't need to tell me."

"It's not that, Raoul, I'm just…"

"Just what?"

"Embarrassed, that's all."

Raoul took her hand in both of his. "I thought we were friends. Am I wrong?"

"No," Lisa was so choked up she could scarcely get the words out.

"Then what was it about? It might be important."

Lisa cleared her throat. "She saw you with me Wednesday night and thought we were on a date. Seeing me with a man other than her father upset her. She had a meltdown and left the house for several hours. When she came back, she apologized and we talked about it. I told her you were my boss and that we were only friends. She seemed to accept my explanation. Then she asked my advice about a man she's attracted to."

"I thought she was engaged."

"She is. That's the problem. She's confused and doesn't know whether to break off her engagement and see where this attraction leads, or do, what she terms, the right thing and put a stop to whatever's going on."

"And who's this other man?"

"I'd rather not say, I mean, I hate to involve him in all this. I don't even know how far that so-called relationship went."

"Have they gone out?"

"Not as far as I know. She said they kissed, but I think that was the extent of it." Lisa breathed a long unhappy sigh. "But what do I know? Her friend, Molly, told me she wanted to go to Boston to visit her grandparents. Imagine that. She wants to see people who in over twenty years haven't so much as sent us a Christmas card. And I have to hear about it from Molly." She wiped away a few tears that had found their way down her cheeks.

* * * *

It was getting late and there was still no sign of Annie. Raoul had taken charge. He notified the staff at work about the situation and had Lisa's name removed from the schedule; then he ordered takeout from a local Chinese restaurant.

Drained of every possible emotion, Lisa appreciated having someone make decisions for her. When he insisted on ordering food, she said she wasn't hungry and couldn't eat a bite; the thought of food made her nauseous. Acting like a parent who knew what was best, Raoul ordered anyway.

The sumptuous mix of fried rice, Moo Shu vegetables, egg rolls and sweet and sour chicken reminded Lisa she hadn't had a thing to eat since the previous evening. She was surprised at how quickly her appetite returned, despite the circumstances.

They had finished eating and were cleaning up when the sound of a car motor came from the front of the house. Lisa dashed to the window, and in the moonlight saw Nathan's car.

"It's Nate," she said. A surge of excitement ran like electric current through her body. "Annie must've showed up in Tampa, and he's brought her home." She was so relieved that she gave Raoul a big hug and rushed to the door to welcome her. The scolding she deserved would have to wait.

"Annie, you're back…" she said throwing open the door. The sight that greeted her was not at all what she anticipated.

The solitary figure standing in the dim porch light was not that of a young woman. It was Nathan, disheveled and wearing a worried expression.

"Mrs. Whitaker?"

They spoke simultaneously, "Have you heard from Annie?" and "No."

Once again Lisa's heart dropped.

Chapter 54

It was dark. Annie had retired to what she now considered her room, after a long day of cooking and cleaning. She had to be careful not to let her contempt for Johnson show or he'd take it out on her with blows to the face, arms, shoulders, back or wherever was most convenient.

Bobby wasn't so bad. She could tolerate him. He had some kind of condition that made his body shake and his speech difficult to discern, but in spite of it all, his personality showed through and he seemed kind. He'd stopped Johnson from hitting her several times and for that she was grateful.

She winced as she touched the latest bruise on her upper arm. Yes, she was extremely grateful to Bobby; she'd be even more grateful if he could get her out of this hellhole. But that didn't seem likely. It was increasingly clear that the only way she'd get away was an escape of her own devising. With those monster-dogs outside, she couldn't figure out how to do that. If only she had some rat poison.

She stood at the window and looked out. A dim light in the yard threw shadows across the drive. All at once the front door opened and Harold Johnson walked down the steps and over to a small shed. He had something in his hands. Annie squinted to make out what he was doing.

As she watched, the rottweilers dashed up to meet him, leaping and barking. He yelled something and they stopped in their tracks. The son of a bitch had trained them to obey his commands. He must have beaten them the way he did her. They didn't behave like dogs who loved their master; they feared him, as much as she did.

Was there any way she could get those dogs to trust her? She had no experience with dogs, and didn't know if it was even possible, but considering she might have some time on her hands, she might as well try. Their sharp teeth and the way they'd snapped at her, gave her pause. How do you win the affection of an animal that wants to have you for lunch?

She lay awake for a long time tossing and turning in the dark. As she tried without success to fall asleep, Harold Johnson's face continually intruded upon her repose. What was there about that horrible man that seemed so familiar? Had he been at her father's funeral?

Reluctantly she allowed herself to recall the day her dad was laid to rest. Once again she heard the funeral music and prayers, saw the mourners who accompanied her mom and her to the cemetery and back to their home for refreshments.

As she mentally scrutinized the group, she remembered seeing her grandparents for the first time. They seemed nice enough, but why had they rejected her mom?

She yawned. All these sad memories weren't getting her any closer to the puzzle of why Harold Johnson seemed so familiar. Perhaps he'd attended a Waterkeeper meeting.

Annie gasped, and sat up in bed. That was it. He was the man who shot Philip. Stunned at the realization, she turned on the lamp. Could it be true? Was Harold Johnson the gunman who'd burst into the hall that frightful night, shouting and waving a gun?

There was no doubt in Annie's mind. Harold Johnson was not only familiar, he was the shooter.

She was afraid of Harold Johnson before, but now, armed with the knowledge he'd shot his own nephew, she was terrified. A combination of fear and exhaustion left her drained. Mercifully sleep finally took her from the hopeless situation, if only temporarily.

Chapter 55

For a few minutes Lisa lay there, refreshed after several hours of uninterrupted sleep. Thanks to the pill Raoul had given her, concern for Annie was momentarily absent from her thoughts. Then it all came back in a sickening rush. Annie remained unaccounted for; Nate slept in the spot normally occupied by her daughter. Raoul had gone home, but promised to check back the next morning.

Lisa took up from where she left off the previous night: worried sick about Annie, desperate to find her and do whatever it took to get her back. Aware Nate was in the house, she donned her robe and walked into the living room. Soft snores told her he was still sleeping. Of course he would be, they hadn't gone to bed till well after midnight and it was now…she checked the wall clock…only seven-thirty. She returned to her bedroom to get dressed and face another day of torment.

* * * *

At nine o'clock, Raoul arrived laden with donuts, sausage and egg muffins and coffee from Josiah's. Did he know the muffins were Lisa's favorite or had he stumbled upon them by accident? Whatever the case, it lifted her spirits—if only for the moment.

Solemn-faced, the three of them sat in the kitchen chewing, swallowing and saying nothing. Oddly, it seemed to Lisa as though not talking would make the grim reason for their meeting go away: Annie would come bouncing through the door and life would get back to normal.

As seconds turned into minutes and the clock continued marking time, Raoul broke the silence with the last thing Lisa would've said.

"So maybe we should check out the boyfriend."

Nate set his cup down and swallowed his last bite of donut. "Boyfriend?" he said. "What boyfriend would that be?" He looked at Lisa and waited for her to respond.

When she didn't, Raoul said, "That's not what I meant."

The look on Nate's face said he knew Raoul lied. "No, it's all right, you can tell me. I've suspected for a while something was going on." He turned to Lisa, "So, is it that Philip guy, and is he the 'boyfriend?'"

Lisa climbed deep within herself searching for a way out. Hurting Nathan was the last thing Annie would want. How could she explain to this nice young man that his fiancée, the woman he planned to spend his life with, had met someone else, that she'd been weighing whether or not to break their engagement? This was not the message she should be delivering, especially when it was obvious he was worried sick about her.

"Nathan," she began slowly, casting about for just the right words. How to be honest without inflicting pain? And when Annie came back, how could she possibly tell her that Nathan knew about Philip? She glanced at Raoul, begging him to intervene. Taking a deep breath, she was about to plunge in. Then the welcome sound of his deep voice intervened.

"Look, Nathan, I misspoke. I didn't mean to say 'boyfriend,' what I meant was the male friends she has whether here in Moore Haven, back at school in Gainesville, or anywhere else. I'm sorry if I gave you the wrong impression."

Lisa swallowed and took a furtive look at Nathan. Raoul's explanation seemed to satisfy him—at least for the moment.

"No problem," he said. "I still think we should take a look at that Philip dude." Turning back to Lisa, he added, "He's her boss, right? Doesn't it strike you as odd that he hasn't come over to find out why she's not at work? Has he so much as called?"

Lisa tried to think.

What day is it now? Tuesday? Was it only yesterday I went over there?

"You're right. Philip hasn't called. When I stopped by the office looking for her, he said he thought she was sick. He probably figured I'd call and let him know if something was wrong."

"Or he knows what's wrong," Nathan said, a dark look on his face. "We need to have a talk with him. What do you think?" He directed his question to Raoul.

"Couldn't hurt. Maybe he can shed light on what's going on. He might know something and doesn't even realize it's important. Besides what else can we do?"

Lisa thought a moment, holding her arms tightly across her chest. Then she swallowed a sob. "When children go missing, don't people put posters up and call the news media? Somebody around here must know something. We've got to find out what that is."

For the next few minutes they worked on figuring out who would do what. Finally it was decided: Lisa and Nathan would put together some fliers and distribute them around town. Raoul would pay Philip a visit. They'd alert the news media later.

Nate had tried to convince Raoul he should go along with him—probably to get a look at the competition. It took some doing, but Raoul finally made him see that was a bad idea. There being no other issues, they trudged out the front door, their hearts conflicted between hope and apprehension.

Chapter 56

Raoul walked into the Waterkeeper's shabby offices, paused and looked around. The place appeared to be divided into two areas: a large space with several desks, a computer and chairs for what looked like small group meetings. And off to the side, what he thought was a private office, probably for the director—or whatever title the head honcho carried. That was more than likely where Philip hung his hat.

At the sound of the door closing, an attractive blonde with big green eyes looked up from the computer screen. She wore a neon orange tank top revealing ample cleavage.

"Hello," she breathed in a sultry voice, reminiscent of Marilyn Monroe. "I'm Becky. Something I can help you with?"

"I surely do hope so." Raoul returned her flirty smile. "I'd like to see Mr. Buckley. Is he in?"

Becky's gaze flitted over to the closed office door. "I'll check," she said. "And your name is…"

"Raoul Tucker"

"He expecting you?"

"No. I was in the neighborhood and thought I'd stop. I wasn't aware an appointment was required."

That remark seemed to puzzle Becky. "May I tell Phil, or, ah, Mr. Buckley, what this is about?" Again she looked at him with those big eyes and that dimple-filled smile.

"It's confidential."

She hesitated, so he added, "Look Miss, if this is a bad time, I could make an appointment and come back later." He waited as she came to a decision, an exercise she appeared to find difficult.

"Well, okay then. If you take a seat, I'll find out if he can see you." She stood, showing off a pair of tanned legs and well-filled shorts.

As he waited, Raoul recalled Lisa mentioning that Annie was annoyed with a woman she worked with. This must be the one. The girl was gorgeous in a sexy, dumb-blonde sort of way. If they were both attracted to Philip, he could see why Annie felt threatened.

A few minutes later, the office door swung open and Becky, as if inviting him to an audience with the pope, said, "Mr. Buckley will see you now."

Raoul had to stifle the urge to laugh. The self-important bastard would see him now? Who exactly did he think he was? Yes, he supposed the Waterkeeper function was of some importance to the community, but it was hardly up there with the governor or president. Some people were surely full of themselves. He braced himself. Getting all in-your-face with the guy would accomplish nothing. He had to remember why he was here.

"Mr. Tucker, is it? I'm Philip Buckley. Becky said you had a matter of some urgency you needed to speak with me about."

The man behind the desk had risen and extended his hand. Raoul could see why the women were all agog over him.

"Would you like some coffee?"

"No, I'm fine." Raoul sat down and looked at the open door where Becky stood, obviously curious to find out what this was about.

Philip followed Raoul's glance, then as if he suddenly understood, he said, "Thank you, Becky, that'll be all."

Becky abruptly turned, flitting her head with annoyance and returned to her desk, leaving the door wide open.

Raoul stood. "If you don't mind, I'd like some privacy." He closed the door as Becky glanced his way; her disapproval reflected on her face.

Philip sat back in his swivel chair and waited for Raoul to get settled. "Now what's this all about?"

"Annie Whitaker. I understand she works here as a summer intern, is that correct?" He watched Philip carefully, looking for any sign. A facial twitch. A sudden blink of the eye. An urgent intake of breath. Swallowing or clearing of the throat—anything that might indicate the man knew something.

Instead what he got was a puzzled look. "Annie? Yes, she works here. Is something wrong?"

Again Raoul scrutinized Philip's visage as he responded. "She seems to have gone missing, and I'm helping Lisa, or I mean Mrs. Whitaker, find her. She hasn't heard from her since Friday and is concerned, so we'd appreciate if you have any ideas that'd help us locate her."

Philip's forehead crinkled, his eyes leaked concern, his mouth went into a kind of grimace. "Mrs. Whitaker was in here yesterday asking about her. When I didn't hear anything, I assumed she'd been found and was okay. I have to admit, I was puzzled when she failed to come in again this morning, but I thought I'd give her some slack. After all, it's summer and she's young. This job doesn't pay much, so it's not hard to understand if an intern wants a day off here and there. In fact, Annie's hardly taken time off at all since she started. She's a real trooper."

"And when she didn't show up again today, you still weren't worried?

"I was more disappointed than concerned. I figured she was quitting and hadn't gotten around to telling me. You know, we work with volunteers a lot. Some are more reliable than others."

"But didn't you say Annie was a paid intern? I'd think you'd view her more as an employee than a volunteer."

Raoul took note as Philip sat up and folded his arms tightly across his chest.

"That's true, and a valued employee at that."

"But not so valued that you bothered to call and check as to why she hadn't come to work in two days?"

"Actually I was about to do that when Becky interrupted me."

"What exactly were you about to do?"

"Call her mother, of course, and ask if Annie was planning to come back, er, I mean, in. I thought she might be sick or something."

"No, actually, you said you were going to ask Lisa if Annie was coming back. Why would you think she wasn't? I thought you said she was a valued intern, that she was so reliable she took almost no time off, which you admit is unusual for a young person in a job that pays next to nothing. So, Mr. Buckley, why would it even cross your mind she might not be returning?"

Beads of perspiration appeared on Philip's forehead and dark rings soaked the underarms of his pale blue shirt. It was hot out but the office was air-conditioned. Raoul himself hadn't broken a sweat, so what was bothering Philip? Could it be a sign of guilt? Had they had an affair that ended badly and he was trying to cover it up? Something was definitely off, but what it was, Raoul couldn't begin to fathom.

For the next few minutes, he grilled Philip, trying every which way to get information out of him. Raoul's gut said he was not only withholding pertinent information, but knew exactly what had happened. Suspicion and proof are two very different things and Raoul, try as he might, simply couldn't drag anything more out of the man.

Why would he want to harm Annie? That would have to remain a mystery, at least for now.

Promising to let Philip know if they heard anything, Raoul left the office. He didn't look forward to telling Lisa he'd learned nothing and they were now back to square one.

Chapter 57

Raoul shook his head slowly. "Philip doesn't know anything. At least that's what he claims."

The three of them sat around the kitchen table exchanging notes. Lisa and Nathan had put together a flier with a recent photo of Annie and the words, "Have you seen this girl?" with details below. The picture was of her at a family outing shortly before Craig's death. The day was still vivid in Lisa's memory. It was the last truly happy day the family had shared.

"We put these up all over town," Nate said. "I'm thinking we should branch out to some of the other communities around here like Clewiston, La Belle, and Liberty Point."

"How about Pahokee?" Raoul turned to Lisa. "Isn't that where the police found Annie's car?"

Lisa, her last ounce of energy spent, nodded.

"Maybe someone saw her get out of the car or noticed who she was with," Raoul said. When no one responded, he added, "It's worth a shot."

The bedraggled little group had a quick lunch, then fanned out distributing their fliers, each with its sad message.

* * * *

Around five o'clock, tired and discouraged, they met back at Lisa's no wiser than before. They had passed out over four hundred fliers and no one admitted to having seen a thing.

"Oh, by the way, I got stopped by a state trooper over in Fort Centre," Nathan said. "He wasn't happy about what we were doing. Said if she was missing it was a police matter and that we shouldn't be stirring things up."

"That so?" Raoul stopped checking the phone book for the number of a carryout place. They were hungry but too tired to cook. "Since when do you have to get permission from the police to look for your daughter? Next time, give him my phone number. I'll be happy to explain the meaning of free speech. Isn't that guaranteed by your Constitution?"

Lisa was too weary to respond. Besides, she had more urgent things on her mind. Where on God's earth was Annie? What was happening to her? Was she even still alive? She started to say it was time to call the news media, when the phone rang.

Nathan picked up, then nodded and said, "Now's a good time. Come on over." He set the receiver down. "A TV reporter saw our fliers and is on her way."

Ten minutes later, a van with "WINK-TV 11" emblazoned on the side drove up. Upon seeing it, Lisa flashed back to the day Craig was found in the lake. The media was all over the story and now, here she was again.

She watched through the window as a man and woman approached. He held a large camera and was dressed in cargo shorts and a navy-blue polo shirt with what looked like the TV station's logo on it. Dressed in a tan business suit and heels, the attractive young woman was, no doubt, a reporter.

Before the bell rang, Raoul opened the door and ushered them inside. Lisa began to tremble; goose bumps erupted up and down her arms. After glancing around, the cameraman, who said his name was Greg, asked permission to set up on the patio.

"It'll make for a nice background shot," he explained.

Background shot?

What did Lisa care about that? She wanted her daughter back. The reporter said something else, but she didn't understand what. Suddenly everything seemed to go in slow motion; she felt as though she was wrapped in cotton. Raoul stared at her. So did Nathan and Greg. What did they want? The reporter, whose name Lisa couldn't recall, appeared to study her notes.

Raoul took her by the shoulders, sat her down and pressed on her back until she leaned over. After a moment, she recovered.

"Are you all right?" Raoul said.

Lisa nodded.

"You looked like you were about to pass out." He handed her a glass of water.

"I'm okay now," she said and took several sips.

After positioning Raoul and Lisa and checking for the right angle to avoid the sun's glare, Greg focused his video camera and tipped his head at the reporter, who nodded back and began to speak into a hand-held microphone.

"A young woman from Moore Haven appears to have disappeared over the weekend. Annie Whitaker, twenty-one, was last seen Friday afternoon at the Waterkeeper organization's office and has not been heard from since. Police found her car at the Pahokee airport, but there was no trace of her or evidence she'd taken an airplane ride. Private planes fly out of there so it's possible she decided on the spur of the moment to take a ride and didn't tell anyone.

"I have with me, Raoul Tucker, manager of Josiah's Restaurant, and Annie's mother, Lisa. She's the widow of Craig Whitaker who drowned in Lake Okeechobee three months ago. Mr. Tucker, what can you tell us?"

As Raoul explained what had gone on the past several days and their growing concern over Annie's whereabouts, Lisa fought back emotions that made her throat tight and her eyes blur with tears. She had to get hold of herself, had to get through this, had to do it for Annie. Raoul finished his statement and handed her the microphone.

"Is there anything you'd like to add?" the reporter said.

Lisa took a deep breath. "Annie, darling girl, if you're visiting a friend and just need some space, please call and let us know you're all right. Honey, we're worried sick."

She swallowed hard, then looking directly into the lens added, "If someone's holding Annie against her will, please return her to me unharmed. You can have anything you want, just bring her back." Then she added in a wavering voice, scarcely above a whisper, "Please."

In spite of her best efforts, Lisa choked up and tears began to flow. "Not long ago, I lost her father. I can't bear to lose her too."

The reporter wrapped up the story and assured them it would air on the evening news. Then they departed, leaving Lisa, Raoul and Nathan to hope and pray something good would come of their efforts.

Chapter 58

With the front door open less than an inch, Annie stuck the mop handle out with a cloth tied to the top and wagged it back and forth. In less time than it takes to wish the ordeal was behind her, the rottweilers were at the door barking, snarling, throwing themselves against it and clawing in an attempt to get at her.

After a few seconds, fearful they'd succeed, Annie pulled back, simultaneously leaning against the door and slamming it shut. She breathed a deep sigh of relief and turned around. Bobby stood across the room, looking puzzled.

"Wad ya do that for?" he said. "Those dogs bite. You need to watch out." He continued to stare. "Why poke that mop out there?"

Annie hadn't counted on having an audience and had to think up something fast. It didn't have to be profound, but it had to make at least a modicum of sense. Bobby might be disabled, but he was no dummy. She'd found that out by the things he did and said over the past few days.

He understood Harold Johnson was mean to her and often tried to intervene. For that she was grateful and went out of her way to make his life pleasant—at least for the duration of her stay. Treating him with kindness and courtesy was the least she could do.

"I've run out of things to clean, so I decided to start on the porch. The only way I can do that is by letting the dogs get used to seeing and smelling the mop." That was the truth, though it wasn't the whole story. What she was really trying to do was get the dogs used to her scent, so when she tried to escape she'd be familiar to them. Annie didn't know if it would work, but she had to give it a try. She had no other option.

So she took an old towel and slept with it wrapped around her body every night. Considering she hadn't bathed since arriving, both she and her clothes reeked. Now when Harold left to buy groceries or do whatever else his rotten mind conjured up, she'd work on the dogs. The last few times they seemed less interested, their attacks less ferocious.

"Harry know?" Bobby said.

"I don't think so, but he won't care." Annie lied, hoping she'd convinced him. "He wants the place cleaned up and that's what I'm doing." She glanced at him as he shook from tremors. Could she trust this man? He was, after all, Harold Johnson's brother. Harold took care of him, saw to his every need—she'd say that much for him. No matter how sweet and kind she was, Bobby's first allegiance would doubtless be to his brother. And who could blame him? Bobby owed his very life to Harold.

Trying to come up with a reason to keep her subversive activity a secret, Annie finally said, "Let's not tell him so it'll be a surprise, okay?" She held her breath.

Would Bobby buy it? She desperately hoped so. It was her only chance to get out of this hellhole.

Bobby licked his lips and gave her a lopsided smile. "A surprise? That'd be nice. Harry hasn't had one for a long time." He headed to the living room, then stopped. "Ya know, he's not bad once ya get to know him. Was mean to me when we were kids, but not now." His mind seemed to wander, then he said, "He'll be nice to you too—after a while."

* * * *

Annie was fixing lunch when Harold Johnson came in laden with parcels.

"You. Girl. Come here." He'd taken to calling her "girl."

Annie could only guess that he thought using her name would make it difficult to carry out whatever he had in mind. Like having to care for an unwanted animal, as long as you kept things impersonal, you were less likely to develop an attachment. That must be what Annie was to Harold Johnson—an unpleasant annoyance he had to put up with until…

Annie shuddered as she wondered, once again, why Philip brought her here; if he knew what was about to happen; and if she would get out alive.

"Girlie, I said get over here—now." Harold looked especially vicious. Not wanting to be on the receiving end of yet another punch, Annie rushed over to his side.

"Sit," he ordered, indicating the straight-back chair he'd positioned in the middle of the room.

Annie did as she was told, wondering what new horror the man had in mind. She watched him pull a small camera from one of the bags he'd brought in. It was the throwaway kind she'd seen at a friend's wedding reception.

"Here. Hold this in front of you," he said, and handed her a newspaper.

All at once, Annie realized what he was up to. He was making a demand for ransom, using a picture of her with today's newspaper as proof she was alive. With the paper held firmly across her chest, she posed as he snapped several photographs.

When he finished and fiddled with it, Annie checked the day's headlines, hoping to see her name plastered across the front page. To her surprise, the paper was not the *Glades County Democrat*, her local paper, but the *Boston Globe*. And it wasn't today's edition either. The newspaper was dated June 4, 1961. The headline read, "Whitaker & Sons win pesticide-spraying contract." Her swift intake of breath alerted Harold Johnson and he grabbed the paper.

"Done reading? One of these days your big snout's gonna get you in a boatload a trouble. Now get your butt out there and fix me and Bobby some lunch."

Chapter 59

Media coverage about Annie's disappearance resulted in a barrage of calls: yesterday Annie was spotted at a restaurant in Clewiston; Saturday she was seen in Pahokee at the entrance to Lake Okeechobee; the next day someone was positive they saw her at the cemetery visiting her father's grave. Some even asked for a reward in exchange for information, to which Raoul promptly told them what they could do.

Several reports sparked hope inside Lisa, unfortunately most did not. Still, she passed the tips on to the police, praying one of them would lead to her daughter's safe return.

It was now late Thursday afternoon, nearly a full week since she'd seen Annie last. Lisa sat in the dining room, compiling a list of national media outlets. She knew the police discouraged this type of thing. They claimed it attracted crazies who were in it for either a reward or attention. But what else could she do?

Annie was out there somewhere, alone and scared. Was she injured or in pain? Did she have enough food and a bed to sleep in? Was she cold at night or too hot when the outside temperature reached over a hundred? The questions tortured her with their endless possibilities. Annie, darling, hold on, we're doing everything we can. Just hold on. Lisa's heart and mind overflowed with pleas to God, to Annie—to the universe.

The doorbell rang. It was probably Raoul back from the restaurant. Or maybe it was Nathan. He'd been wonderful, refusing to leave until... She refused to follow where that thought might lead. Resolving to have keys made for them, she got up from her notebook computer and opened the door.

Much to her surprise, it was neither of her anticipated guests. Standing in the hot sun outside her front door was her father-in-law.

"Mr. Whitaker," Lisa said. She could hear the surprise reflected in her own voice.

"Hello, Lisa," Whitaker said. "May I come in?" His face was drawn as if he was ill.

"Where's my manners? Of course. You just took me by surprise." Lisa was stunned.

What's he doing here? Is he involved with Annie's disappearance?

She stiffened as if to brace herself against what he was about to say.

She settled him on the living room sofa and offered him a drink. "Would you like some tea or lemonade? I don't have any liquor in the house."

He declined and, crossing his legs, said, "What's happening with Annie? Have you heard from her?"

Lisa, who'd hoped he could shed some light on what was going on, shook her head. "We've put fliers up all over, contacted the police and the news media. We've had calls from people claiming they saw her, but so far nothing has panned out." She paused. "Are you sure you don't want something to drink or maybe a cookie or sandwich? It wouldn't be any trouble."

Whitaker started to say no, then changed his mind. "A glass of iced tea would hit the spot, thanks."

Lisa went in the kitchen and fixed a tray with a pitcher of tea, two glasses and a plate of cookies.

"Why don't we go out to the patio?" she suggested.

He nodded and followed her. After they were ensconced at the table, sipping tea and nibbling cookies, Whitaker revealed the purpose of his trip.

"I wanted to check on what was happening before I showed you what I got in the mail." He took a photograph from his suit pocket and handed it across the table to Lisa.

There in the picture sat Annie, looking tired and disheveled. In her hands she held a newspaper. Lisa was elated: Annie was alive. She wasn't dead, she was alive. But why was she holding a copy of the *Boston Globe*?

"Annie's in Boston? What's she doing there?" Hope surged through her. She must've gone to visit her grandparents like Molly Jenkins had suggested. But, then what was he doing here? She squinted hard trying to read the newspaper headline, but couldn't make it out.

When Whitaker handed her a magnifying glass, she realized that it was an old story about his company. Her forehead crinkled with confusion.

Whitaker ran his hand through his thinning hair. "There's more." He pulled a wrinkled sheet of paper from his pocket and put it in Lisa's trembling hand.

The note read, *To Craig Whitaker, the rich man who chose money over life. First your son and now your granddaughter. Was it worth it?*

Lisa gasped. "I don't understand."

Whitaker lowered his head and shook it back and forth. "Only thing I can figure is that it's about the crop dusting. The pesticides we sprayed made people sick; destroyed crops and killed animals. When we found out, we stopped, but by then it was too late—the damage had been done."

As the implications of Whitaker's revelation sank in, Lisa was horrified. Whoever held Annie wasn't looking for ransom—they wanted revenge.

"I'm so sorry," Whitaker said, seeming to age even as he spoke. "Back then I put money ahead of everything."

Lisa didn't know what to say. At the moment, she was overwhelmed with concern for her daughter. This man, who was little more than a stranger, mattered not at all. If he was devastated by the ominous turn of events, did it even occur to him to consider how she felt?

"Lisa," he continued, "I know it's too late, but I truly regret the way we treated you when Craig brought you home to meet us. It's unforgivable."

The glacier on Lisa's heart melted slightly. She patted his hand, feigning an effort to comfort him. "That was a long time ago."

"Still, I wonder if you could find it in your heart to forgive me—that is, me and Noreen."

"Mr. Whitaker, I forgave you years ago." What she said wasn't true, but it seemed the right thing to say at the moment. Lisa wasn't sure but she thought she saw tears glisten in the old man's eyes.

"Would you call me Craig? Mr. Whitaker sounds so formal."

Lisa paused and swallowed hard. "I'm sorry but I can't. Craig was my husband."

He nodded. "Then how about calling me CT, those are my initials. The guys in my company called me that back in the day."

"Okay, CT it is." She managed a wan smile.

"So, what now?" He gestured at the photograph as though it was somehow malignant.

Before Lisa could respond, the doorbell rang. "Hold on a minute," she said.

Raoul stood on the porch holding several bags; no doubt containing takeout from Josiah's.

"Hey Lisa. How you holding up?" His dark eyes projected empathy for her painful situation.

Pushing back the screen door, Lisa managed a smile, despite the fear ravaging her soul. "Raoul, come on in." She was happy to see him, especially in view of her father-in-law's unexpected visit. He'd know what to do. "There's someone I want you to meet," she said over her shoulder as they headed toward the patio.

Seeing the old man sitting under the umbrella sipping tea, Raoul gave Whitaker a quizzical look as if to say, "Who're you and what're you doing here?"

"Raoul, meet my father-in-law, CT Whitaker. CT, this is my boss, Raoul Tucker."

The two men shook hands, mumbled "glad-to-make-your-acquaintance" messages and sat down. An awkward silence settled over them for a few seconds, then Lisa said, "Raoul, CT got this in his mailbox. Take a look."

Upon viewing the unsettling image of Annie, Raoul's face dropped. "Good God, what's it mean? Do you know?"

CT handed him the crumpled-up note and explained his company's connections to pesticide spraying decades earlier. With an embarrassed expression, he concluded,

"We managed to poison the water, damage trees—and, I later learned, cause some people to come down with diseases like cancer and Parkinson's."

Lisa could see anger reflected in Raoul's face. "And were they compensated for their losses?"

CT shrugged. "My firm was relatively small, so my insurance company insisted we fight the claims. Hell, the chemical companies did likewise and they were more to blame than we were—it was their product, after all. We were just a cog in a much larger machine."

"So what happened to the people who got sick and lost their property?"

CT shook his head. "The lawsuits were consolidated; the chemical companies used high-priced lawyers and successfully argued the people were collateral damage, that no one knew what the outcome would be and that they owed the farmers nothing. Unfortunately that's exactly what they got."

The room grew silent. Lisa bit her lip to keep from telling CT what she thought. She stood and said, "I'm going to start supper."

When she was alone in the kitchen, her tears began to flow. Not only had that man rejected her simply because of her race, denying her little girl the joy of knowing her grandparents, uncles, aunts and cousins, but now she learned that more than likely because of what he'd done, she'd lost her husband and soon may lose her only child.

She stopped pulling plates from the shelf and began to sob. How do you forgive something like that?

She was so deep in thought she didn't hear the doorbell ring or notice Raoul hustle through the living room to answer it.

"Hey." Nathan appeared in the doorway, a sheepish look on his face. "You all right?"

Lisa wiped her face on a dishtowel. "I'm fine. What've you been up to?"

She wasn't sure but thought he wore a guilty expression, kind of like when a dog poops on the carpet.

"Oh, nothing, just an idea I had. I'll let you know if anything comes of it. Who's the guy on the patio?"

"Annie's grandfather, CT Whitaker. He got a picture of Annie in the mail."

Nathan looked confused.

"Go out and introduce yourself. He'll explain." She couldn't bring herself to repeat the sordid story. Better to get busy unwrapping and heating the food Raoul had so thoughtfully brought. It'd give her something to occupy herself with besides the nightmarish vision of what Annie was enduring—and the possibility of yet another funeral.

Chapter 60

As soon as Annie heard Harold Johnson's car back out of the drive, she went to work. Now, in addition to the towel stinking of her scent, she'd added scraps of meat left over from supper. It was easy to hide them from Harold. She'd simply wrapped them in a napkin and stuck it down her blouse.

She tied the towel to the broom handle with threads unraveled from where the dogs had ripped it. Accustomed to her scent, they merely sniffed. Her plan was to make them her friends by having them associate the towel and her scent with food. It appeared to be working. Now, if only Johnson didn't catch her.

Bobby watched as she worked her magic.

"Now, remember don't tell Harold."

"Why not?" Bobby looked confused. "Tell me again."

"Because I want to surprise him by giving the porch a good cleaning? Since the dogs try to bite when I open the door, I'm trying to make friends with them."

"Whyn't tell H… Harry? H… he'd put the dogs

away." Bobby's eyes lit up as though he'd come up with a great idea.

"No, Bobby, don't say anything. Remember it's a surprise." Annie looked Bobby in the eye, trying to communicate with him on the deepest level she could. "Promise you won't spoil it by telling. Please. Promise, Okay? Promise?" She urged and bobbed her head up and down.

Bobby hesitated, then nodded his head in rhythm with Annie's. "Okay," he said. "Promise. Keep it a secret. Surprise Harry w… when done." He put his finger to his lips and said, "Ssshh. Don't tell."

Annie went back to work training the dogs. She'd run out of meat and decided they were ready for the next phase. Taking a deep breath, she slid her hand down the mop handle. For the first time, part of her body was outside where the dogs could sniff her. If she miscalculated, she'd pay a heavy price. Not only would they mangle her, possibly ripping off several fingers, but she'd have a hard time explaining her injuries to Harold Johnson.

For a few seconds the dogs pawed at the towel trying to find more meat. As Annie continued to slide her hand down the extended handle, they began at first to growl and then whine. She was about to pull back when she felt something soft and wet. Almost as rough as sandpaper, the dogs' tongues tickled her.

Oh my gosh, they hadn't mistaken her fingers for dessert, but as she'd hoped, recognized her scent. She was the one who provided yummy treats; sang softly to them through the door; and told them what good boys they were. Harold Johnson never did any of that: all he did was beat them and yell.

Annie was thrilled. She was about to take the next step and open the door all the way when Harold Johnson's car came barreling down the drive. Panicked by his unexpected return, she yanked the mop handle back, slammed the door and sprinted to the sink filled with dirty dishes. Only then did she realize the towel she'd been using had fallen off the handle and was probably on the porch.

She breathed a silent prayer that he wouldn't notice what was little more than a soiled rag as he walked up the steps to the front door. If he did, there'd be hell to pay.

Quickly filling the sink with warm water, she began to wash dishes left over from lunch, then she stopped and pulled out several covered containers from the fridge. Maybe he'd think she'd started supper early. She glanced at the clock on the wall. On its face was an advertisement from a farm supply catalog. It looked old, like it had seen better days. It was probably left over from when Harold and Bobby were children. She hadn't seen anything like that in Moore Haven.

It was a little after four, not really all that early. She'd tell him she wanted to try something new. She grabbed the cookbook from the counter and flipped it open. Annie'd been surprised when he gave it to her. She realized it wasn't so much that he wanted to please her, he just wanted something to eat besides the same old burgers and chicken she knew how to fix.

"I thought you'd have that done by now," Harold Johnson blustered as he walked through the door. The towel had caught on the heel of his boot. Annie held her breath. Would he figure out what she'd done?

"What the hell's this?" He pulled the rag off his foot and looked at it for a second. "Those damn dogs're always getting into something." He tossed it aside and sat down. "When'll supper be ready?"

Annie was so relieved she could scarcely speak. "In about an hour," she said and began to flip through the cookbook for the simplest recipe she could find.

* * * *

Supper was thankfully uneventful. Annie managed to fix meatloaf, mashed potatoes and a green bean casserole. She had the ingredients for them all and it wasn't too hard to figure out. For dessert, Harold had brought home an apple pie. He specified that he wanted a slice of cheese on his. Bobby would have his with a dip of ice cream. If there was any left over, she could have some too. Despite Bobby's repeated urging that Harold allow Annie to eat with them, he'd adamantly refused.

"The help don't eat with their masters," he'd said and that's how it remained. Annie didn't care; she preferred to eat alone. It was the only time she had to herself during the day except when Johnson took off on some errand or other.

Finished eating, she was cleaning up and thinking how delicious the meatloaf was. After finishing her chores she'd look for more recipes that weren't too difficult. In the back of her mind she reminded herself that keeping Harold Johnson well fed, might stop him from killing her. The photo session of her holding that old newspaper came to mind, and she wondered what he'd done with it. As she mused, Harold Johnson bellowed.

"Hey, girlie. Get over here"

Startled by his sudden demand, Annie jumped and dropped the cookbook.

"Yes, Mr. Johnson, what can I do for you?"

"What d'I tell you bout calling me that?" He stared, his eyes drilling her as he awaited her response.

"I'm sorry, I meant, Harold."

"That's more like it." He didn't seem to recognize the incongruity between insisting Annie address him informally and making her work as a servant. She, of course, did and had to bite her tongue to keep from pointing it out.

"Sit," he barked, indicating the disheveled sofa with his head.

As Annie crossed the room to do as she was told, she noticed a number of cartons and bottles piled on the cushions. A space had been left in the middle where he obviously wanted her to sit.

"What's this?" she said.

"Was anyone speaking to you?"

"No."

"No, what?"

"No, Harold."

"Then shut up and do as you're told."

Clamping her mouth closed, Annie sat down amid insect killers, rat poison and weed eradicators. When she was settled, Harold Johnson thrust a newspaper into her hand and ordered her to hold it across her chest as she'd done before.

"Now, where'd I put the damned camera?"

Harold glanced furiously around the cluttered room and spotted Bobby at the window, his trembling hands up at his face. He dashed over and snatched the camera from him.

"What'cha think yore doing?"

With a crestfallen look, Bobby retreated to the kitchen.

"Oh, come on, don't pout. I just need it for something important."

"You not mad at me?" Bobby said.

"I'm not mad but from now on keep your hands off my stuff. Okay?"

Bobby nodded.

Harold turned his attention back to Annie, who'd continued to eye the deadly stuff. He pointed the camera at her, only this time the paper she held was today's—and it had Annie's photograph on the front.

Chapter 61

Fear and grief had taken a heavy toll on Lisa; she could scarcely get out of bed. This was the eighth day Annie had been missing, and she was beginning to lose the optimism that had kept her going until now. With no demand for ransom, or any other communication from the kidnappers, she feared the worst was either about to happen or already had.

It was after nine and she finally forced herself to get up. Nathan was already gone on whatever secretive mission he'd concocted. Raoul was, no doubt, at Josiah's making sure the restaurant was running smoothly. And CT, who hadn't made an appearance yet, must still be at the motel.

Lisa sat in the kitchen trying to force food down her throat. It was awful with no appetite, but if she didn't eat, she'd get sick and things would be even more difficult. So she picked up the spoon and shoveled in one mouthful of cereal after another, chewed and swallowed, washing it down with stale coffee and orange juice.

She was nearly finished when the doorbell rang. She

no longer greeted such intrusions with soaring anticipation of Annie's imminent return; by now she realized how unlikely it was. No, it seemed each ring of the bell only brought more disaster.

Lisa set her cup down and, grasping the edge of the table, wearily stood. Then she headed through the living room to greet the latest bearer of doom.

Expecting to see CT, Raoul or in the very least, Nathan, Lisa was puzzled when she opened the door to a whole lot of nothing. Nobody was there. She looked to either side of the door, thinking perhaps her visitor had gone to check out the bougainvillea blooming profusely on a trellis at the side of the house. But no, not there either. That's when she glanced down and saw an envelope on the stoop where it had been delivered—or rather, dropped.

She picked it up by the corner, careful not to disturb whatever fingerprints, DNA or other evidence may have been left behind. She knew not to do that from what she'd been through over the past week, as well as from watching all those police shows on TV.

This may be nothing more than an over-eager salesperson, but she doubted it. From the bulge, she could tell there was something more than a brochure inside. She brought it in and set it on the table next to the photograph CT had left behind. They had agreed to give it to the police but since it was late had decided to wait until this morning. The rumpled note with its cryptic message lay beside it. Now she had another something to add to the collection.

Trembling in anticipation, she fervently wished the kidnapper would simply demand money, or let her be sacrificed in place of her daughter. In her gut she knew neither of those things was going to happen. They weren't after her; they were after CT. And they didn't seem to want money; they wanted to make him suffer by hurting those he loved. It was odd. He'd only set eyes on his granddaughter the one time, so she hardly qualified as a loved one. She guessed the kidnapper hadn't considered that.

She stared at the sealed envelope, holding herself back from ripping it open. Better to wait for Raoul and CT. They'd know what to do and how to handle it. As she sat there unable to tear her eyes from whatever it held, she couldn't wait any longer. There'd been no name on the outside, so it may, in fact, have nothing to do with Annie.

She got a scissors from the drawer and slit open the end opposite the sealed portion, thereby preserving whatever DNA might be present.

Inside the padded envelope was a disposable camera. Lisa's breath caught in her throat. What would it be this time? Rushing for the door, car keys in hand, Lisa headed straight for the one-hour photo place. There was no time to waste.

* * * *

An hour later, she gasped as she stared at a photograph of Annie sitting on a couch holding yesterday's *Glades County Democrat*, surrounded by bottles and boxes of something. Thinking the stuff around her daughter must be significant, Lisa grabbed a magnifying glass and took a closer look. That's when she realized the containers held different kinds and brands of pesticides. A cold chill went down her spine. Of course, it was a not too subtle message for CT.

She shook the envelope to see if there was anything more was inside and sure enough a folded sheet of lined notebook paper fell out. Carefully unfolding it, she read the scrawled handwriting.

It said, *Whitaker: Plants. Animals. My mom and dad. Your son. All dead because of you. Too bad your pretty granddaughter also will soon pay for your crimes. Time's running out.*

Lisa dropped the note and let out a scream. "No-o-o. Please, no-o-o." She sobbed so hard, she didn't hear Raoul come in through the door she'd left open.

"What's this all…" Seeing the photographs on the table and the note in Lisa's hand, he stopped in mid-sentence. Grim-faced, he reached out and said, "Let me see".

* * * *

Nate, Raoul and Lisa sat around the kitchen table pondering their next move when CT arrived. Looking every bit his seventy-five years, he was haggard, as though the mere act of walking might drain him of what little strength he still possessed.

"Hey," he said, in a raspy voice, "what's up?"

The little group barely acknowledged him.

"Hey, CT," Raoul finally said.

"Anything new?" Hope that they would have something good to report seemed to infuse CT with at least a bit of strength.

Raoul looked at Lisa as if asking her permission to reveal the latest communication. She inclined her head. What could it hurt?

"This morning this was left on the doorstep along with a note." Raoul ripped off a section of paper towel and placed it around the piece of notebook paper. "Be careful, we don't want to mess up any fingerprints or DNA that might be on it."

Lisa watched as her father-in-law examined the photo. "What the hell's he doing? Well, I'll be a son of a bitch." He picked up the note by a corner and read it. The look on his face could only be described as pure grief. "Craig was murdered?" he added softly. "It wasn't an accident."

As he carefully set the note down and leaned back in the chair, something deep inside him seemed to collapse.

"And now they've got Annie." His eyes filled with tears. He looked from Lisa to Raoul. "They're doing this to get back at me, aren't they?"

"Looks that way," Raoul said.

"So what're the police doing about it?"

"We called awhile ago to let them know about the photographs. They'll be here pretty soon, though what good it'll do, who knows." Raoul shrugged. "At least now they'll take it seriously."

"So, we just gonna sit around and wait for the next one?" Nate spoke up.

He looked so desolate Lisa had all she could do to keep from giving him a hug. She wanted so badly to reassure him that Annie would be okay, but although that's what she wanted more than anything in the world, she had to admit she was no longer sure the outcome of all this would be good. Who knew what those horrid people would do to Annie, especially since they'd apparently gotten away with murdering her husband?

A little while later, the police arrived and not only took the pictures of Annie and the notes but delivered something for Nathan: It was a restraining order along with a stern warning. He was to leave Philip Buckley alone—no more sitting in front of the waterkeeper's office and following him around. The order required him to stay at least a thousand feet from Philip or suffer the consequences.

Lisa was surprised to learn what Nathan had been doing the last few days. She thought he was up to something—his long absences from the house told her that, but what, she didn't know. When she'd inquired where he was, he'd been vague. Now it all came out. On the one hand she was pleased he cared enough about Annie to do more than sit around putting together fliers and comforting her. On the other, she was aghast that he'd put himself in jeopardy.

"But don't you see," he argued to the Raoul, Lisa and anyone else who would listen. "Philip knows something. Don't you find it odd he hasn't come over and offered to help? I mean, the man's her boss, maybe more than that. I don't know, but if I had someone working for me and they just up and disappeared, I'd move heaven and earth to find them."

Lisa had to admit he had a point. It was strange she hadn't heard from Philip. He certainly hadn't been shy about pursuing them when he thought they'd stolen that money. Although truth be told, all his communication had been through Annie. He'd never confronted her personally. Maybe for reasons of his own, he didn't want to get involved. Or maybe, like Nathan said, he knew more than he let on.

"Nathan, you have to stop harassing Philip or you'll land in jail," Raoul said, adding with a smirk, "but that doesn't mean *I* can't look into what the guy's up to."

"Raoul," Lisa said, "let the police handle this. If Philip's involved, they'll figure it out."

"Sure, like they're so concerned about what happened to Annie that they're doing what? Oh that's right. Nothing. Instead they decide she took an airplane and went on vacation."

"At least now that they have those photos, they can't deny she was kidnapped. When you showed it to them, they seemed genuinely concerned, don't you think?" Lisa said.

"As well they should be," Nathan said. "If Annie's… I mean, if we don't get her…" He couldn't seem to finish his thought, as if not getting his fiancée back was unthinkable. "I'll sue the pants off them for not trying to find her."

Chapter 62

It was late and the room was stifling. Annie tossed and turned, unable to sleep. The photo Harold Johnson had taken earlier weighed on her mind. Why would he put her smack-dab in the middle of a bunch of pesticides? It was clear from the picture he'd taken before, he had some kind of bone to pick with her grandfather, but what that might be, and how it involved her, Annie had no clue.

This latest picture with the herbicides and insecticides seemed more ominous, as though Harold Johnson was gearing up to prove something. The underlying message was obviously that pesticides were dangerous. That somehow her grandfather's use of them had killed. But who? What? Harold Johnson's pet dog? Something he'd been fond of as a child?

What could her grandfather's crop-dusting possibly have done to affect Harold Johnson so profoundly he'd be willing to risk going to prison to get even? Is that what this was all about? Getting payback with her grandfather? Is that why her father was dead?

Annie had long suspected her dad's death wasn't an accident despite the fact no one else seemed bothered by it. She'd just not been able to figure out who was behind it—that is, until now.

It was Harold Johnson. Maybe Philip as well. Much as she hated to think the man of whom she'd been so enamored was in cahoots with a kidnapper, and possibly a killer, she had to concede it was possible.

And where did that leave her? In mortal danger, that's where. She shivered. Despite the heat, cold chills worked their way up and down her spine. The realization of how precarious her situation was destroyed any prospect of sleep. Hour after hour, Annie pondered her options. By dawn she arrived at a decision: Her only choice was to escalate her work with the dogs and attempt to escape the following night— that is, assuming she was still alive by then.

Chapter 63

It was well after midnight when Annie finally summoned the courage to try and escape. Nearly a week ago, she'd convinced Harold Johnson he needn't bother locking her in at night since the dogs would eat her alive if she so much as stuck a foot out the door. Besides, she'd argued, it was a bother using that stinky chamber pot then emptying it every morning—and for what? She wasn't going anyplace, especially not at night in the middle of nowhere.

At first he'd resisted, saying she was trying to pull something, but little by little she brought him around to her way of thinking. There again, it wasn't so much that he wanted to please her, he was just tired of locking her up every night and then letting her out to cook in the morning. As he'd put it, if she was to have breakfast prepared when they woke up, she'd have to be able to leave her room. He resented having to get up to let her out like a damn dog only to go back to bed and get up again when she called. And she was right about the dogs, he said. If she so much as put her little toe outside they'd snap it right off. Hell, even Bobby was scared of them.

So, Annie had managed to win a concession from Johnson. It was her first, and most likely the only one she'd win, but it was important and may well mean the difference between surviving her ordeal and perishing.

She heard the clock strike one as she got up and went to the bathroom. It was a good test to determine whether or not the men were asleep. She'd gotten used to their distinctive snores: Bobby's was fairly quiet while Harold's sounded like the buzz of a chain saw.

Imagine sleeping next to someone who snored like that all night long.

For her purposes, however, it was a godsend.

As she crossed the hall, she paused long enough to recognize both sets of snores. She could only hope the rhythmic sounds meant they were in a deep sleep. What would happen if Harold Johnson discovered her trying to get out was unthinkable. Death might be preferable.

Glancing around, Annie was ready. Now, if only the dogs would cooperate. She had contingency plans for them as well. She'd managed to purloin some rat poison and bury it in a few scraps of meat she'd put down her blouse. If the dogs decided to have her for lunch, she'd toss it their way. She really didn't want to kill them. It wasn't their fault they had a master like Harold Johnson. But if it came right down to it, and she had to choose between her freedom and those dogs, the decision wouldn't be difficult.

With her shoes in hand, she quietly closed her bedroom door and started down the steps. From observation, she knew exactly which ones creaked and carefully avoided them. She made it to the first floor and was about to open the front door when she heard Bobby call out. "Harry, I need you."

She froze. Looking around, she ducked behind the old rocker-recliner just as the hall light went on.

"Hold on, I'm coming," Harold Johnson called out in a voice heavy with sleep.

Annie thanked God she'd had the foresight to close her bedroom door. There was no reason for Harold to suspect she wasn't in there. For a second, she panicked, fighting the urge to sneeze. She pinched her nose and swallowed.

It seemed like hours before the house was finally settled. Harold handled whatever had disturbed Bobby, got him a glass of water and went back to bed. Annie had to admit, for all his faults—and they were countless—Johnson took good care of his ailing brother. She never heard him complain or speak disparaging of him. And that was something, considering he'd no doubt spend his life caring for him. Too bad he didn't have it in his heart to show her some compassion as well. Like it or not, she represented her grandfather. And if Harold Johnson got his way, she'd pay for that with her life.

Once the rhythmic snores again bounced back and forth between Bobby and Harold's rooms, Annie stood. Her legs had cramped from the uncomfortable position she'd squeezed into. She massaged them, running her hands deftly up and down as she'd done countless times after a particularly strenuous run. As the pain subsided, she patted the packets of meat she'd stuffed into her pockets earlier. These would occupy the dogs while she made her escape. The one down her blouse was for use as a last resort.

Walking on tiptoe, Annie made her way to the front door and, oh, so carefully turned the knob and pulled it open. "Please God," she prayed, "Don't let Harold

Johnson—or those dogs hear me." She didn't realize it but she held her breath, half expecting to hear Johnson demand, *"Where the hell do you think you're going?"* and feel sharp blows across her back.

When that didn't happen, she managed to take a deep gulp of air and put one foot out on the porch, anticipating the rottweilers to attack, sinking their teeth deep into her leg.

Outside it was pitch black. That was a mixed blessing for, while the moonless night protected her from being seen, it made finding her way difficult. She felt like she had on a blindfold and had to feel her way down the steps. The hush of the post-midnight hour was broken only by the occasional hoot of an owl and the screech of its prey.

Annie made it down the steps and was halfway between the house and the drive when the dogs bounded up from the shed and began barking, growling and lunging at her. Scared nearly out of her mind, Annie hastily tossed several scraps of meat their way, desperately hoping Johnson hadn't heard the ruckus. Unfortunately that was not to be the case.

A light flicked on in a second floor window. Tossing several chunks at the dogs, she dove behind a nearby bush as floodlights illuminated the yard and the front door banged opened.

"What the hell's going on out here?" Johnson shouted.

Annie curled into a fetal position as the man went out on the porch and directed his flashlight beam around the yard. It fell on the dogs that were growling and competing for the meat she'd tossed.

"So you got yourself a fuckin' critter," Johnson growled. "Big deal. Ya gotta wake up the whole house?

Shut the hell up." He switched off the flashlight, went back inside and doused the lights, leaving Annie to tremble with fear and relief.

Disoriented, Annie stumbled in the dark; going first toward the house, then making a wrong turn and ending up at the shed. Fortunately the dogs still scrapped over the last remnants of the meat she'd tossed. When, at last, her eyes adjusted, Annie headed down the drive toward the main road.

Vaguely recalling her trip to the house with Philip, she estimated it was around five miles to the highway. That meant walking on what was little more than a dirt trail, hoping she didn't happen upon any of central Florida's wildlife. Visions of boa constrictors and ten-foot alligators floated in her imagination as she forced herself to overcome her fear and keep going.

By her reckoning, it would start getting light soon and although that would enable her to see where she was going, it also would expose her to the possibility of discovery.

A gentle breeze swayed sugarcane leaves on either side of the road. Soughing sounds made them seem almost alive. Spooked at first, Annie soon realized what it was, calmed down and began to hear the other night sounds surrounding her. The occasional screech of a wild animal no longer seemed threatening. The real danger to her was from mammals of the two-legged variety.

It was still dark when she heard what sounded like a car motor in the distance, and thought it was likely a farmer getting an early start on his chores.

As the vehicle approached, its headlights illuminating the road, her only thought was to beg whoever had come this way to provide her with the assistance she so desperately needed. With that in mind, she stepped into the middle of the road, letting the car's headlights wash over her. Then she waved her arms high in the air and screamed, "Stop. Help me. Please. I need help."

The car squealed to a stop. Annie rushed to the driver's side. As soon as the door swung open and the dome light illuminated its driver, she realized she'd made a terrible—possibly fatal—mistake.

By his astonished look, Philip said it all. The last person he expected to see alone at this hour on the dirt road leading to his uncle's house was Annie Whitaker.

Annie momentarily froze then turned to run, but Philip was faster. Reaching out he grabbed her arm and held it in a vise-like grip.

"Let me go." Tears spilled down her cheeks. "Please. I won't tell anyone. Honest. Just let me go and that'll be the end of it."

Philip hesitated as if considering. Then he squeezed her arm so tight she could almost feel bruises starting to form. He shook his head. "Sorry, Annie, wish I could, but I just can't. Now get in. Don't make this harder than it has to be."

When she planted her feet firmly on the ground, he simply swept her up in his arms and tossed her into the vehicle as though she was nothing more than a bag of flour.

Not willing to give in so easily, Annie screamed, pulling at his hair and kicking wildly. Philip cuffed her. "Want to make things difficult? Fine. Kick my dashboard again and see what happens."

He paused, as if waiting to see what she'd do next. When she folded her arms tightly across her chest and glared, he pushed the button locking both doors and said,

"That's more like it." Then he started the car engine and began to drive the few miles back to the place Annie had tried so hard to escape.

Filled with despair, her face awash in tears, Annie cast about to see if there was anything she could say or do to get Philip to change his mind.

"I thought we were friends," she whined. In the faint light dawning on the horizon, Annie could see Philip's face. Her words seemed to have made an impression.

He winced. "I was, er, am…fond of you, Annie. That's not what this is about."

"Seriously? You say you like me and yet you deliver me to a man who keeps me captive, beats me when I do something wrong and treats me like a servant?" She swallowed and took a deep breath, "And I'm pretty sure he's going to kill me."

When Philip didn't react, she said, "Why are you and your uncle—if he's really your uncle—doing this? What did I ever do to you?"

Philip took his gaze from the road and gave Annie a penetrating look. "Nothing—you didn't do anything. And yes, Harold Johnson really is my uncle. Annie, I'm sorry you have to go through this, but don't you realize it's not about you?" He stopped talking and turned his attention back to the road.

Dawn was fast approaching as the dark melted away and the sky began to lighten up. Annie noticed some birds hovering over the sugarcane fields.

"So, it's about my grandfather? Your uncle and him have some kind of feud?"

"That's not it at all. There was no feud," Philip said.

The grave expression on his face scared Annie even more. She expected some kind of an explanation but none was forthcoming. "If I'm to lose my life over this, don't I at least deserve to know why?"

Heaving a sigh, Philip pulled to the side of the road, and jerked to a stop. "Not that it changes anything, but I suppose you have a right to know."

He cleared his throat and gripped the steering wheel with both hands. "Back in the '50s, my dad, Uncle Harold and my grandparents lived on a farm back in Michigan. I'm told it had been in our family for over a hundred years. You told me you're majoring in environmental studies, right?"

Frowning, Annie wondered what her education had to do with this.

"So you probably read the book, *Silent Spring*?"

Annie nodded.

"Well, you read about it. My dad and his family lived it."

Ripples crossed her forehead. "What are you talking about?"

"Our farm was sprayed with pesticides back in the fifties and it ended up killing our orchard, crops and livestock. My grandmother died a hideous death from cancer. My grandfather went broke and killed himself. My dad was a toddler in the yard when the spraying took place. He ended up with Parkinson's, which we now know is the result of pesticide exposure."

Annie gasped. "Oh my God, Philip, Bobby's your father?"

"Yes." Philip said it softly as if pained.

"But your last name's Buckley. Isn't Bobby Harold Johnson's brother?"

"I assumed my mom's maiden name to prevent people from putting two and two together."

Annie's heart fell realizing her kidnapping wasn't some a spur of the moment act, but had been carefully planned.

"I'm assuming you're wondering what this has to do with you," Philip said.

"No," Annie replied, "I get the picture. My grandfather owns the company that sprayed your dad's farm and Harold Johnson's getting even first by killing my dad and now me. Right?"

Philip's silence was her answer.

Her heart racing, Annie slid her hand to the door handle, hoping Philip had forgotten and unlocked it. She could bolt from the car and get lost in a field of dense sugarcane.

"Don't even try," Philip said, revving the motor.

"You're really taking me back?"

"I have to, Annie, I got no choice."

"Of course you do," she pleaded. "Just unlock the door and drive away. Harold won't even know you've been here."

"Is that what you'd do?" Philip put the car in gear and stepped on the gas.

"You mean if it was my dad instead of Harold, and you were the one in trouble? Would I turn my back on him and let you go?"

"Yeah, would you?"

Annie hesitated.

"Didn't think so."

Recognizing Philip's SUV, the dogs raced from the shed, teeth flashing and generally raising hell. There were no lights on, so Annie assumed Harold Johnson and Bobby were still in bed. It was their habit to get up when she called them around seven and not a minute before.

The clock on the car dashboard read six.

Philip opened the door and reaching across to the passenger side, yanked Annie's arm, pulling her from the car.

"Let's go," he said. "We can't put it off any longer.

Realizing this was her last chance to escape, Annie went limp and fell to the ground with Philip's hand still clamped firmly onto her wrist. Then, hoping against hope that there was a workman of some kind in the area, she began to scream.

"Let me go! Help! Help! Someone, help me! They're going to kill me! Help!"

Philip yanked her to her feet and said, "Stop that right now. There's no one around for miles. That's the reason Uncle Harold rented this place." Putting his face inches from hers, he added, "You might as well accept the fact you're not going to be rescued, it's too late."

Those words, "You're not going to be rescued," and "it's too late" struck a chord. The optimism Annie'd held out for the past week, that she'd win her freedom and regain her former life, drained away and she slumped in defeat.

As they made their way up the walk, the dogs continued their noisy greeting, jumping up and licking both their hands. They, no doubt, hoped for another helping of meat, but all Annie had left was the baggie of poisoned chicken parts stuffed down her blouse. With Philip holding both hands behind her back, she couldn't access it and in any case saw no reason to bring the rottweilers harm. Unlike Harold and Philip, they'd done nothing to her.

Philip was about to open the door when it flew back revealing a livid Harold Johnson.

"What the hell's going on out here," he blustered, then as if it suddenly registered who stood facing him, added, "You. Girl. Who said you could go outside? Don't you know those dogs'll rip you to pieces? Ain't you supposed to be makin' breakfast?"

"And Philip, what're you doing here? Thought we agreed you'd stay away 'till this was over."

"She tried to escape and nearly made it too. I was on my way here when she flagged me down."

Harold glared, then punched Annie, slamming her into the doorjamb. "That's what I get for letting you keep your door unlocked."

Annie's skull vibrated as her head, colliding with the frame, exploded in pain. She gasped, struggling to breathe.

He turned back to Philip, "I still don't get what you're doing here. Sure you weren't followed?"

"I'm sure. That's why I came so early. If someone was following me, I'd have seen their headlights."

"So, you have a reason for coming out, or you just wanna wake us up?"

The expression on Philip's face changed from a scowl to an all-encompassing grin. It was the first time since the ghastly affair began that Annie saw the handsome man with whom she'd been so obsessed.

"No, Uncle Harold, I didn't come out here in the middle of the night to interrupt your sleep. I just wanted to warn you that someone's on to us. I did a little digging and discovered it's Annie's fiancé." Philip said the word "fiancé" as though it was distasteful.

Upon hearing what Nathan had done, the smallest glimmer of hope sprouted in Annie's breast. She touched the diamond ring on her left hand and breathed a silent prayer.

Oh, Nate, I'm so sorry for what I've put you through. I don't deserve you. If I get out of this alive, I'll be the best wife you could hope for.

Philip continued. "He's staying at her mom's house, I assume to help with the search. I got a restraining order claiming harassment, but it probably won't stop him." He glanced around the room. "Uncle Harry, you'd best get the show on the road. I'm afraid if you keep this up, you'll get caught—and take the rest of us down with you."

Annie silently beseeched Philip to rescue her. He pointedly avoided her gaze. Obviously he'd decided his family was more important than a friend—even one he supposedly cared about.

Chapter 64

Hundred degree heat beat down mercilessly in the midday sun. The unhappy group inside Lisa's air-conditioned house found respite however temporary it might be. With each passing day their confidence in a positive outcome sank a little more until it finally hit rock bottom. Raoul was out of ideas, CT out of strength, Lisa out of tears.

"What more can we do?" CT said. They'd passed out fliers, done media interviews, and generally made pests of themselves continually checking with the police, all to no avail.

Raoul was about to say something when the phone rang.

"I'll get it." Nathan jumped from his chair as though relieved to have something to occupy him.

Raoul, CT and Lisa fell silent, awaiting whatever news the call might bring. Maybe it was the police. They heard Nathan thank the caller and hang up. Maybe they'd located Annie. Maybe… Maybe… They could only hold their collective breath and hope.

The look on Nate's face when he came back into the living room said the news was good.

"So?" Raoul said, as if unable to contain himself. "Let's hear it."

Nate took a deep breath and smiled. It was the first time Lisa had seen anything other than a sick expression on the young man's face since he arrived.

"It was some lady at Flora & Ella's Restaurant over in LaBelle. Said she saw a woman that looked like Annie there Friday night. And," at this he frowned, "she was with some guy. From her description, he sounded like Philip."

"Flora's?" Raoul said. "I know that place. Some of us used to eat over there all the time." Then he stopped himself as if he realized this was hardly the time to reminisce. "So, what'd she say?"

"Just that she was almost positive the girl was Annie and that she looked like she was enjoying herself. She didn't appear upset or anything, so she must've gone willingly."

"And when was this?"

"Last Friday night. Friday's the last day you saw Annie, right?" Nate directed his question at Lisa.

"Yes," Lisa had a hard time squeaking out her answer. It was the first lead they'd had and she could feel a mix of anxiety and hope resurging inside. "Should we call the police and let them know?"

"No, she said she'd take care of it. Said she was sorry she didn't realize sooner Annie'd been in the restaurant, but she hadn't really looked at the flier until today. Said the man was a real looker, that's what made her remember them. They'd made such a cute couple." With that, Nate's voice fell off and he slumped into a chair.

"Nate, honey, first of all we're not sure it was Annie and Philip. And second, if it was them, the only thing we know for sure is that they were having dinner."

"Yeah? So why didn't he tell us?" Nate crossed his arms tightly across his chest.

"Because it might not have been them," CT offered. "Don't get me wrong. Annie's a beautiful girl. But there's lots of lovely young women out there, and where there's a pretty girl, there's often a good-looking man hanging off her arm. So a handsome couple having dinner on a Friday night isn't all that unusual, now is it?" He took a deep breath as if saying all those words had robbed him of his last reserve of energy.

Lisa didn't know what to think. "I'm sure the police will sort it out." Turning to Raoul, she added, "Before the phone rang, you were about to say something. What was it?"

A twinkle found its way into her friend's eyes. "In that stack of photos you had developed, I found some that were taken before the ones of Annie. You'll never guess what I saw."

Chapter 65

Attempting to recover from Harold's vicious blow, Annie struggled to her feet only to realize the meat she'd stashed down her blouse earlier lay on the floor in full view. In an effort to keep Harold from noticing, she quickly stepped on it. Unfortunately, she was too late.

"What's that?" He pushed her aside and picked it up. Unzipping the baggie, he sniffed. "Chicken? What're you doing with that? Don't you get enough to eat at dinner that you need to steal?" He raised his hand to cuff her, but Bobby intervened.

"Wh-why hit her for being hungry?" he said. "If sh-she wants f-food, l-let her have it. We have pl-plenty. 'Sides, she's the one c-c-cooked it."

Harold lowered his hand and took a closer look at the meat. "You're right little brother. If she's so hungry she's taken to stealing, then she should eat it—now." He stretched out his arm and waved the packet in Annie's face. "Well? Go ahead, eat up."

"I-I was hungry earlier, Harold," she lied, adding his name in the hope it would defuse his anger, at least to a degree. "I'm not hungry anymore. Maybe I could save it for later, if it's all right with you?" She said it in her most humble and almost little-girl tone of voice. "Besides, I need to start breakfast." Her eyes swept the room. Philip and Bobby stood as if waiting to see what would happen next.

"Well, all right then. Get to it, girl." Harold put the tainted meat in her hand. Then he went into the living room. "Make yourselves comfortable, boys. Breakfast'll be ready 'fore long. It's easier to decide what to do on a full stomach."

Annie decided not to rush the cooking process. If Philip's comment about being followed was to be taken seriously, her time may be running out. Perhaps if she made a fancy, time-consuming meal she could buy herself some more.

Consulting the cookbook several times, it dawned on her that a little rat poison might be just the thing. She glanced over to where Harold and Philip were deep in conversation. After sneaking a box of D-Con from the pesticides he'd surrounded her with during that awful photo session, she'd managed to hide it under the sink behind a bottle of dishwashing detergent. Harold, who never bothered with cooking or cleaning, hadn't gone near it. Now, if she could only manage to mix some into the pancake batter without them noticing.

She retrieved the box and glanced over her shoulder to make certain she hadn't been seen. They were still talking—no doubt deciding exactly how and when to dispose of her.

Annie knew from her studies rat poison contains a deadly compound which causes death from internal bleeding. Then she thought of Bobby. He'd been nothing but kind to her and surely didn't deserve what was about to happen. She set the D-Con down. Her eyes filled with tears as she realized that she'd be responsible for Bobby's death. But what other choice did she have? There was none. Isolating Harold and Philip's food or drink would be far too risky. It was clear she had only the one chance to get it right. If she failed, Harold would kill her—no question about it. With great regret, she blinked her eyes, picked up the box and began to pour.

After mashing the pellets, she stirred the powder into the pancake batter and had just finished when Harold poked her on the shoulder. She jumped, nearly spilling the mixture, and caught herself just in time.

"Hey, girlie, we're starving, when we gonna eat?"

"It'll be a few more minutes. Everything's done except the pancakes. I'm about to start them now." Annie forced a smile and nodded in the direction of Bobby and Philip. "Harold, would you tell them breakfast's almost ready?" She added, "Please?" to make sure it was clear she knew her place.

Harold grunted and went to give his brother and nephew the news.

A few moments later Annie put out platters of bacon, eggs and pancakes. She'd already poured glasses of orange juice and placed butter and syrup out along with salt and pepper. All that was left was to pour the coffee—and hope the poison did its job.

The men had settled around the table when Bobby said, "This looks good. Harry, l-let her eat with us." He threw an appreciative grin Annie's way as if he'd done her a favor. Only she knew the disaster his kind words were about to cause.

"Thanks, Bobby, but I don't mind waiting." Annie

realized too late her refusal might alert Harold Johnson's finely tuned instincts to the fact something was amiss.

Harold looked from Bobby to her and back. Then, as if reading her mind, he said, "Why that's a fine idea. Girlie, pull up a chair and join us."

Annie was so frightened she seemed frozen in place.

"I said get your butt over here. Food's getting cold."

Now all three men waited and watched as Annie snatched a plate and cup from the shelf. Philip brought in an extra chair from the living room.

"Great, now let's eat." Harold lifted the platter of eggs and bacon and helped himself. Then he passed it to Bobby who sat next to him. When it reached Annie she put several pieces of bacon and an egg on her plate and handed the platter to Philip. Next came the pancakes. She hesitated, then took the smallest one she could find.

When everyone had filled their plates and was about to dig in, Harold, as though a light bulb had come on inside his head, said, "Girlie, since we're being such gentlemen and you're the only lady here, you start. In fact, take a bite of each and every thing on your plate. Go ahead."

Annie wasn't sure if he was being polite for a change or if he'd figured out what she'd done. "Harold, thank you but that's not really necessary. The food'll get cold if you wait."

Harold gave her a look that said *do what I say or suffer the consequences*. Bobby started to pick up his fork, but Harold stopped him.

"You heard me. Nobody eats nothin' till girlie here does."

Annie hesitated, finally taking a bite first of the eggs, then the bacon. She chewed as slowly as she could without making it too obvious, hoping all the while Harold would realize he was spoiling breakfast for everyone. But he leaned back in his chair, folded his arms across his chest and waited.

When it was time to start on the pancake, her hand trembled. She slowly cut off a piece, brought the fork to her mouth and inserted it. Knowing the bite's lethal contents, she couldn't make herself swallow.

Harold, who had been watching her performance, stood and took her face in his hands. "Open your mouth," he said and forced her jaw apart. "My, my, what do we have here? You didn't swallow. I wonder why."

He turned to the two men. "Don't eat the pancakes. She's done something to them."

He yanked her from the chair and shoved her into the kitchen. "What'd you do, you little bitch?"

"N-n-nothing," Annie stammered. "I cooked them like I always do."

"Oh, yeah, then why didn't you swallow?" He got up in her face, nose to nose, "Look here girlie, I ain't stupid. You tell me what you did and tell me this minute—or else."

What went through Annie's mind at that moment was sheer terror. If she admitted what she'd done, the least she'd get was a severe beating; if she didn't and he discovered what she'd done anyway, she couldn't begin to imagine what he'd do. As it turned out, the decision wasn't in her hands after all. In her rush to mash up the pellets, she'd left the D-Con box on the counter in plain sight.

"Hello. What's this?" Harold Johnson took a step toward the sink and picked up the empty carton. Then he looked at Annie with fire in his eyes. "So you cooked the pancakes like you always do? Like you al-ways do-o-o?" The volume of his words increased until he shouted. "And do you al-l-l-ways mix pancake batter with rat poison?" To say he was furious at her treachery would be no exaggeration. To Annie, it seemed as if his very skin, unable to contain his wrath, might split apart,

She lowered her head and looked at the floor.

"You look at me when I'm speaking to you." Harold yelled.

Annie took a deep breath. If he was going to kill her, there was nothing she could do to stop him. She'd tried everything and nothing worked. All she had left was her self-respect and that he could not take. She wouldn't cry, beg or plead; she'd meet her death with whatever dignity she had left. Having made that decision, she squared her shoulders, raised her chin, looked him square in the face and steeled herself for what would happen next.

Chapter 66

Lisa waited for Raoul to divulge his "discovery." Her heart no longer soared optimistically the way it had with every new revelation. She'd been disappointed too many times, and it was beginning to take its toll. She forced herself to feign interest. "What'd you see?"

Raoul, acting like he could hardly contain himself, said, "A barn. I saw a picture of a barn,"

"A barn? What's so great about that? There're hundreds of barns around here." Nathan had reached the end of his patience. "Why're you wasting our time with that?"

Personally, Lisa agreed with Nathan, but didn't say so for fear of offending Raoul. She needed his help, and if indulging him in a little foolish banter made him feel as though he did something useful, who was she to disparage him?

"But don't you see? It wasn't just any barn; it was very distinct. I've seen it before. Now, if I could remember where it was, we might be able to figure out where Annie's being held."

"But how do you know she's anywhere near the barn? Maybe the kidnapper was passing by and snapped a picture."

"I thought that for a minute too, but then I looked through a magnifying glass at the window in the background of the first photo they sent. You could barely make it out, you had to know what you were looking for, but it was the same barn. I'm sure of it."

"Great, so what do we do now?" Nate sounded less dismissive.

"I told the police, but they weren't impressed. Maybe after that call from the waitress, they'll have enough information to start looking in the right direction. Until then…" Raoul seemed to have run out of steam; the rural area around Lake Okeechobee was large with fields of tall sugarcane that kept most barns from view, making discovery next to impossible.

Before he could finish his thought, CT jumped in. "I have an idea. Why don't we fly over? If it's as distinctive as you say, it shouldn't be hard to spot from the air."

Nate sighed. "We don't have the money to rent a plane and even if we could afford it, where would we find one on such short notice?"

The grin on CT's face made him appear years younger and even a little handsome. "Son, you don't realize who you're talking to," he said and, taking out his cellphone, began to dial.

* * * *

Realizing CT meant it when he said he had a friend who'd loan them a plane, Raoul was too embarrassed to admit he'd never flown before. The thought of being so far off the ground gave him the willies. Now the two of them were at the Palm Beach County Glades Airport in Pahokee, standing next to what seemed to be little more than a toy.

CT had said it was a Cessna 150, which meant absolutely nothing to Raoul. To him it looked more like a hopped-up car with wings, a propeller and wheels that appeared way too fragile. Despite being tied down, it seemed to wobble in the breeze. What if, upon landing, the wheels snapped off? He'd heard about planes landing on their bellies. Didn't they usually explode?

He was about to get into such a flimsy plane with an old man at the controls. Was this really a good idea? The thought of Lisa and how distraught she was crossed his mind. Could he turn his back on what was most likely their last chance to find Annie alive? Driving around looking for that barn would take too much time.

Reluctantly, he put his foot on the narrow step and climbed inside. The cockpit was even more cramped than it appeared from the outside. Being literally shoulder to shoulder with CT made him even more uncomfortable.

After they strapped in and began to taxi, CT started to drone on and on about the plane's features. The gleam in his eyes told Raoul the man was in his element. He tried to listen, but, distracted as the plane vibrated and bounced its way into the air, he wondered if it would keep them safe. He had serious doubts, but couldn't back out now.

CT said the Cessna 150 had a high wing which made for better downward visibility; that it typically flew in the eighty-five to ninety-five mph range and held enough fuel for about three to four hours.

"We'll use the headset intercom with the transponder off. The FAA doesn't need to know what we're up to."

When Raoul gave him a look, he shrugged and added, "We don't know who we're dealing with. Best to be on the safe side."

Adding what sounded like a reminder to himself, "Flying this low, we'll need to watch the altimeter closely."

"So we'll be able to see the barn from the plane?" Raoul managed to ask.

"Our vision down will be unobstructed except directly over the nose and very slightly by the wing struts. Got that?"

Raoul had stopped listening. All he could think about was what would happen if the engine stopped working in mid-air. His body rigid, his feet dug into the floor, his fists were clinched tight making his knuckles turn white.

CT poked Raoul in the ribs. "Hey, buddy, you all right? You don't look so good."

"This is my first time, you know, in a plane."

"Relax, I've done this once or twice before," CT said with a laugh.

"When did you start flying?" Raoul figured if he could engage the old guy in conversation, it might distract him from the butterflies whipping up a storm inside his stomach.

"Started when I was a kid. My dad used to take me with him crop-dusting. I loved flying right off the bat. Couldn't wait to learn. When I took over the company, I assumed Craig'd feel the same way." He sighed. "Some things don't work out the way you expect."

For a few minutes neither man spoke. Raoul assumed CT was thinking about his dead son and didn't want to intrude. He looked out the window as the plane gained altitude.

They agreed that in order to locate the barn, they'd have to fly low. CT explained the plane could be flown ten feet off the ground, "that is, if you have the chutzpa."

He gave his terrified companion a wicked grin, "Below fifty feet's risky, so we'll stay above that, okay?"

Raoul swallowed hard and nodded.

They headed over to LaBelle, then, using a GPS, began to fly back and forth in a grid pattern, as if it were a search and rescue operation, which, in fact, it was. Fly so many miles east, turn and fly west. They made their way little by little, hoping to spot the barn before they ran out of fuel.

Raoul glanced at CT who seemed at ease behind the controls, handling the plane as though it was no more complex than driving a car. He began to relax. The man might be old but he obviously knew what he was doing.

"So, how come you know about flying search and rescue?" Raoul said, looking up from the binoculars.

"We were sometimes called on to help out if a boat went missing."

"Oh that's right, you're from Massachusetts. I imagine ocean rescues are common."

"That's more the purview of the Coast Guard, but over the years we helped when they needed us, especially spotting someone in trouble."

Raoul could tell by the way CT spoke, he harbored fond memories of those times. As they continued to search, the buzz of the engine got inside his head, mesmerizing him. This flying thing was all right. He could get used to it. Back and forth they went, over sugarcane fields, lakes, and the tops of swaying palms. He scrutinized barn after barn, comparing them to the photograph in his hand, none remotely similar.

Before long, a look of concern replaced CT's former jovial mood. He didn't have to say anything. Raoul knew: Time and fuel were running short; and they still had to get back to Pahokee some fifty miles away. He couldn't bear the thought of facing Lisa with nothing to show for their efforts.

Raoul had scrutinized so many barns they began to look alike. Perhaps he'd been wrong, wasting precious time, along with CT's money. They might as well head back. He started to say as much, when it appeared right in front of them in all its glory.

The two men spotted the barn at the same time. "There, that's the one," Raoul almost shouted. "That's it," he said again.

Built of grey weathered stone with a slate roof, the barn was as different from the typical red or white barn as a castle is from a cabin. The main portion of the rectangular structure contained a loft. A long narrow addition with a double-sized door extended at right angles and included a walkway. It appeared at least a hundred years old.

CT dipped and circled the area. "You sure that's it?" he said.

Raoul held up the photograph. "Absolutely. Take a look." He handed the snapshot to CT, who nodded.

"That's it all right. Can't possibly be another one like that."

"What do we do now? Call the sheriff and have them storm the place?"

"And how long do you suppose that'd take?" CT said.

A cold chill crawled down Raoul's spine. It would take at least several hours and if the tone of that last note was any measure, they might be too late.

"What else can we do?" he said. "We'll be out of fuel soon, right?"

A mischievous grin crossed CT's face. "How about this? You contact the police and give them the GPS coordinates of the barn. Tell them what we found and to get their butts in gear. Meanwhile, we'll land in a pasture and pay the bad guys a surprise visit. If we're wrong, we'll just tell the farmer we ran out of fuel and offer to pay for any damage the plane causes. If we're right, we'll hopefully save my granddaughter's life."

"What if there's rocks? Wouldn't that rip the plane open?"

CT looked amused. He nodded. "It could."

"Or what if the farmer doesn't take kindly to trespassers and decides to take a shot at us?" Raoul said.

CT laughed. "Man, where's your spirit of adventure? Lisa said you're a Seminole?"

Raoul nodded.

"And that's the only tribe that never surrendered?"

"That's right." His ancestors, who'd been vastly outnumbered by the U.S. Army, managed to escape into the swampy Everglades numerous times. The government finally gave up.

"Enough said. Make your people proud." CT began his descent.

Raoul held his breath. Better to die for a worthy cause—like so many of his ancestors had, than play it safe and let a young woman pay with her life for his cowardice.

"Okay," he said. "Let's do it."

Chapter 67

Shoving Annie ahead of him into the living room, Harold steered her to a straight-back chair and, placing his hands on her shoulders, pushed her down as Bobby and Philip looked on.

"Phil, get the hell out of here while I take care of this."

"You sure?" Philip glanced from Harold to Annie and back.

"Yeah. Thanks to you things are under control. I hate to think what might've happened if you hadn't paid us a visit. Girlie here might've escaped."

Annie sat stick-straight in the uncomfortable chair, staring ahead, her expression as solemn as a stone statue.

"Go on, get on out of here," Harold repeated. "We got to finish and be on our way. I'll meet you later, like we agreed."

Realizing that in a matter of seconds Philip would be gone along with whatever slim chance she had to stay alive; Annie managed to quell her fear momentarily. "Before you leave, would you answer a question or two?"

Philip looked from Annie to his uncle. Harold Johnson said, "Go on, but be quick about it."

For starters how in hell had she fallen in love with this jerk?

Where's that nice guy gone?

"So, when you got shot, it was your uncle here who did it, right?"

Philip gave Harold Johnson a quick glance and said, "Yes."

"Well, I wondered why he'd do something like that—I mean, the two of you seem close, so close you'd risk going to jail in order to help with the plan to kill me and my dad. I mean, Philip, think about it. He shot and nearly killed you. Doesn't that make you the least bit angry?" Annie tried to stretch this out, buying as much time as she could before Philip left. Once he'd gone, Harold Johnson would lose no time disposing of her.

"Here we go again," Philip sighed. "Not that it's any of your business, but it was an accident."

"An accident? How could it of been an accident? He walked in, pointed the gun right at you and shot. I saw him with my own eyes."

At that point, Harold spoke up. "The plan was to fire once, not hit anything, grab you and leave. I never intended to hit anyone, certainly not Philip." He shrugged. "It was a half-assed idea. I was lucky I got away." He laughed as if he'd pulled a prank. "Imagine that. Those yokels were so scared they couldn't come up with a decent description of me. What idiots." His voice softened, "I really do feel bad about shooting you, Phil."

Philip nodded. "That's okay. I knew it was an accident." Turning back to Annie, he said, "That all?"

"No," she said. "What about your girlfriend?"

Crinkles formed on Philip's forehead. "My girlfriend? What girlfriend?"

"Becky. She's your girlfriend, isn't she?"

"Becky?" Philip and Harold both laughed. "She's not my girlfriend, she's my sister."

"Your sister?"

"Yes, my sister."

"But, I don't understand. The lovey-dovey way the two of you acted." Suddenly she understood. "It was a setup, wasn't it? You did it deliberately to make me jealous. Right? The whole thing was designed to get me attracted to you and make it easier to…" she couldn't finish her thought. What a damned fool she'd been. She was played and had been too stupid to see what was going on right in front of her. She deserved to die.

"Don't feel bad," Philip said. "I really was beginning to have feelings for you. If Uncle Harold here hadn't insisted I get you out here that night, and we'd gone any farther, I don't think I could have, you know, done what I did."

"You mean kidnap me and leave me here to die? That's what you did, you know." For the moment, anger and indignation replaced Annie's sense of foreboding. "You're a real son of a bitch."

Philip just nodded and looked away as if unable to meet her angry gaze.

"So, that it?" Harold said. "Chop chop. Time's awastin'"

"One last question," Annie said. She heard a plane buzz overhead. Probably a farmer checking his crops. She knew for certain it wasn't her grandfather. He didn't care about Mom and for sure didn't care about her.

Harold was exasperated. "Fire away girlie. Let's get this over with."

"It's about the money. How'd it get in and out of my closet like that—and why?"

The look on Philip's face was one of amusement. "That was Becky's idea. She thought if your mom got arrested, you'd be alone in the house making it easy for us to grab you." He shook his head. "How stupid."

"How'd she manage to get it into our house without being caught?"

"Simple. After the funeral there were so many people coming in and out of the place, she slipped it in your room and left. In fact, she said she even expressed condolences to your mom." He laughed again. "After you started locking your windows and doors, things became more difficult, so she took your keys from your purse and had a copy made while I talked to you in the office. Then it was a simple matter of going in when you and your mom were out."

Annie's head spun. She'd been duped. It had been planned the whole time and neither she nor her mother had the faintest idea. They'd even begun to suspect her father embezzled the money.

"Where'd she get ten thousand dollars? Does she have that kind of money to just toss into my closet? And how'd she know I'd find it in the first place?"

"She didn't. It was just a chance she took. As far as the money was concerned, all except the first few bills were bogus."

Annie sighed. It never dawned on her the money wasn't real. Not for a minute.

"Okay, that's enough," Harold interrupted. "You asked your questions and got your answers. Philip, we got a job to do. Get out of here now. I'll see you later."

Philip nodded and gave Annie a look that before now would have melted her heart. "I really am sorry about all this," he said, "You're very special."

The fire inside Annie had nothing whatever to do with affection. "I'm special?" she shrieked. "Far as I'm concerned, you can go straight to hell!" Then before either man realized what was happening, she stood and punched Philip in the belly.

Chapter 68

As Raoul expected, the bumpy landing jarred him from head to toe. The fuselage didn't get ripped open by sharp rocks embedded in the soil, as he'd feared—and for that he was grateful.

CT got his cellphone out and dialed nine-one-one. "This is CT Whitaker. I need to talk to the sheriff." He listened then said, "It's concerning my missing granddaughter, Annie Whitaker." Again a pause. "Yes, I'll hold."

He glanced at Raoul who looked at him with questioning eyes. "It'll just be a minute," he said. "Sheriff, I'm about five miles outside LaBelle. We think we may have located my granddaughter, Annie Whitaker. No, we haven't actually seen her, but remember that barn Raoul Tucker told you about? We located it and if we're right, she's being held in that farmhouse."

He listened a moment.

"What makes me think so? As Raoul told you, the barn's in the background shot of that first picture the kidnappers sent me. How'd we locate it? I'm a pilot and we flew around 'till we found it. Now, can we stop wasting time? Her life may depend on getting there in time. Judging by the cars we saw in the drive, people were there when we flew over. One vehicle was a black SUV, the same model driven by that Waterkeeper guy. No, we won't do anything stupid. Okay, here's the location."

He provided GPS coordinates and a rough address, then, reminding him to hurry, he ended the call. "I don't know, but if we're right and she's running out of time, I think it's going to be up to us to save her. Only thing is, we've got no weapons."

Raoul laughed. "You supplied the plane. I'll supply the guns." He reached in his pocket and pulled out a revolver. Then he stooped down and produced a twenty-five automatic from his ankle holster.

"Yep, you're a Seminole, all right," CT said and laughed.

They quickly locked up the plane and began their trek in the direction of the old barn which was clearly visible in the distance.

As they jogged across the open field, Raoul wasn't sure if CT could manage to keep up. After all, he was well over seventy and unaccustomed to Florida's heat and humidity. He glanced back and asked how he was doing.

Somewhat out of breath, CT said not to worry. "I work out every day." He added, "Last year I ran the Boston Marathon."

Raoul was impressed. The man was in better shape than he was and it wasn't long before they arrived at their destination. That's when Raoul's hunting instincts took over. He put his finger to his mouth, shushing the older man and pointed at him and the back of the house. CT nodded and ran in a half-crouch from building to tree.

As Raoul headed toward the front, the door opened and the man from the Waterkeeper's office came out. He put his hand on the butt of his gun, then changed his mind. He couldn't risk alerting whoever remained inside to his and CT's presence. Best to hold off till they got the lay of the land. If they were lucky, the sheriff would catch him on the road.

Besides, premature action on his part might cause them to kill Annie on the spot—that is, assuming she wasn't already dead.

Chapter 69

Harold Johnson grabbed Annie and shoved her into the straight-back chair, then let out a loud belly laugh. "I'll say this for you, girlie, you got spunk, hauling off and punching Phil like that." He shook his head.

Smarting from Philip's unsavory revelations, Annie sat as docile as a whipped dog. There was nothing more to be done. She'd used up every trick in her toolbox: tried to escape and got caught; was unable to convince Philip to let her go; and had been unsuccessful trying to kill them with rat poison. Nothing worked.

She'd sworn and punched Philip as a farewell message; one she hoped he'd remember long after Harold Johnson murdered her. With no more fight inside, preparing to die was all that remained. Hopefully she'd meet her Maker with some kind of dignity. Whining like a pathetic baby and begging that son of a bitch for her life was out of the question. No matter what, she wouldn't do that.

Harold stood a few feet away. "You're a pain in the butt for damned sure, but you cook and clean real good.

I'm gonna miss that." He stepped over to the kitchen counter and picked up a jug filled with green fluid.

It crossed Annie's mind that she could make a run for it, but she was all played out; her spirit broken. Exhausted to the core and tired of being frightened, she just wanted to get it over with.

He approached with a glass full of the foul-looking liquid.

"What's that?"

Harold groaned. "What the hell difference does it make? It's gonna kill ya' either way." He gestured to her with the glass.

Annie surprised herself by reaching out and knocking it from his hand. The sound of breaking glass echoed across the living room as liquid splashed onto the floor.

A look of surprise crossed Harold's face. He seemed to have taken her lethargy for submission and thought she'd simply do as she was told.

"Goddamn it. Now look what you've done." He smacked her, knocking her clean out of the chair. "Didn't do you no good," he growled. "I got plenty more."

The blow caused Annie to see stars. In spite of her resolve, she screamed as her head jerked back and forth. The chair collided with her back causing pain to shoot throughout her body.

Harold yanked her up and secured her with a rope he'd been using to tie stacks of old newspapers. Then he went to the kitchen, took another glass from the shelf and filled it with the vile-looking stuff.

Her spirits somewhat revived, Annie decided since she'd probably end up dead anyway, she wasn't going to make it easy. She clamped her mouth shut. Each time Harold attempted to force her lips open, she wagged her head back and forth like a toddler refusing to eat. She even managed to bite him a couple times.

"Ow, you little witch. Okay, fine. You want to make it hard? I can handle that." Going into the kitchen, he opened several drawers before he found what he was looking for. Then he came back with a tablespoon and a small funnel.

"This better work or I'll be a son of a bitch," he muttered.

He grabbed a handful of Annie's hair and yanked it hard, forcing her head back. Then he wedged it between his upper arm and sturdy barrel-shaped body. She couldn't move; it felt as though a vise held her in place. Trying to keep her mouth closed, she clinched her jaws so tightly she feared her teeth might crack.

But Harold prevailed, jamming the tablespoon into her mouth and prying her jaws apart, he stuck the funnel inside and picked up the glass.

Expecting the chemical cocktail to begin burning its way down her throat, Annie held her breath and closed her eyes.

Chapter 70

As CT headed for the rear of the house, Raoul crept toward the front, zigzagging back and forth behind trees, bushes and outbuildings. He'd just passed a shed when two rottweilers, big as Mack trucks, burst out and began to bark up a storm. If the people inside weren't alert to their presence before, they most certainly were now.

For the most part, Raoul wasn't afraid of dogs, regardless of their size. But these seemed intent on doing him harm. Lowering his head in the most submissive pose he could muster, he began to speak in soothing tones, masking the fear that rose inside.

"Well, hey there boys. How're ya doing?" He opened his hands palm down to let them sniff and see he meant no harm. Raoul had spent years hunting on his people's tribal land, determined to carry on his heritage of independence despite the steady march of modern civilization. Now, that skill might save him from being mauled and possibly killed by two vicious dogs.

The dogs calmed down and continued to sniff him for any hint of danger or fear. Raoul forced himself to breathe slowly, tamping down his rising "fight or flight" adrenalin.

"That's a good boy," he said. Just as the dogs began to lose interest, CT moved from behind a tree at the side of the house and off they went—heading in his direction, snapping, snarling and baring their teeth.

"Oh god," Raoul said under his breath and crept toward the rear of the building, hoping he'd somehow save the old man who was no match for those powerful jaws.

Fearing what he was about to see, Raoul was amazed at what happened next. Half a yard away, CT stood over the dogs. They'd come to a standstill and whimpered at his feet. Looking up he grinned, shrugged and held up what appeared to be some kind of spray he'd apparently brought with him. Raoul gave him a "thumbs up" signal, pointed toward the house and began to retrace his steps. If they were to save Annie, there was no time to spare.

Chapter 71

Harold Johnson heard the dogs making a ruckus. "Good god, what now?" The glass, filled with pesticides, was positioned over Annie's mouth. He began to tip it.

"Stop. Harry stop now." It was Bobby. She couldn't move her head, which remained wedged between Harold Johnson's arm and his body, but she understood his garbled speech.

Harold lowered the glass and looked up. "What? You know we have to do this. Remember, I told you all about it?"

"Don't care. She never hurt us. Keep her here. Don't kill her."

"We have to. It was her grandfather that flew over our farm, killing our plants and animals, causing Dad to lose the place. He committed suicide because of that man. Our mom got cancer and died, and you—it's his fault you got Parkinson's."

"Yeah, I know. What's that got to do with her?"

"Don't you understand? Somebody's got to pay. If she dies, her grandpa will suffer the same as we suffered after Mom and Dad died."

"Not right," Bobby said. "You got to stop right now."

"Sorry Bobby," Harold Johnson said. "I know you have a good heart, but I've made up my mind. If you don't have the stomach for it, go in the other room. It'll be over soon enough."

"No," Bobby said. "Stop or I'll shoot you."

Harold dropped Annie's head and they both turned around to see Bobby standing there, a revolver between his palsied hands.

"You gonna shoot me, boy?" Harold said. There was a note of disbelief in his voice. He set the glass of liquid on the table. As he did so, Annie managed to spit the funnel and tablespoon out of her mouth.

"Now look at that," Harold said. "All that work and I got to start over." His eyes blazed with anger as he turned toward Bobby. "You're not gonna shoot your big brother, the guy who takes such good care of you. Besides, what'll happen to you if I'm not around?"

He waited a few seconds for his question to sink in, then said, "C'mon Bobby, stop this nonsense and gimme the gun. We don't have time to waste. The police'll be here any minute. We got to leave before they show up."

"Then let's go. Leave her here. Don't need to kill her."

"Bobby, give me the gun. I don't have time for this shit."

"No." The gun remained in Bobby's wobbly hands pointed directly at Harold Johnson.

"Bobby, give it to me. I'm not asking again." Harold Johnson had begun to shout. "We can't wait any longer."

He took several steps toward his brother and the gun went off.

Chapter 72

Raoul reached the dilapidated porch, scrambled up the side and no sooner put his ear to the wall to determine what was going on inside, when several gunshots rang out. His heart sank. They were too late. Annie was surely dead. Before he had a chance to react, CT came from the back at a dead run. Raoul kicked in the door and they rushed inside, their guns drawn.

To say the sight before them was unexpected would be an understatement. A man bled on the floor, a second man held a gun which trembled dangerously in his hands. Off to the side, Annie sat bound hand and foot to a chair.

"Drop it," Raoul pointed his revolver and hoped he wouldn't be forced to use it. The palsied man looked from CT and Raoul to the man lying on the floor. "He dead?"

Raoul ignored the question. "Drop your gun. Do it. Now."

Slowly, with obvious difficulty, the man bent down and set the weapon on the floor.

CT rushed to his granddaughter's side. "Annie, you all right?" When she flinched, he said, "I'm your grandfather. We've come to get you out of here."

Tears bubbled up in her eyes and ran down her cheeks. "Grandpa, you came," she said, her voice nearly inaudible.

"You bet I did," he said and began to work on the knots that tied her up.

The man on the floor groaned. Raoul stooped down to see what he could do. Blood flowed from a wound in his shoulder. "Get me a clean towel," he said to no one in particular.

The man with the palsy made his way to the kitchen and returned with several clean towels. Tears ran down his face. "He gonna die?"

Unable to understand him, Raoul gave Annie a questioning glance.

"Bobby wants to know if his brother's going to die. He shot him 'cause he was about to kill me."

Raoul looked over at a distressed CT who'd finished teasing out the last of the knots. With a mix of grief and embarrassment, he said, "And I know why. Fifty years ago, all we cared about was making a buck. We've been trying to make things right ever since."

Harold Johnson, eyes blazing, somehow found the strength to retort, "How convenient. After killing my parents, destroying their farm and even…" he groaned, "…even Bobby here has suffered because of you." He shifted slightly and sat up. "All the time you were living the good life. Now, after you lose your son and damned near lose girlie, here, you want to 'make things right?' Here's what I think of that." He cleared his throat and spewed a wad of spittle at CT.

Raoul waited to see how CT would react. The older man hung his head. "I understand why you're angry."

Those words seemed to take Harold Johnson by surprise. His bluster gone, he was at a loss for words.

Bobby, who'd been patiently awaiting a verdict as to whether his brother would live or die, spoke up. "He gonna be okay?"

Finally able to decipher the man's garbled speech, Raoul nodded. "He'll live."

Bobby extended both arms, wrists up. "You can arrest me now."

Raoul had to suppress a laugh. "Arrest you? What for? First of all, we're not the police and second, you deserve a medal. You saved Annie's life."

Bobby's face brightened. "I did do that, didn't I?" Then as if realizing the implications of what he'd done, he said, "What about Harry?"

Raoul started to respond when the door opened. Several sheriff's deputies walked in, a grim-faced Philip in tow: his suit ripped; blood spilled down his cheek; his wrists in handcuffs.

Harold Johnson's face said more than any number of words. His look expressed surprise, disappointment and, yes, guilt.

"I'm sorry, Uncle Harry," was all Philip was able to spit out before the burly officers took over and demanded Raoul and CT surrender their guns along with Bobby's.

"Now what's going on?"

Raoul had to admit the scene was two steps past bizarre: A man lay on the floor pressing a blood-soaked towel against his body; a second man held his arms up in a gesture of surrender and a young girl, battered and bruised, appeared on the verge of collapse.

Fortunately, CT stepped up to the plate. "I'm Craig Whitaker, this here's my granddaughter, Annie. She's the one that was kidnapped. Raoul Tucker…" he pointed to the younger man, "…and me got in a plane and rescued her." A look of satisfaction crawled across his face, his eyes sparkled. "That guy on the floor over there's the one held her captive and planned to kill her to get even with me for, well, that's another story."

"So, who shot him?" the sheriff's deputy asked.

"Me, I did that." Bobby spoke up in his quivery voice. "Did it to save her. Harry wanted to, you know…" He made a slicing gesture across his throat. "Didn't wanna shoot, but had to; he wouldn't stop." He again held up his wrists.

The officer in charge looked over the motley group, then turned to Philip. "And what part did you play in all this? Don't say you're innocent because we found that young woman's purse in your SUV."

Philip looked sheepish and more than a little bit frightened. "Like I told you, her purse was in my car because we went out to dinner. Afterward I dropped her off at the office and didn't see her again until now."

"That what happened, Miss?"

"Officer, that's not what happened at all." She glared at Philip, then took a deep breath and recounted the events of that fateful Friday night, including the fact that Philip left her with Harold Johnson despite her pleading with him to take her home.

The deputy smiled and said, "I get the picture. Thank God for your grandfather and Mr. Tucker here. If not for them, I hate to think what we'd be looking at." He paused, "Are you okay, Miss Whitaker?"

Annie nodded. "Yes, I just want to go home. My mom's probably out of her mind with worry."

"You need to be checked out at the hospital first. After that we'll take your statement." He frowned at Harold Johnson and Philip, "This scumbag'll be taken to the hospital too. We'll call your ma and let her know you're safe."

Annie's eyes glistened with tears as she nodded and voicelessly thanked him.

Raoul was so relieved he scarcely heard Harold Johnson and Philip being Mirandized as they were handcuffed and led away.

Chapter 73

Lisa sat in the living room, got up, went into the kitchen and poured herself a glass of water, then without taking even the tiniest sip, set it on the counter, retraced her steps and sat back down.

She stared at the phone willing it to ring. Where were they? What was happening? Had the plane gone down? It'd been more than three hours since they'd departed and still she heard nothing.

Had they managed to locate that barn? Raoul had been certain he'd seen it in the area. What if he was wrong and the barn in the photograph was in another part of Florida, or for that matter, another state? What if they couldn't find it? What then?

Realizing the barn represented their last best chance to find Annie alive, Lisa shuddered and, for what seemed like the one-millionth time, began to beg and bargain with God for her daughter's safe return:

"Please God, you have my husband, don't take Annie too. I won't complain any more about anything if you just bring her back to me. I won't tell you how much I miss

Craig, or how hard my life is now, how lonely it is without him; how much my feet hurt from waiting tables; won't mention how hurtful Annie's thoughtless comments sometimes are."

Annie's comments—oh, what she'd give to hear those snarky remarks one more time. She missed her so much it hurt inside. Created a hole so deep she could scarcely breathe. Just when she thought her eyes were dry of tears, they began to flow once more. She buried her head in her arms and sobbed.

Alone in the house, she didn't have to keep up her stoic demeanor. Instead she gave in to a crumbling fear, and finally acknowledged that most likely Annie was dead and that the lengths to which CT and Raoul had gone to find her were futile.

She cried so hard and so loud that, at first, she didn't hear the phone. Finally the sound came through and she got control of herself. With a sense of dread she reached for the receiver and steeled herself for news that would change her life forever.

She took a deep breath and said, "Hello."

As she'd anticipated, a deep male voice was on the other end of the line. This was it. No doubt the man was from the sheriff's office. He'd tell her they found Annie and that she was dead. He was so sorry. Or else he'd say the plane went down and not only had they not found Annie but that CT and Raoul were either badly injured or dead. She felt lightheaded.

Then through the mishmash of thoughts buzzing inside her head, she thought she heard the word "found" followed by "your daughter." Had she heard correctly? Was it true? Had they found Annie?

"Wait. What did you say?" The muscles in her throat constricted to the point she could scarcely make herself heard. "You found Annie?" The words came out in strangled gasps.

The man on the other end of the line said yes indeed they'd found her and that she was safe. They'd be at the hospital in Clewiston in about half an hour if she wanted to meet them there. Not to worry, it was a precaution after what she'd been through.

As Lisa tried to hang up she trembled so violently she couldn't replace the receiver onto its cradle. It kept missing and falling on the floor.

"Oh my gosh. Oh my gosh. She's alive. The man said she's alive." She let out a loud squeal and said it again. "My Annie's alive. I can go pick her up." Cold chills went up and down her spine as she finally managed to hang up the phone. "Thank you God, thank you. Thank you. Thank you." Tears of gratitude streamed down her cheeks as she went to get her purse and car keys.

She was halfway out the door when Nathan's car pulled into the drive. He'd been at a TV station, providing an update. He looked exhausted—and puzzled. "What's up?"

Overcome with joy, Lisa could scarcely speak. She kept waving her arms around trying to get the words out. Finally, she said, "They found her, Nate," tears again swelled and overran her eyelids. "She's alive." Only then did it dawn on her the officer hadn't said a word about CT and Raoul.

* * * *

Fifteen minutes later, Lisa and Nathan sat in a waiting room at Hendry Regional Medical Center in Clewiston. She was so nervous she felt as though she might jump out of her skin. She reached for the pitcher of water, hoping it would calm her down—at least a little. It wouldn't do to embarrass Annie after all she'd been through. But it wasn't every day that she regained the child she thought she'd never see again. Still, she'd make every effort to stay in control.

Her fingertips drummed the plasticized tabletop, making clicking sounds in the quiet room. As if that wasn't enough, she began to tap her foot. Every moment lasted an eternity. Annie was coming home. She wasn't dead. She was safe. Her Annie was alive. The chant echoed in an endless loop inside her.

The door opened, interrupting her thoughts. Two officers walked in, grins as broad as all outdoors plastered across their faces. As Lisa stood, a disheveled figure tore from behind the men and shouted, "Mom!"

Lisa's resolution to maintain some kind of decorum went by the wayside as the two women squealed and embraced. The happy reunion went on for several moments then Nathan, who'd been waiting his turn, stepped in and joined the celebration.

Finally, an officer cleared his throat. "I'm sorry to interrupt, but we have to take Ms. Whitaker's statement. You can wait here if you like." Lisa nodded, then noticed CT and Raoul standing quietly nearby.

"Thank you both from the bottom of my heart," she said as they approached and enfolded her in their arms. "I'll never be able to repay you for what you did today."

"It was only a down payment on what I owe you," CT said and hugged her again. "I can't begin to tell you how sorry I am for what I've done to you and your family. But I promise you this: If it takes the rest of my life and every dime I have, I'm going to make things right."

Raoul didn't say a word. The relieved expression on his face said it all.

Chapter 74

Several weeks later, Annie and her mom sat on the patio enjoying the cool evening breeze. Most of her bruises had faded. She'd even said her nightmares were becoming less frequent.

Lisa took a sip of lemonade. The glass filled with ice made a puddle on the table top. As she sopped it up, Lisa said, "How are things with Nathan?"

Annie glanced at the empty space on her left hand. "I gave him the ring back."

"Oh, honey, I'm sorry. Are you all right?"

Annie nodded. "You know, I really am. Mom, I care for Nate, I really do—but I'm just not ready to get married. I think that's what I learned this summer. I mean if I can't even be around an attractive guy like Philip without throwing Nate overboard, then what does that say about me?"

Lisa smiled and patted Annie's hand. "You've done a lot of growing up."

Annie nodded and put her feet up on the patio rail. "I called Molly Jenkins to see if she wants to share an apartment next year. It so happens she's available. She's flying down from Boston to look. I told her I'd meet her in Gainesville next week."

Lisa smiled at her daughter. Things finally seemed to be getting back on track. "Remember you have to come back and testify at Harold Johnson's and Philip's trials," she said.

"I know. That won't be a problem. I'll talk to my counselor about it." She stood and stretched as only a twenty-one year old can. "That was really nice of Grandpa to take care of Bobby like that, wasn't it?"

Lisa drew a blank for a second. "You mean paying for assisted living? In a way it was, but assuming Harold Johnson's convicted for Craig's murder and attempting to kill you, he'll probably spend the rest of his life in prison." She didn't want to say that since CT's pesticide spraying most likely caused Bobby's Parkinson's, it was the least he could do. It would've sounded spiteful and she really didn't feel that way, at least not anymore.

"And he and Grandma invited us up for Christmas. That's nice, don't you think?"

"It really was," Lisa said without a whole lot of enthusiasm. She wasn't sure whether or not she'd go. Perhaps it was time to contact her own family. It had been so many years.

"What?" Annie said.

"I didn't say anything."

"You didn't have to. You had that faraway look you sometimes get. Who were you thinking about? Raoul?"

"Raoul? No."

"Oh, c'mon Ma, I know he's sweet on you. Look how far he went to find me: risking his life like that. You think he did it all for me? Please."

Lisa smiled as a warm flame ignited inside. "Actually I was thinking about your grandparents."

"Yes, I love that we're finally getting to know them. And the way Grandpa was able to fly that plane. Raoul told me what a cool dude he is, you know, for an old guy."

"I meant your other grandparents."

Annie looked puzzled, then it sank in. "You mean your mom and dad?"

"Yes, my parents, and my sisters and their families. You have a whole bunch of relatives in New Mexico you've never met."

"I do, don't I?" Annie's expression took on a somber tone. "So what're you thinking, Mom?"

"That it's time I did something about it."

With that she went into the house and came back with a cellphone in one hand and her personal phone directory in the other.

"I don't know if they're still in Acomita Lake, but there's only one way to find out."

ABOUT THE AUTHOR

Joan Mauch's background ranges from teaching and working for nonprofit organizations advocating for the poor to a career in marketing and public relations. Over the years, her nonfiction has appeared in a variety of publications. Joan has a bachelor's degree in chemistry and a master's in urban studies. Her first two novels, HALIFAX (2013) and THE MANGLED SPOON (2014) were published by Whiskey Creek Press. Visit her website at www.joanmauch.com or her Facebook author page at facebook.com/joanmauch.author.